His Return

by

Sheila Kell

HIS Series, Book 3

Cover Art by *Lea Schizas*

The Wild Rose Press, Inc.
PO Box 708
Adams Basin, NY 14410-0708
Visit us at www.thewildrosepress.com

Publishing History
First Edition, 2024
Trade Paperback ISBN 978-1-5092-5658-7
Digital ISBN 978-1-5092-5659-4

HIS Series, Book 3
Published in the United States of America
Previously Published 2016 by Cunningham Publishing

Dedication

To Helen McNabb

This is the book that brought us together as partners in my writing and co-authors in later HIS newspapers. I never would have survived the entire series without your encouragement and support. Thank you for being the best beta reader and co-author around.

Prologue

Three. Two. One. Midnight.

Emily Hamilton knew exactly what she would do since she'd turned eighteen–seduce Jake Cavanaugh. She'd loved Jake since the day he'd walked through their door twelve years earlier. Sure, it began as a child's infatuation, but it morphed into a love of him as a man. When she'd turned sixteen, she'd attempted to capture his attention, dressing to impress him, flirting, acting like a woman instead of a silly teenager.

Yet, he'd continued to call her "sprite," the stupid childhood name he'd given her. When he'd done so, she'd escaped to her room and cried. He hadn't seen her as a woman.

Sometimes she'd catch a weird look in his ice-blue eyes before he'd frown, which she took as disapproval. Emily banished whatever outfit she'd worn when he gazed at her that way. She'd tried everything to turn that gaze to desire. She'd seen it flash through his eyes a few times, only to quickly disappear before a look of indifference flooded them.

In an attempt to keep him to herself, she'd told women who had shown up to see him or phoned, that he was in his bedroom with another woman. Jake never understood why some women stopped speaking to him. But Layla Stevens, his on-again, off-again girlfriend, always came back.

In her heart, Emily knew he wanted her, but he wouldn't act on it because of her age. In fact, last week she *accidentally* fell into his arms, hoping he wouldn't push her away. Being that close to his body had set hers on fire like she'd never felt before, giving her a hint of what could be between them.

She'd witnessed the blaze of heat in his gaze too as he'd pulled her into a sensual embrace. Emily had wanted to cheer because she thought he'd finally kiss her, and he almost had. Instead, he'd groaned and pushed her away, saying she was too young. She'd wanted to scream, to beat on his chest and make him quit denying them. There was only a four and a half year age difference between them, and many people had an even larger one.

"I'm no longer jailbait, Jake," she whispered to her empty bedroom. He'd called her that often enough, but now, he no longer had a reason to ignore what was between them. She didn't care that she'd make the first move. He'd follow along. She felt it.

Stripped down, she rubbed a jasmine-vanilla body cream on her petite body. It was advertised to heighten sensuality. She wanted all the help she could get. She double-checked her appearance in the full-length mirror, pleased that her long blonde hair had cooperated with her and fell in smooth waves down her back. Finally, she dusted on a light touch of makeup. He'd always said she looked best with little to none.

Satisfied that she'd passed her inspection, Emily picked up the short, light pink, silk robe from her bed, slipped it on and reviewed her plan, searching for potential flaws.

Could she actually do this? Could she seduce her

brother's best friend?

The creak of the front door opening and closing reached her ears. She cracked her door open a few inches, listening for footsteps on the stairs and a specific bedroom to be occupied.

Hearing Jake enter his room, she closed her door without a sound, tiptoed to her bed and then sat on the edge, waiting for him to settle in for the night. She released a pent-up sigh of relief. Her brother, AJ, hadn't come home with him, and her father was out of town. With only the two of them occupying the house, it couldn't be more perfect.

A crash and then a curse reinforced her belief that he'd been drinking. He, AJ, and a couple of their college buddies had been out celebrating their graduation. Jake had majored in international studies, specializing in Middle Eastern affairs. Emily knew with the languages Jake now spoke and the countries' problems he'd studied in depth that he would be a valuable asset against terrorism. This worried her, especially since Jake and AJ would leave to join the FBI in the morning. Would they deploy him to some far-off land? Would she ever see him again? She shuddered at the thought of his being in harm's way.

She pushed those images from her mind, banishing them for the evening. She couldn't allow herself to be brought down that miserable path. She had a mission of seduction and love to tackle, so she had to stay on track.

What if he turned her away or treated her like a child?

Her rapidly beating heart plummeted to her stomach, squashing the dozens of butterflies fluttering around. Their pitiful attempt at convincing her to abandon her plan, to let Jake leave without knowing her feelings, without an opportunity for him to humiliate her by turning her away, failed.

Emily stood and straightened her shoulders. "I am a Hamilton, and Hamiltons don't back down or quit." It was now or never. She exited her room and walked down the hall to Jake's bedroom. After inhaling a deep, calming breath, holding it a moment before releasing it, she opened his door, stepped in, and silently closed it behind her. The room was dark with only a sliver of moonlight shining in the middle of the room through a part in the curtains. But she knew her way around, knew where each piece of furniture was located, but most importantly, knew where his bed stood.

Her body trembled as she slowly approached him, her pulse jetting through her body. At the last moment, she missed crashing into his luggage. "Jake." She hadn't expected the slight hitch that entered her whisper.

Oh, how she loved this man. She'd remained a virgin for him, wanting him to be her first and only lover. She couldn't help but wonder if he would appreciate it.

His only answer to her call was snoring.

Emily nibbled on her bottom lip. *What to do? What to do? He's supposed to be awake.*

She attempted to view his expression, but the moon had slipped behind a cloud, plunging the entire room into near darkness.

Feeling for his shape, she touched his shoulder lightly and called out his name again, but that also failed to rouse him. This had to happen tonight. She wanted him to know she was his before he left for training.

Although inexperienced, she knew a way to wake him, hoping he wasn't in a deep, alcohol-induced sleep. Emily removed her robe and slid into bed beside him. His body heat drew her closer while nervous energy rippled through her, her body quivering. She whispered his name and then hesitantly glided her right hand up and down his naked chest. The excitement of finally being this intimate with him ran rampant through her with overwhelming anticipation.

Jake didn't wake to her touch, but his muscles tensed under her palms. She would not back down.

Emily pressed a light, lingering kiss to his neck, savoring his taste. She whispered his name in his ear, nipping at the lobe, hoping to turn up the heat inside him enough to rouse him. Jake's response was unintelligible, so she continued her assault, lightly kissing him and whispering his name. As she explored his body, he moaned, reached out and pulled her close, rubbed his hands up and down her back, and then clutched her buttocks tightly, feeding her desire.

The moonlight entered the room again, casting a shadowy light on Jake's face and his closed eyes. His hand moved to her breast, and passion gripped its shimmery hold, intensifying her burning need for him. She didn't resist when he grabbed the back of her head and pulled her to him, slanting his lips over hers in a deep, heated kiss with an intensity that left her breathless and craving more.

Their first kiss, his warm lips on hers, had been better than she'd imagined. And she'd dreamed of it for years and pursued it just as long. In her romantic fantasy, they were in the gazebo, alone, a light rain sliding off the roof, driving the remainder of the family indoors. Jake would walk to her and pull her into his arms, slowly lowering his lips to hers, admitting he loved her.

Pulling away to look into his eyes, disappointment tugged at her seeing they remained closed. Her heart hammering in her chest, Emily called to him again, receiving no response, but one of his hands kept running through her hair while the other fed the tingling taking over her body as he played with her breast and taut nipple.

Emily glided her arm downward, and her small hand encircled his growing hardness, feeling the shuddering response flow through him before she began caressing the length of him. He groaned, and his hands tightened in her hair, pushing her head down, leaving no doubt of his request.

Never having attempted the task, she'd heard about it, read about it, but had never been curious enough to attempt it until now. As heat pulsed stronger between her legs, she maneuvered herself down his body, uncertainty attempting to shove its way through her. She wanted this to be perfect for Jake.

His tormented groan spoke to her, giving her the courage she needed to pleasure him with her mouth. Exhilarated, she continued the movement of her hand on his fully rigid cock, slowly and tightly, her tongue swirling around the engorged head before she took him into her mouth.

Jake's head fell back on the pillow, and he mumbled something that sounded like, "God, yes, Em!"

Passion and love pounded through her blood, urging her onward when she heard her name. She continued the rhythm, reached down and cupped his balls, and moaned when he urgently pulled her up his torso.

With a growl, he covered her lips, devouring them, leaving the throbbing between her thighs in desperate need of relief. He pulled her astride him, reached down, and slid a finger inside her. "You are so hot and wet." The words were slurred, but she understood him.

She halted. This wasn't right. He wasn't fully awake. Releasing a heavy sigh, Emily climbed off Jake. "I'd best go." Disappointment dropped to the pit of her stomach. This had been her chance, and she'd blown it.

A hand clamped around her wrist. "No. Stay."

She couldn't make out his face in the dark, but his words were clear. A cheer raised itself inside her, and she slowly climbed on top of him.

Emily's breath caught in her throat at the heady sensation that Jake would finally make love to her, leaving her euphoric and anxious. She'd closed her eyes and tensed as he guided himself to her slick entrance, slowly sliding inside, making her feel like a woman. She almost cried out in disappointment when he withdrew, leaving her empty, lost, her future with him fading away. Then he'd slid himself inside her again, withdrawing and nudging inside her deeper with each move until he was fully sheathed. After the initial discomfort ceased, a new wave of heat flooded her.

He groaned, clenched her hips and moved her slowly up and down his length, setting a rhythm that sent warm pulses to her core, and each stroke increased the intensity. Her attempt at reining in her erratic heartbeat and breathing failed miserably. She finally knew what it was like to have him inside her body, and she loved it.

With a hand behind her back, he'd pulled her down for what she'd expected to be a kiss. Instead, he took her sensitive nipple into his mouth, tugging, sucking, and nipping, building urgency inside her, awakening a sexual hunger that was new to her.

She arched her back and sighed in pleasure, turning herself over to him completely. The dreams of his hands on her, his filling her, had never been this wonderful, this satisfying, tempting her to the very peak of ecstasy.

Shifting, she saw his eyes half open, hooded, and she placed her lips on his and outlined his bottom lip with her tongue, tugging on it with her teeth, teasing him as she whispered his name.

"You feel so damn good. Just like I knew you would, Em."

Her heart filled with joy. He may have mumbled, but it was her name on his lips. Goosebumps burst forth on her flesh.

Mumbling something new, he shifted his position, driving deeper and deeper, overwhelming her senses, and confining all her needs in one place, ready to explode.

Her breath caught in her chest as she reached the brink, spiraling out of control. The immense orgasm ripped through her body and soul, carrying her away on a cloud of bliss, leaving her sated and weightless, a limp, rag doll draped atop him.

"Fuck!" He pumped into her a few more times and then shuddered and groaned as she felt him release himself inside her.

A moan brought her head up, but the darkness had

returned, preventing her from seeing his face. She knew making love with Jake would be incredible. "Jake."

"Mm." He pulled her closer to him, tucking her against his chest with a possessive arm. "You're mine now."

With thoughts of their wedding playing in her head, Emily fell asleep wishing she could stay together like this forever.

A loud noise jarred her awake to the early morning light filtering through the curtains. She opened her eyes and smiled, remembering she'd spent the most glorious night with Jake.

"You bastard!"

Emily jerked her head to the booming noise and bolted upright in bed, belatedly grasping the sheet to cover her chest. *Oh God.* "AJ!"

Sitting beside her, Jake's bewildered look at seeing her, and then his wide-eyed surprise when he noticed they were naked, brought reality crashing down around her. He hadn't been awake, or at least not fully awake. *But he'd cried my name and told me to stay. He'd said I was his.* She paused, struggling to hold on to her emotions. *Maybe he regretted sleeping with me.*

Tears pricked her eyes, and despair weaved its way through her heart. This could not be happening. Her brother was ruining everything.

At AJ's approach, Jake jumped from the bed, quickly stepping into his pants. He stood, and she waited for him to tell her brother to mind his own business, but AJ plowed his fist into Jake's jaw before he could speak. Panic rushed through her. *No. No. No. This is not how things were supposed to happen.* She was to wake to Jake's handsome face while he whispered sweet nothings to her, and they made plans for their life together. Heck, he'd taken her virginity.

Rubbing his jaw, Jake looked at her once again and drew in his eyebrows, confusion written all over his face. Sorrow swam into his eyes and it shot right into her heart. He opened his mouth to speak to her, but instead, a loud breath escaped him, and he doubled over after he received a punch to the gut.

Emily jumped from the bed and wrapped the sheet around her. "AJ, no! Stop!"

"Stay out of this, Em. This son of a bitch has gone too far." Several punches followed that statement, all from AJ to Jake. He wasn't fighting back. He just stood there, taking the beating.

Tears streamed down her face; her stomach had soured, ready to toss everything. She pushed past AJ and threw herself over Jake, who lay on the floor, bleeding. She screamed at her brother again, "How could you? This is not your business, AJ. I love him."

He scowled at her and then looked back at Jake while rubbing his hand. "Grab your shit and get the fuck out of our house and never return, or I'll tell Dad that you tricked Em."

She'd never heard her brother sound so angry. "I'm eighteen, AJ, and he didn't trick me or force me. I came to him."

AJ turned on her. "I don't give a fuck! Come on, we're leaving." He reached for her, and she jerked away.

"Dammit, Em! Get away from him." His strong arms pulled her upright.

She cried out for Jake, but he remained quiet, only looking at her with an expression she couldn't decipher.

Fighting her brother every step of the way out the door, she continued to rant at him for butting in and at Jake to not leave without her.

AJ hurried her into her room and blocked the door so she couldn't exit.

"Get out of my way."

"No. Emily, I'm sorry, but this is for the best." He ran his hand through his hair. "Christ!"

"Best? Best for who? You? Because it certainly isn't best for me." He'd always teased her about her crush on Jake. Why couldn't he understand? She was old enough now for her brothers to leave her alone, to let her live her life.

The slam of the front door shocked her.

She raced to the window and flung it open. "Jake!"

He looked up for a moment, then entered his car and drove away.

With a shaky hand, she covered her mouth and dropped onto her bed. "No."

Sobs erupted from deep within her, tremors of despair flowing in her veins as she murmured his name.

Jake had left her.

Chapter One

Four Years Later

Jake Cavanaugh wondered if one's life flashed before their eyes moments before they died, but he hadn't planned on finding out the answer this early in his life. He had to find another escape option, or the next morning, terrorists would kill him in a gruesome fashion, so they could brag to the world that they had outsmarted America.

"Oomph." He tried not to show how painful the punches to his gut affected him, but he had yet to recover from the torture he'd received regularly over the past few months. Each strike shot severe bolts through his already broken-down body, radiating through each muscle, each body part, with excruciating intensity. He hung with his arms in chains above his head, his feet high enough off the floor so even his toes couldn't touch the concrete. He remained trapped while the leader took his fists to Jake's stomach.

"Who are you really?" Mohammed bin Shakaran turned the beating over to the man who had been his guard since they'd caught him snooping. He'd realized Jake wasn't truly one of them, that he didn't believe in their mission and was a threat to their plan. A plan Jake had to get to Arthur immediately, but he couldn't see how he'd make it in time.

The force of a solid kick connecting with his gut

sent him swinging back from his attacker. Jake sucked in a deep, hissing breath between clenched teeth, and, with significant effort, he held his grunt back, barely, the hellacious pain in his body almost overwhelming him. He'd never thought he'd consider something like this, but he wished they'd beat a different part of his body. If it weren't for the give, the swing of the chains, he had no doubt that he'd be suffering from internal bleeding instead of only deep bruising.

He needed to make a jailbreak. He couldn't allow the terrible things to happen tomorrow the way this group planned it. Lives were at stake. Needing a clear head, Jake shut his eyes and struggled to block out the white-hot pain overtaking his body and mind.

Inhaling a deep, ragged breath, Jake opened his eyes and saw a chance to free himself. His guard, Mohammed something or other—in actuality, his name was Greg Jenkins, another American, who'd turned against his country—Greg moved closer with a gleeful smile on his face. It was his turn to use his massive fists in this session. Forcing his weak, right leg to move, Jake kicked out at the man, pushing him back and off-balance, leaving Greg holding his throat where Jake's foot had made contact. If he'd had the strength in his legs, his torturer would be breathing his last instead of only gasping for more air.

With the man temporarily out of commission, Jake worked the chains to free himself.

The leader moved within his reach and with a will of power that until that moment he had no idea he wielded, Jake lifted his shaky legs and encircled the waist of the maniac. He squeezed with all the strength he could muster, trapping the man while continuing to work the chains. He'd almost succeeded in releasing his wrists when Greg pulled his leader free of Jake's grasp and then proceeded to beat the shit out of Jake.

Fists rained down on him, hard and unrelenting. Skin split, ribs cracked, Jake was sure he'd be lucky to ever reopen his eyes.

When they finally gave up on his saying anything new, they released him from his bonds. Jake crumpled to the straw-covered floor, in too much pain and agony to move to attempt another escape. He had to find the wherewithal to do it. If they'd leave him there in the barn, he could steal a horse until he could acquire a phone or any way to call in to the bureau. Although, in his current health, if he made it on the back of a horse, he'd probably end up dropping the phone and then hearing it crunch under the horse's next step.

"Tomorrow." The leader's evil laugh grated on Jake's nerves; a shiver danced down his spine with what the comment meant. "You'll be an Internet sensation. Shame you'll miss it."

Miss it, my ass. I haven't given up yet, asshole. He might not be able to move, but the night was not over. He would find a way out of here.

Unable to walk, they dragged him back to his little prison. The big burly man shoved him forward, and the sound of Jake's knees cracking on the concrete floor reverberated in the tiny room. He bit back a groan at the sharp pain that rocketed up his legs, jarring him all the way to his molars. With determination, he fought the darkness rimming his vision, refusing to pass out, refusing to let them win. Slowly, he turned his head to face Greg, wishing the venom in his eyes could actually seep into the man's bloodstream.

"American pig." The man that had once been an American from Wichita, Kansas, had given up everything to believe in the fight. "You all think you're so smart. We'll succeed and purify the world, beginning with you." The jihadist slammed the door to Jake's room and locked it from the outside. The lack of retreating footsteps told him Greg stood guard. They knew he wouldn't give up attempting to escape, no matter how weak and injured he was.

Jake had remained on the floor, curled into a fetal position against the pain. He eventually managed to stand and shuffled across the room and dropped on the edge of his rugged cot, placing his bruised and swollen face in his dirty hands, wincing at the pain in his wrists. Resignation attempted to overtake him, but he fought it and won. A knot wove its way to his belly, tightening with each moment he wasn't free to warn his boss about tomorrow. This was not how things were supposed to end.

For four long years, he'd worked hard to be the best undercover agent the FBI had ever known. He'd become someone he barely knew so that he could make a big difference in the world.

He shook his head, grimacing at the pain. It didn't matter how well he'd infiltrated this group or that he'd found their plans if Mohammed bin Shakaran was to win. He scoffed, his focus drifting to a time when perhaps his need for punishment stemmed from. His best friend's sister. Emily. He groaned at the memory.

Hell, he'd thought it was an erotic dream. The woman of his dreams. His little sprite had surprised him with her passionate responsiveness, drawing him deeper into his dream, allowing him to push aside his reserve.

If he couldn't have her in real life, he'd be damned if he'd kick her out of his dreams.

He closed his eyes. But it hadn't been a dream. Standing up for her is what he should've done. That was what he'd wanted to do, but he'd broken the Hamilton family's trust and knew they'd never forgive him.

Then again, he wondered if she'd ever forgive him. Her devastated face haunted him, and he knew it wouldn't be easy to regain her trust.

He caught his breath at the painful squeezing of his heart. It was too late to apologize and let the family know he loved them and appreciated their taking him into their home. He had no idea how AJ had explained his absence to everyone, if he even had. All Jake knew was that he had shattered his relationship with them because of his actions and by leaving without a word. He'd acted just like his father, and they deserved better. Emily didn't deserve to be abandoned that way, without an explanation from him, without trying to make amends.

After he'd left the only home he'd ever felt loved in, Jake had appeared on the doorstep of Arthur Hall, a family friend who was also the FBI Deputy Director. He'd recounted to Arthur what had happened, not in detail, of course, and asked Arthur to help him disappear for a while. He'd planned to let things cool off and then return to repair the damage he'd caused. Jake had been expected at FBI training the next day, but couldn't face AJ there. He'd needed time to think, to figure out what to do.

Arthur hadn't been pleased with his actions, announcing that he should beat the hell out of Jake himself. Emily was like the daughter he'd never had, but, eventually, he'd sat with Jake, discussing his options. "I have something that could work, but I'm not certain you're ready for it."

"I can be ready for anything." He'd fly to the moon at this point for a quick way out of his dilemma.

He'd briefed Jake on a new group the bureau believed was linked to a large terrorist group, but they had no proof. It was a group of refugees who had set up their own settlement of believers who wished to establish a true Islamic state. They were based on a large plot of land in the desert of Arizona, and had been extremely careful. They were law-abiding citizens, but the FBI believed the group was actually a terrorist organization. They hadn't crossed any lines and had not, as far as the FBI could find, had any contact with other terrorist groups. That lack of evidence kept the bureau from storming the compound and breaking up the group, arresting everyone to keep them from harming Americans.

The agent who had been assigned to go undercover had broken his leg, so Arthur had been contemplating an alternate plan. The agent who'd accepted the assignment had to disappear from society with no ties to the FBI or any family or friends, plus they had to pretend to believe in their Muslim leaders.

In college, Jake had specialized in Middle Eastern studies, anything Islamic, including studying the Quran to ensure he'd be useful in the war on terrorism. He firmly believed that every person had a right to their own religious beliefs, but committing atrocities in that name was something he wanted to help defeat.

Excitement had flooded him. His reasons for

wanting to disappear no longer mattered. He was a perfect fit for this assignment. "I can do this, Arthur."

The deputy director had raked his hands through his hair. "We'll conduct your training in secret to ensure no one knows you. This is too important for any slipups or leaks." He'd narrowed his eyes at Jake. "I won't release you from training until I'm sure you're ready to tackle this assignment. It has to be more for you than just wanting to disappear."

"Arthur, even if I weren't in my current situation, I'd want this. Give me the chance." The thought of destroying a terrorist group and thwarting a possible plot against America fired his blood, pushing his determination to make a difference.

Arthur made a few phone calls and then Jake had been whisked away to a secluded location with only two agents who provided his FBI training and mission preparation. By not entering him into the system as an agent, a necessity in case of a system breach, and with no future activity in his own name, he wouldn't expose his family. His cover as Jake Jenson, aka Abdullah Alim Shah, had passed through the background checks the paranoid community leader had conducted on more than one occasion.

That same damn agent who had been the initial undercover agent, Bryant, had later joined them. When Jake had been captured, he'd thought the man would get word to their boss for a rescue. That was when he'd found out the agent was a true believer and wanted the group to succeed, leaving Jake to his fate.

He swallowed hard. It had started out with his seeking space from Emily. Little had he known that he couldn't immerse himself in a mission deep enough to forget the memory of their time together. Each night, it replayed in his mind, wrapping him in happiness and love.

Jake's head popped up at the sound of voices outside his room, but he couldn't make out what they were saying. Not that it mattered at this point. He couldn't transfer any new information to the FBI unless he could get the hell out of there.

Infiltrating the group had been simple as they'd been eager to grow the community with not only Muslims but also converted Americans who weren't afraid to live that life. After more than three years, Jake had believed it was just a band of overzealous jihadists who wished to live together until Judgment Day. The only brow-raising thing had been the arms training that everyone had been required to complete. The leaders waved it away, stating it was so they could protect their compound from outsiders who didn't understand their ways and wished them harm.

Finally, Jake had discovered their plans to attack numerous locations simultaneously in the U.S., to make their statement. Once it happened, the world would know America brought in a terrorist group and allowed them to live in plain sight, growing their number of followers into the hundreds while plotting against the U.S.

Jake had just discovered the plans when he'd been captured. He'd been careless, so engrossed in what he'd found, that he hadn't heard the leader sneak up behind him. Unsuccessful interrogations had turned into torture. Untrusting, they wouldn't release him even though he'd answered their questions to what should have been satisfaction. Once he'd realized they had no plans to let him go, he'd attempted his first escape. He'd failed, but hadn't given up and tried again and again, failing each time, but the only bright side was they hadn't figured out he was FBI, and Bryant, keeping his own cover, hadn't outed him, which meant one less humiliation to the bureau when they murdered him.

He snorted. Bright side? There was no damn bright side.

The voices rose. Jake listened intently and released a heavily burdened sigh. They spoke of his execution. It was set to air live on the Internet. It would be the kickoff to seventy terrorists attacks throughout the U.S. He shuddered at the impact of that many explosions.

Jake removed the orange jumpsuit and bit back the excruciating pain in his body as he reclined on the bed, wishing he had the energy to attempt another escape. He was so emotionally and physically exhausted, he couldn't think of another way out, couldn't even put together a possible plan.

He swallowed hard, his pulse throbbing rapidly against his neck. He hoped his family never caught wind of the video. A beheading was gruesome and something he hoped Emily would never witness, especially if it were his death.

His death. *Will I feel pain?* He touched his throat. *I hope they make one clean cut. Will anyone care that I've died? Will Em care?*

He needed to speak, and reached out to the one person he'd been closest with most of his life. It didn't matter that no one was there to listen. He just had to say the words. "Well, AJ." Heavy emotions mixed in Jake's raw voice as he spoke aloud. Taking a deep swallow, he pushed past the lump in his throat and continued, "This may finally be it. If I can't escape, I won't have a chance to tell you how sorry I am for what happened. You were the best friend any man could have. I'm sorry I ruined it. I swear if I'd have realized what had been happening, I would've stopped it."

He rubbed his hand over his face and then stroked the scraggy dark beard that he hated. He had to get his emotions off his chest. "I know you may not believe me. You were right when we were in college about me wanting your sister. She'd grown up at some point, and I knew I felt more for her than just a sisterly affection." He took a deep breath, ignoring the pain in his ribs. "But, you were also right that I should've stayed away. But, brother, she's all I've thought about these last four years."

A smile touched his painfully dry, cracked lips. "I don't know when she grew from the little pixie in ponytails who followed us around, trying to steal kisses from me, to the young woman she was when I left. I imagine you noticed, as I did, that she had a special smile for me."

Thinking of Em made his body feel light with less pain. He grabbed onto that relief. "I don't know if you want to hear this, but it was the toughest thing for me to do not to kiss her every time I saw her." The image of their kisses, even in his dream, had kept him warm at nights, before and after his capture, thinking of how they'd feel when he was awake, and his lips against soft ones, drinking in her sweetness.

"I'm not sure when I fell in love with her. Hell, I didn't realize it until I was here and had sorted out my feelings." His throat tightened, making him unable to swallow for a moment. "I love her with every fiber of my being and know I will love her in whatever afterlife there might be for me. Take care of her, AJ."

Jake closed his eyes; a shiver bled into Jake's body, and an unchecked tear slid past his temple into his hairline.

Composing himself, he slipped his hands behind his head, linking in his dark hair in desperate need of a wash and cut, and a chuckle erupted from within him.

"Do you remember the time we caught Matt skinny dipping with his girlfriend, Caitlyn? I'm not sure how he found out it was us who took off with their clothes." Shaking his head slightly, he winced at the pain radiating through it with each movement. It had been hilarious watching Matt come back to the house, cupping his jewels and searching for clothes for his girlfriend. Of course, Senator Hamilton hadn't thought it was funny. "I guess we deserved all the trouble the twins gave us as we gave them back more. If not, it sure wasn't for lack of trying."

Jake was on a roll and couldn't stop. He had things he needed to say, and while he lay upon the cot, allowing his body to recover enough to escape, he continued, "I know I've told you before, but I can never thank you enough for rescuing me after my mother died and my father left me to fend for myself. If you hadn't found me and convinced your father to take me into his home, I have no idea what would've happened to me. I can't imagine I'd have found a foster home so loving and caring. Not many people would want to associate with the son of a murderer."

His heart squeezed at the thought of his mother. Remembering the smile she would give him each morning spread a warm, loving feeling through him, having her love lifting his spirits briefly. He hadn't spoken about her in years, but she was regularly on his mind. "Mom, I hate how your life turned out with and without Dad. I'm sorry I couldn't save you. I know I was young, but I was puny for my age. Maybe if I'd eaten all of my vegetables like you told me to, instead of feeding them to the dog, I might've been strong enough to break down my bedroom door." A humorless laugh escaped him. He wouldn't think about that night.

"You always told me to do something that makes a difference and helps people who need it. I had hoped to make you proud when I stopped this group from killing others for no reason." He fought the heavy sob grappling to be released and then stiffened, feeling his mother's comforting presence. *I will not allow despair to overtake me.* "I will try to escape one more time and salvage this mission." He had to or the consequences were dire. "But, if I fail and there is a God and a heaven, I will see you tomorrow. I love you, Mom."

His mother's presence lingered, and he used it to beat back the darkness. Without thought, he did what he felt she would want him to do, what they had done together daily. He slipped off the bed to his knees, clasped his hands together, and did something he hadn't done since she'd passed. He prayed. He prayed for the family that had treated him as one of their own. He prayed for Emily and her future. He prayed for another opportunity to escape and save all the people who would unknowingly walk to their deaths tomorrow just for being in the place targeted by this vicious, unstable group.

Jake startled at the sound of the lock to his room

turning. Terror seized his body, tightening every muscle, pumping his blood fast through his veins while his heart pounded in his ears. This was it. This was the end. But he'd be damned if he'd show his fear.

The guard grabbed his arm, but Jake wouldn't go without at least one last fight…one last attempt for freedom. He may be beaten down, but no matter how resolved to his current fate, he wouldn't just give up. He wanted to live.

He rammed his elbow into the man's stomach with everything he had. With his guard bent over, groaning, he attempted to stand and run, but that final surge of energy faltered. Dizziness overcame him, and he would have fallen to the floor if not for the man who caught him. He struggled in the guard's hold.

"Dammit, Jake!"

He snapped his head up at the angry whisper in his ear and looked at his guard. Either his mind had decided to play tricks on him in the end, or AJ Hamilton stood in front of him, dressed in full combat gear and a grim expression on his face. "AJ," his voice, all choked up, cracked, "is it really you or am I hallucinating?"

"It's me. Can you walk?"

Irrepressible relief washed through Jake, and he struggled with the strength to stand on his own. "I may need help, but I'll make it." He'd make it even if he had to crawl to leave this hellhole. "Did Arthur send you?" He had wondered how long before his boss would figure it out and dispatch someone to find and extract him if necessary.

AJ wrapped an arm tightly around Jake's waist. "Don't mention that fucker's name to me right now."

He paused at the door. "Hold on."

Two large figures emerged from the darkness, and Jake tensed. The idea of a successful escape surged an unexpected dose of adrenaline through his veins, but he wasn't sure if he could overpower either of the men, but damn if he wouldn't try. "I think I can handle one on my own."

AJ chuckled. "I don't recommend taking out our escort. Besides, you never bested either of the twins."

The twins? The other men he'd grown up with, Brad and Matt, had also come for him?

Brad looked Jake up and down. "Motherfucker." He shook his head, anger tracing his features. "Ready?" He stepped over the prone body of Jake's guard to lead the way.

Both he and AJ nodded. With his best friend supporting his weight, they quietly slid through the building, around bodies on the ground, to the back of the compound, and out to safety. Jake stumbled, his legs threatening to collapse on him, and his world grew fuzzy, but AJ held on to him. He fought with everything he had to remain conscious, but he started failing. It had been too long since he'd eaten and not long enough since his last beating.

"Shit! Matt, grab his other side. He's passing out."

Someone put an arm under his shoulder, helping AJ support his weight.

"We're clear." The affirmative came before shooting and yelling commenced behind them.

As the darkness pulled him down, Jake realized that he luckily hadn't found out the answer to his question of if one's life flashed before one's eyes before they died. He'd gladly wait to find out.

****

Waking was the last thing Jake wanted to do. Being conscious meant it would be time for his execution. He preferred the darkness and his dreams. In them, he wasn't alone.

"I told you only two at a time," a woman's voice remarked disapprovingly over a series of beeps. "I count five."

"You can count six now."

Jake's heart pounded at the familiar, deep voice. It was the man who had always been there when he needed him, the man who'd given him a chance at a life with a loving family and to grow into a man his mother would have been proud of knowing.

"Oh, Senator Hamilton, sir, I, um, well, I guess it'll be okay as long as you're all quiet and allow him to rest."

In his dream, his family was there until the end. He only hoped that he didn't bring Em into it, knowing it was about to turn into a nightmare. Before he allowed himself to pull her in, he slid back into oblivion.

Sometime later, the beeping and whispering brought him back to the surface. He tried to swallow against the lump constricting his dry throat. It must be time for them to take him away. The fog in his mind began to clear, lifting the fuzziness from his memories. AJ had rescued him, hadn't he? Or had that been just another dream?

Jake slowly opened his eyes, but bright light forced him to slam them shut, but not before he'd captured a glimpse of his blessed surroundings.

Reopening his eyes, Jake surveyed the hospital room. Two men huddled near the door, their backs to him, in deep discussion. He only captured bits of two sentences: "Not all of them," and "Be careful." He turned his head to the side and saw AJ asleep in the chair beside him. Even after what had happened, his family had risked their lives to save him. His heart squeezed at the time lost with them, the love he had missed.

"Jake, you're awake."

At Senator Hamilton's statement, AJ startled and almost tumbled out of the chair.

Jake bit back a smile at the sight and turned his head to the speaker, fighting the racing of his pulse and the heavy beating of his heart. He focused on the man who'd been a father to him. "Sir," he responded, unsure of what else to say. What did the senator know about him and Em? What had AJ told him?

"Here." AJ pushed a button on the remote by the bed that tilted it upward, until Jake was sitting up. His best friend put a cup of water to Jake's lips, pouring slowly so the drink could wet his parched throat. "I'll let the nurse know you're awake." He set the cup on the bedside table and exited the room.

"Special Agent Cavanaugh. I'm glad to see you."

He turned his gaze on Arthur. The man had aged while Jake had been on assignment. Gray flecks peeked out of his short, brown hair, his face lined faster than what he would consider normal for four years. He wondered if it was the pressure of the job or something else. His pulse spiked, and he tensed. "The attacks! I couldn't get you the information in time." His stomach soured, threatening to toss the water back up. He'd survived, but how many had died because he'd failed to do his job?

The FBI deputy director walked to him and patted him on the shoulder. "It's okay. We got them, son."

He loved how both of these men called him son and treated him like he belonged to them, something his own father had never done. "But, how?"

"You told us." Arthur chuckled. "You were pretty adamant even though you couldn't hold consciousness to finish a sentence. Once you told us about Bryant, we were able to pull the information from the weasel. You're a hero, son."

Jake groaned. How the hell could he be a hero? He'd been captured, had to be rescued, and had almost allowed hundreds, if not thousands, of people to be murdered. "I'm no hero."

"Semantics." His boss winked at him. "As for your rescue—your father, and your brothers refused to leave your rescue to the FBI, and since I'd kept your existence secret, I agreed with them, despite drawing significant anger for not contacting them sooner." Arthur flicked his head toward Blake. "After they had extracted you, we raided the compound. We believe we captured most of the terrorists sent out for targets throughout the U.S. We had one minor attack, but we'll get all the information we can and ensure they can't start over."

A heavy weight lifted from Jake's chest. He hadn't failed completely. He caught and held his breath for a moment. "How many died?"

Arthur turned sorrowful eyes to him. "Only the bomber, but there were several serious injuries."

"Thank God." He wished no one had been hurt at all, but at least they'd survived.

A woman with gray hair pulled into a tight bun

leaned into the room. "The doctor is on his way to examine him." She quickly disappeared.

"We'll talk more when you're ready." The deputy director smiled and exited the room.

Senator Blake Hamilton placed his hand on Jake's shoulder. "I'm glad you're okay. I've missed you."

The emotion in the man's eyes and voice almost broke Jake, making him feel like the vulnerable child he'd been when he'd first met the man. After what he'd done, Jake didn't believe he deserved the love this man was showing him.

"Sir." A multitude of emotions clogged Jake's throat, threatening to release in the form of tears that he no longer needed to shed. "I'm sorry."

The senator squeezed his shoulder, and a smile lit his face, which allowed Jake to feel only the love this man was attempting to provide with that touch and smile. "There's nothing for you to be sorry about. I'm happy you're finally home."

Further conversation was halted when a doctor entered the room. This was the man who had helped him? He looked like he'd just graduated high school. Jake was still alive, so that was saying something for the kid.

Jake was relieved to finally leave the ICU. That was until he'd been wheeled into a private room where five men stood waiting for him. Five rather large, imposing men who resembled each other and who hid their expressions so well that he couldn't tell if they were happy to see him or pissed that they'd had to rescue him. Maybe they wanted to let him know that even though they'd rescue him, he was no longer welcome in the family.

Jake tensed and did a full sweep of the room. He closed his eyes and breathed a heavy sigh of relief. No Em. He wasn't ready to see her, to explain things, to tell her the truth, and beg for her forgiveness.

After the nurse settled him comfortably in the bed, checking all machines connected to him functioned properly, she left, leaving him alone with the men.

The Hamilton brothers' expressions had changed to angry scowls. *Fuck.*

"Well?" Jesse, the oldest of the Hamilton brothers, always took the lead when the men were together. When their father had to travel, he'd taken the role as head of the family seriously. Sometimes, too seriously.

A long, awkward moment of silence sat stagnant in the room while Jake glanced at each brother, gathering his wayward thoughts. Shame, love, and relief battled for a prominent position in his emotional bank. His brothers had risked their lives to rescue him, even after what had happened. He had to speak with AJ and find out if everyone knew the truth.

Jake cleared his throat and locked gazes with his oldest brother. "I can't thank you enough. You saved my life."

Jesse waved his hand nonchalantly. "Yeah, yeah. That's what we do for family. What I want to know is what do you have to say for yourself for running away?"

A vise grip tightened its hold on his heart, squeezing it in its nasty claws. Was there even a right answer to that question? No matter what, he'd abandoned the family that had basically raised him. Jake looked at AJ, hoping to read his expression to learn what the others knew.

AJ solemnly nodded. "They know."

Damn. Now he had to figure out if they were more pissed about him sleeping with their sister or his leaving without a word. The fuzziness in his head from the medications needed to clear so he could think more deeply and say the right things and not blurt out the first thing that came to his mind. He hadn't prepared to explain himself to all of them at once. Hell, he'd only thought of apologizing to AJ and Em. He had hoped his brother had kept it to himself. No such fucking luck. He should've known. They were too close-knit of a family to keep that kind of secret from each other.

Lying on the bed in a damn hospital gown that left his bare ass clinging to the not-so-soft sheet didn't boost his confidence. Not to mention the needle sticking in his arm, taped down with tubes chaining him to a machine. Hell, he may as well be unarmed in a gunfight with all six brothers pointing their weapons at him.

"Emily told us she came to your room, and AJ stated that he kicked you out." Jesse's lips narrowed into a thin line of disapproval.

What could Jake say without being beaten to a bloody pulp? That was what he'd have done to someone he'd found with Em. Yet, he knew his anger would be born more of jealousy than of a big brother protecting her.

"You should've contacted us, Jake." Devon, the second oldest Hamilton brother, stepped toward him. "We searched for you, worried about what had happened to you."

Jake closed his eyes against an unfamiliar ache welling inside him. He'd never truly expected to be away from them this long. Many times he'd considered sending word, but he couldn't risk his identity being compromised and possibly putting their lives in jeopardy. "I thought Arthur might eventually tell you."

"Don't mention that goddamn motherfucker," AJ growled. "He knew we were looking for you. He knew the toll it took on us. On *me*."

The hitch in AJ's voice on the last statement didn't go unnoticed.

AJ cleared his throat and turned to his brothers. "I'll call Em and let her know he's alive."

"No! Don't tell Em." Jake gripped the bed sheet tightly at AJ's statement, hoping they would allow him this.

Their gazes drilled into him. His body trembled, but he wasn't sure if it was from his weakness, the medicine, or the anger in their eyes; either way, he couldn't control the noticeable movement. "I don't want her to see me like this." He hadn't meant it as a plea, but that was how it sounded to his ears.

The looks that passed between his brothers worried him. He struggled to interpret them. Would they let Em see his beaten body? The brothers he knew would protect her better than that, but they also wouldn't want to keep this heavy secret from her.

Jesse appeared to decide for the group. "We won't hold this from her for long, so you'd best get better fast."

He sighed and dropped his head briefly, relieved at their kindness. "Thank you."

The men filed out of the room, AJ bringing up the rear. He stopped at the door and looked back. "Jake, I'm sorry." He cleared his throat. "I, um, don't know what to say. I–"

Stunned, he looked at his best friend and couldn't allow him to suffer through his apology. "I'd have done the same." Catching him as he turned back to the exit, Jake hesitantly asked, "Where is Em? Is she all right?"

Before the door closed, he heard AJ answer in a pain-filled voice, "She moved away."

Moved away? Em would never have left her family. She loved them too much to live elsewhere. What the hell had happened after he'd disappeared from her life? Good God. Had she married someone and moved away with him?

The nurse barreled back in while he'd attempted to leave his bed to chase after AJ. He had to know. AJ couldn't just drop that bomb and walk out. It took little for her to have him back down and injecting something into his IV bag. He wanted to fight, but his fight had been exhausted long before the men he'd considered his brothers had appeared.

He had to find out what was happening with Em. What if she didn't want to see him? He hadn't thought of that until that moment. How would he handle it? He had to apologize to her whether or not she wished to hear it. Apologize for leaving…for being the bastard his father had been by abandoning her.

Her name escaped his lips in a whisper as he succumbed to the drug rushing through his veins, leaving him unconscious.

Chapter Two

Please, please let me have this right. I can't afford to screw up this early in my job. Emily Hamilton's small, hesitant steps were a direct result of how much her confidence wavered.

She grasped the overflowing manila folder, which contained printouts of her first full-client audit, protectively to her chest. She'd triple-checked her figures, and the results were the same. Her coworker had made two major errors with reporting the client's money. She hadn't figured out where the money had disappeared to; that would be her next step if her boss wanted her to dig deeper or hand it over to his assistant, who seemed to have her hands in everything.

As a new accountant, not even a CPA yet, Emily couldn't afford to report anything incorrectly. And to turn in her colleague for something as grievous as this wasn't how she'd expected to begin her career. She'd been extremely lucky to be offered this job at Wright Accounting in New York City. Although she didn't know for sure, she suspected her father had something to do with it. He hadn't wanted her to leave Baltimore, but he also knew she wouldn't stay. There were too many memories of growing up with Jake. Falling in love with Jake. Making a fool of herself and being rejected by Jake.

The crushing pain in her heart that she'd fought to

break away from these past four years returned. She'd thought immersing herself in college and her family would help clear him from her mind, and purge the memories. But, every time she looked at her daughter…their daughter…she couldn't escape, and she loved her daughter all the more for who her father was.

She held onto hope, refusing to believe he was dead despite the lack of contact. No matter what had happened between them, she wanted her daughter, Amber, to know her father at some point. Sooner rather than later would be preferable. If only her brothers could find him. Then what? How would she handle things? He'd walked away.

Reaching Mr. Wright's door, she heard two distinct male voices inside his office and stopped. With Teri, his bossy administrative assistant away from her desk, Emily didn't mind waiting. A small sitting area that reeked of power and wealth, because her boss wanted to impress his high-profile clients, reached out and invited her to sit on one of the soft leather chairs. She picked her foot up and then dropped it back in place. If she sat, that'd be when Teri would return from wherever she'd disappeared to and berate Emily for slacking off.

She hadn't planned on eavesdropping, but she'd been curious about how her boss handled his clients, how he spoke with them, what they talked about, how he explained things. One day, she'd have her own firm, and she'd learn everything she could here. Mr. Wright was reputed to be one of the best in the city. He'd kept his business small and was selective about his clients.

Two words reached her ears, and the world crashed around her. Panic followed right behind it. *No. No. No.* Hurrying back to her desk, she fought the shiver worming its way up her spine before she was confronted with Teri, who was leaving Emily and her colleague's work area.

Taking no time to worry about why the woman was there, Emily prepared to depart. "Teri, please tell Mr. Wright that the daycare called and my daughter is sick." How easily the lie spilled from her lips. She had to leave. Now.

Teri Sheppard pursed her bright red lips. "You know, if this becomes a habit, Michael will let you go." She loved to flaunt she'd been given permission to call their boss by his first name. Or if not, she did it anyway, out of his earshot. Emily couldn't care less. Especially now.

Quickly shutting down her computer and grabbing her purse, Emily ignored the woman standing beside her desk. After raising her eyebrows at Teri and receiving no answer, she maneuvered around her and out the door. She almost wretched once she'd reached freedom.

What the hell was she to do now?

Everything continually played out in Emily's mind on the subway ride when she picked up her daughter and on their cab ride home. Maybe she should call her brothers. She bit her lip, nibbling while she considered the option. No. She would handle this on her own. If not, how could she show the family that she could live independently if she had to run to them whenever a problem arose? She loved their overprotectiveness, sometimes, but they needed to understand she was a grown, twenty-two-year-old woman and mother. Now she had to prove it.

"Mommy?"

Her three-year-old blonde-haired daughter stared up at Emily, her head cocked to the right and her hands on her hips. Emily reached down, and little chubby arms automatically grabbed hers to be lifted. She slung the toddler on her hip, and Amber's arms wrapped around her neck, almost choking her. "Sorry, baby, Mommy was thinking. Now, what did you want to tell me?"

"Nemo did *twick*!" Amber squirmed to be let down. "Come *tee*."

Although difficult, Emily held back her laugh. A big smile pushed its way through. Nemo was a beta fish and did nothing but swim in place or hide, and had also been replaced three times without her daughter's knowledge. "What trick does he do?"

Amber pointed at the SpongeBob influenced, decorated fish bowl with a pineapple house in the middle of the bowl. "Float."

Dammit. Not another one. Grabbing her daughter's hand, she pulled Amber away before she realized the fish floating was not a trick. "I see. How about we start on dinner? You want to help Mommy?"

"I want *pasghetti*." Nemo forgotten, she raced to the kitchen and grabbed her small, ruffled apron that matched her mother's. "*Hep* me."

"Here, baby, let me do that for you." Good grief, it was like putting an apron on a kangaroo; the girl never held still. "How about you grab the noodles from the pantry?"

Amber nodded. "I want *PongeBob*."

Emily sighed. She should never have purchased those noodles. Her daughter wanted them for everything. She'd have them as a full meal, plain, if allowed.

After a quick, messy meal, Emily relaxed on the couch with her little girl lying across her lap. Amber stuck her chubby thumb in her mouth while watching *The Backyardigans*. They had to purchase more DVDs. No matter how many times her daughter watched them, Emily didn't think she could sit through this particular one another time.

She brushed a piece of hair from the little girl's face. "Big girls don't suck their thumbs." Being called a big girl like her cousin Reagan, Emily's oldest brother Jesse's seven-year-old daughter, seemed to be important to Amber, so Emily used the tactic whenever she needed it. Okay, it wasn't the best way to break habits or behavior, but it had been working.

A small pop sounded as the thumb was removed and hidden in the cute pink shirt Santa Claus had given her for Christmas. The clothes hadn't gone over well at the time, but now that she wanted to pick out her own outfits, which rarely matched, the shirt became a favorite.

By the time the movie ended, the thumb was back in Amber's mouth, and she was sound asleep.

After settling Amber in bed, Emily's mind returned to her dilemma—not that it had fully left it. If what she'd heard was true, she had to report it. She really had no choice. But, by working there, would she be considered an accessory? A party to the crime?

Settled with her decision, she fell into a fitful sleep and woke with a tension headache knotting her neck, making her wish she could stay in bed, under the covers, and sleep until everything in the world was right.

The following morning, after Samantha, the mother of another girl at Amber's daycare, left to drop both girls off, Emily made the call she'd been dreading. "I need to report a possible Ponzi scheme."

****

The cool wind accompanying the dark stormy clouds gliding toward Central Park provided Emily a temporary reprieve from the oppressive heat wave that had hit the city. The scent of rain in the damp air and thunder rumbling in the distance sent many park visitors scurrying to find cover before Mother Nature ended the drought.

Maybe this isn't such a good idea. She scanned the area, battling strands of hair that whipped in the breeze, impairing her vision. Being too nervous during her conversation, her tattling, she hadn't thought to ask what the man she'd be meeting would be wearing, even though he'd asked about her clothing.

She sank on the newly vacated park bench in her fitted gray skirt. Keeping herself from fidgeting and appearing guilty instead of nervous was more difficult than Emily had imagined. Yet, she'd done nothing wrong. She was actually doing the right thing. Still, guilt ate at her, gnawing its way through her stomach that churned painfully at the knowledge she would soon ruin possibly hundreds of people's lives, but they'd truly already been ruined, just no one was wise to it yet. Except those involved in the scheme.

"Are you certain about this, Miss Hamilton? This is a serious accusation," the U.S. Securities and Exchange Commission employee had asked her during the phone call.

She'd hesitated. What if she'd been wrong? She'd

lose everything she'd just started building for her small family, and she would make a fool of herself, ending her career as an accountant before it truly began. She had no proof. "Trust your instincts," her brothers had always told her. Her instincts screamed there was foul play, and her ethics refused to allow her to ignore it. "Based on what I overheard, yes."

Dipping her head, she glanced at her silver watch, and with her mind so preoccupied she'd had to do a double take to actually register the time. The SEC agent, Paul Thompson, was late. She'd wait five more minutes before she'd abandon this idea.

More people raced by, some in business attire, some in workout clothing and some in outfits she couldn't even describe, but none looked in her direction or stopped to address her.

The fraying of her nerves stripped the serenity she'd usually felt when in the park with Amber. This was the little girl's second favorite place in their new hometown. Nothing could compete with the animals at the zoo.

Giving up her wait, she stood and looked skyward, hoping she'd beat the rain since she hadn't thought to carry an umbrella with her. She'd rushed here after replacing her daughter's fish. She hoped this one didn't do any float tricks.

"Miss Hamilton."

The rough male voice, close to her left side, startled her. She reached her right hand inside her black purse, grasping the pepper spray her brothers had insisted she carry with her at all times. While Emily knew many moves to protect herself, courtesy of those overprotective brothers, her tight skirt and three-inch stilettos prevented her from doing one of the most important things—running away as quickly as possible.

Knowing better than to respond to her name from someone unfamiliar, she stood and turned, acting as if just scanning the area, and glanced at the man who had spoken. That was the plan until her mouth dropped open at the sight of the drop-dead gorgeous, blond-haired man in an expensive, charcoal suit beside her. He was not what she'd been expecting. He looked more like a CEO than an underpaid, overworked government employee. This couldn't be him. Her hand tightened its hold on her weapon.

A crooked, charming smile stretched across his face, and his green eyes captured her in a sensual embrace. "Let me try this again." He held up official identification for her to see. "Miss Hamilton? I'm Paul Thompson from the SEC. We spoke earlier." He replaced the identification in his pocket and held out a large hand in an offer of a handshake.

Embarrassed, she closed her mouth, removed her hand from her purse, and shook his as a smile crept on her face. "Please, call me Emily." The wind gusted, almost pushing her into the man, which may not have been such a bad thing.

"Would you like to sit?" He gestured to the bench she'd vacated. "I'm not sure how long the rain will hold off, but since you just wanted to meet each other first, this won't take long. When you're comfortable, we can go to the office."

Nodding, she sat on the bench, smoothed out her skirt, and dropped her hands on her purse, which now lay in her lap. The butterflies in her stomach bounced off the walls, increasing her anxiety about the meeting, about the subject, about the potential fallout.

He sat and turned to her. "I looked over the audits of your employer, and frankly, I couldn't find anything that stood out." He held up his hand, forestalling her from commenting. "But I'm sending it to the forensics team. I'd like any evidence that you have before it possibly disappears."

Emily's relief at his believing her that something might be amiss was short-lived when he asked for anything she'd collected. She thought they'd do that when the time came. Would her not bringing the SEC anything prevent them from exposing her boss? "I didn't hang around to look for any evidence. I only know what I heard."

"Are you sure you didn't recognize the voice or see who it was?"

"I already said I didn't."

The menacing look that developed on Paul's face had her reaching into her purse again, clutching the cool, metal cylinder for comfort. A chill slowly crept through her. Something was off about him.

"Ah, but you downloaded information that you shouldn't have."

Her pulse raced, and her hands grew clammy. She had no idea what he was talking about. She'd told him everything. "I didn't download anything." Why was he accusing her of that? Did he think she was in on it?

"Let me try this again. Files were downloaded on your computer. Until you provide me with the information you stole from your employer, your daughter remains with us."

Her heart stopped for a moment. *Amber.* Emily's breath caught, and her heart jumped, almost clogging her throat. "What do you mean?" *Oh God.* They couldn't have her daughter. Was this some kind of sick joke?

Scooting closer to her, Paul lowered his voice, creating more turmoil to run rampant through her system. "Let's just say that little Amber checked out of daycare early today. She'll be returned to you as soon as you comply."

No! No! No! This was not happening. Emily jumped up from the bench, her hand moving from the weapon to her cell phone, quickly auto-dialing her daughter's daycare as she turned to sprint to find a cab. Blood surged through her veins, everything around her turned to a blur. Her only focus was to get to Amber and make sure her baby was okay.

A firm hand on her forearm halted her forward momentum. "Don't do anything foolish."

Narrowing her eyes, Emily wished she could claw out his for having anything to do with her daughter.

Please, not my beautiful, sweet, innocent daughter.

"Big Hope Daycare."

"Maureen, it's Emily Hamilton. I just wanted to check on my daughter." Her throat closed. She'd contacted a crooked SEC agent, who obviously knew what her employer had been doing.

"Your cousin picked her up already. He said you wanted her home. Funny, I didn't remember a man on your pickup list, but it was in the computer."

A wave of fear rolled down her body. She closed her eyes. "Thank you, Maureen." With trembling hands, she lowered her phone. "Where is she?"

He flashed her a crooked, and not so charming smile. "She's safe. Now, where is it?"

Emily had to think fast. She didn't have whatever it was he wanted. This was pure madness. She had to do something to get her daughter back. She wanted to scream for help, but feared he'd run, and she'd never see her daughter again.

Her cell phone was now at her side. She discreetly slid her fingers over a preset number that, when answered, would be silent on the other end. She slid it in her pocket, out of sight, in case he noticed and took it away.

She cleared her throat. "How do I know you have my daughter and that she's unharmed? How do I know that once I give you what you want you'll release her?" Emily spoke loudly enough that Paul darted his gaze around and then narrowed his eyes at her.

"I'll let you speak with her, but I am serious about this. If I don't return within the hour, you will not see your daughter again, so I'd recommend no games with a passerby."

Rage and fear for her daughter made her struggle for control. Everything her brothers had taught her about survival jumbled in her mind. All she could think about was her precious Amber in the hands of a kidnapper. And Emily didn't have what they wanted in exchange for her. "Until I speak with her, I won't believe it's you who has her."

The SEC agent removed a cell phone from his pocket and dialed. Staring into her eyes with hard threatening ones, he spoke, "Her mother wishes to speak with her."

Emily reached for the phone with shaky hands. "Hello."

"Mommy? *Tinky* man picked me up."

At the sound of her daughter's voice, Emily almost collapsed with relief that was quickly replaced by a resolve to find a way to save her daughter. "I'm sorry, baby. I had something to do. The stinky man will bring you to me soon. Will you be good for Mommy until then?"

An exaggerated sigh came across the phone. "*Otay. I big gurl, not baby.*"

Paul snatched the phone from her and ended the call.

Emily grabbed at it. "No! I want her back! You have no right to her."

He leaned close. "Cry out an alarm and I run. Remember what happens if I don't return."

She wanted to slap the smirk off his face and then shoot it full of pepper spray before running as fast as she could, but didn't. She'd put Amber's life in danger by doing the right thing and calling this man to oust fraud at her workplace. "You'd best not hurt her, or I'll kill you myself."

He chuckled. "Enough dramatics. Where is it? And don't even try to tell me the office."

Obviously, they'd searched her desk. He said it had been downloaded, so it must be small, like a CD or thumb drive. She had to delay him until she could think of how to get herself out of this mess. "It's at home."

"See, that wasn't so difficult. We'll take a ride to your place."

After a short walk and climbing into a cab, Emily still wasn't sure what she should do. Bringing him into her home wasn't smart, but she had to get help, and all she could think of was the silent alarm and her handgun waiting for them at her home. He wouldn't be able to run then, and Paul, if that was even his real name, would tell her where her daughter was being held. He'd obviously never seen a pissed-off mother bear, and especially not a Hamilton one.

Nowhere close to calm, but with a plan in place, Emily watched the storm break. The rain shower turned into a heavy downpour, rapidly filling the potholes on the roads, leaving puddles behind that would be splashed upon unsuspecting pedestrians from passing cars. In the distance, a split limb of lightning cracked the sky, lighting it enough to see the dark gray clouds moving away. She'd swim through the streets of New York City for her daughter, buck naked if it were necessary. She closed her eyes, and a tear slid down her cheek. This had to work. She couldn't imagine anything happening to her baby.

Stepping from the cab in front of her home, Emily was thankful the rain had slowed to only misting in the air. She took a step forward and then abruptly stopped, shock reverberating through her. *It can't be.*

Chapter Three

Dark gray to almost black, water-laden storm clouds engulfed everything outside of Jake's water-spotted window, creating the turbulence that jostled the airplane to and fro in the sky. Suddenly, they dropped into a seemingly bottomless air pocket. Jake's stomach lurched, and his fingers dug into the seat rests, his heart pounding with fear. When the pilots finally leveled the plane off, he slammed down the shade on the window and attempted to do the same with the cries of passengers screaming they were about to die. Something that hit a little too close to home.

He'd spent the past week recovering at Jesse's home, with several women treating him as if he'd been helpless. Initially, walking from the bedroom to the kitchen had exhausted him, so he hadn't argued with them. But, he'd pushed on so he could strengthen enough to see Em. Amazingly, her brothers had allowed him the time he'd requested before she would be made aware of his presence. Who would inform her had been an ongoing battle.

The changes that had happened in the family during his absence left Jake's head swimming. While he'd imagined Jesse would have remarried, for his daughter's sake if nothing else, he'd been floored to learn that AJ had taken a wife and was soon to be a father. Jake and AJ had been best friends growing up, and he remembered everything about the man. One thing that stood out was that his brother had an unspoken rule of never dating a woman for more than a month. After he'd met AJ's wife, Megan, and witnessed them together, he'd understood. They had the kind of closeness and love he wanted to have with Emily.

Thankfully, before he'd been discharged from the hospital, AJ had updated him on the changes in the family to help him not stick his foot in his mouth.

"All your brothers have left their alphabet agency. They work with Jesse at Hamilton Investigation and Security. Jesse and I both met our wives through there. Although, I was technically still FBI at the time. A fugitive FBI agent, but that's for another time."

Warmth had poured through him when AJ had called them Jake's brothers. Jake had furrowed his eyebrows, trying to discern the information. He'd had a hard time believing none of their brothers still worked for the government. That was all they'd talked about growing up, their dreams to make a difference. Four years had obviously been too long to stay away.

Jake had shook his head at the changes in his family's lives.

"I'd be careful asking why they left. Some are a little touchier than others about it. Especially Brad."

Well, hell, that had only intrigued him more, but Jake had made a mental note to hold on to his curiosity until things settled with the family. Alienating any of his brothers before he'd repaired their relationships wouldn't be wise.

Jake had cleared his throat, nervous at the reception of the question that had been burning inside him since he'd woken. "What about Em? You said she moved away."

He hadn't wanted her to see him in his current state, but not being around? For so long, he'd envisioned her running into his arms and never letting go. But she wasn't even near him. Had she given up on his ever returning? He'd given her no reason to wait. He hadn't said a word to her before he'd left. The cloying emptiness inside him had expanded in an attempt to suffocate him at the thought.

AJ's smile died as he stood, thrusting his hands into his front jeans pockets. He'd walked to the window and looked out. The bright afternoon sun highlighted his tall profile. Just like his brothers, AJ had inherited the Hamilton family trademark—jet-black hair, golden-brown eyes, and strong facial features. Emily had been the only one to take after their mother. Thank goodness.

An image of the blue-eyed wildcat had tugged at his heartstrings, awakening a ghost of a smile to his face. His little sprite.

AJ had remained silent for so long, Jake feared he wouldn't respond to the question.

"Like she'd planned; she went to college to be an accountant. Then she surprised us all and took a job in New York City." AJ had turned back to the hospital bed and captured Jake's gaze; an amused look had overtaken his features. "Oh. You'll never believe this. We think Dad is finally serious about someone."

The abrupt change of subject had hit Jake like a slap in the face, closing the conversation on Em. He had sensed something was missing but knew it wasn't the time. There had to be a reason for her to move away. He wondered if she'd found someone else, and AJ hadn't known how to tell him.

After nearly a week, his impatience at not regaining his strength fast enough had taken over, and he'd decided it was time. It irritated him to not be 100 percent, but he wouldn't wait any longer. The Hamilton brothers could be angry all they wanted. He didn't need their permission. He and Em were grown adults.

As if they'd read his mind, his brothers had asked to speak with him. He owed a great deal to these men, but he couldn't remain there with them. He needed to move forward with his life. Whether or not that included Em, he wouldn't know until after they'd spoken.

They'd each found a space to lounge, filling the couch and the chairs in the family room. Before he sat, AJ had dropped a piece of paper on Jake's lap. "It's time."

Puzzled, he'd lifted the paper and read it; his hands still had an annoying light tremble to them. His breath had caught. An airline ticket to New York City. Em. He took it as their blessing for him to visit her. Not that he'd planned to wait for it, but it would be welcome.

Devon, who'd left the CIA to work with his brothers, had ran his hands through his long curly hair and cleared his throat. "Just like things have changed with us, they've changed with her, Jake. She's not the girl you remember. We can't say how she'll receive your sudden appearance, but we do know it needs to happen before she finds out you're here."

Still looking at the Navy SEAL that he'd been, Matt had leaned forward. "And, you need to decide how you feel about her, and what you plan to do about it. We won't tolerate you messing with the life she's set up for herself."

So, finally sitting in a large metal tube, rocketing through a thunderstorm, he remained unsure of what he'd say to the woman he loved. It had been four years, and he'd yet to find the words that would make things right. And what was right for the two of them? There was no doubt in his mind that they belonged together.

Flight attendants hustled through the cabin collecting trash as the captain announced their final descent.

When he'd queried her brothers as to what they thought her reaction at seeing him might be, he'd received five shrugs that now ate at him. She had every right to be angry with him for acting as he had, leaving without a word, but would she at least allow him to explain why he hadn't returned before now?

After checking into his hotel, he strode toward the address AJ had provided, and when it started to drizzle, he stopped to purchase a NY baseball cap from a small tourist shop. After receiving no answer at her front door, Jake sat on Em's cement front steps as the drizzle turned into a rain shower, the fat droplets beating loudly on the striped awning that barely covered him, coursing to the ground like a waterfall. He didn't care if his jeans, T-shirt, and tennis shoes were soaked. He had to see her. Had to see if she still loved him.

As much as he hadn't wished to admit it, she had a reason to detest him for leaving her like he had. Begging her forgiveness was what he'd intended to do, and he wasn't above groveling when it came to Em.

He folded his arms over his knees and leaned his head down atop his forearms, hoping this bad turn of weather wasn't a sign of how their initial meeting would go.

Jerking awake, Jake looked up and spied a shapely leg slip out of the door of a cab, followed by another. He followed the vision up a figure that made his mouth water. Four years without a woman was a long time.

He caught the woman's gaze and couldn't think, couldn't speak. Em had been a beauty growing up, but she was a stunner as a woman. Were her curves and breasts that pronounced before? And had her bottom lip always been that full? How had he not noticed?

Standing, ready to speak, Jake faltered when he caught sight of a man, reeking of power, stepping up behind her. Was this a boyfriend? A lover? A husband? Was this what her brothers had meant about her changing? Had they been trying to prepare him for the fact she'd tossed aside her childhood infatuation for him?

"Jake," Emily's soft voice broke. "Did Aunt Betsy send you?"

He stiffened. *Son of a bitch!*

Chapter Four

Of all the fucking luck! This was not how Jake had pictured his reunion with Emily. Hell, several scenarios had run through his mind, but witnessing her with another man had at no time entered his dreams, especially one she had just warned him was a threat.

As the daughter of a U.S. senator, the family had worried about Em's safety, so they'd instilled in her to make a statement with "Aunt Betsy" in it if she felt under duress and needed help. A small shiver jostled up Jake's spine at hearing it from her for the first time. Especially as those were the first words spoken between them for so long.

Jake swiveled his head and assessed the man accompanying his Em. While still not at full strength, he knew he could take the man who placed his hand intimately on the small of his sprite's back and whispered in her ear like a lover. He narrowed his eyes at her unwelcome reaction to the man, and it took almost everything he had to hold himself back from ripping the man's head off. Jake didn't yet have a right to Em, but this guy would not touch her again.

Composing himself, he controlled the rage that had skyrocketed to the surface after burning a path through his veins, vaporizing the lust-filled jolt he'd initially felt upon seeing her. Smiling, he hoped his words soothed her, letting her know he understood and wouldn't allow anything to happen to her. "Of course she did, sprite."

"Tell her I'm okay. But, Jake, would you come back later? I can't chat right now."

The look of fear in her eyes almost undid him. Reining in his emotions to detach himself enough to think strategically was a challenge. This was Em. The little girl who had followed behind him. The teenager who had flirted with him. The woman he'd found in his bed. The woman he'd thought of constantly since he'd left.

Jake turned back to the man beside her, slowly approached, and reached out his hand. "Jake Cavanaugh. I'm Emily's brother." The man didn't need to know he wasn't related by blood. He only needed to know someone was there to protect her.

He extended his hand to shake the one Jake offered. "Paul Thompson. Look, buddy, we're in a hurry. She can chat with you later."

Raising his eyebrows in question, Jake gripped Paul's hand and squeezed until he saw the asshole wince. "Is that so?" Before the man could issue a response, he twisted the threat's right arm behind his back, pushing up until the fucker cried out in pain.

Em's scream broke through the red haze of rage and jealousy that held him. "Enough, Jake! Just hold him for a minute."

Puzzled, he turned his attention to her and wasn't prepared for the man to use his left elbow to deliver a painful blow to Jake's stomach, doubling him over while he lost his grip on the man. "Oomph." A sudden vision of fists hitting him while being tortured flashed in his mind and an unwelcome shiver surged through him. Before it could grab hold, he stomped down on it.

This was about Em, not him.

Had Jake misread her signal? Was this a man she loved and the threat wasn't to her, but to him, if he interfered?

Jake ignored the rain that had begun to fall in earnest again, sliding off the bill of his hat. None of them moved to take cover. He didn't fucking care if this was her lover. This was not a man he'd allow her to be with, and he knew her brothers would agree. How the hell could they have let her move here alone?

The handgun suddenly pointed at him didn't faze him, but the scream that ripped through the air took his breath away. He almost couldn't push Em behind him fast enough.

Paul quickly glanced around, probably ensuring there were no witnesses, giving Jake the opportunity he needed. He put his weight into the swing with his right arm and every bit of strength he could muster. His opponent made a slight move, and Jake's fist connected with the man's temple instead of his jaw. Em's threat dropped like a stone, his head smacked on the sidewalk, and blood trickled from underneath it, diluted with the water mixing with it.

Emily rushed to the man's side, kneeling ,and grasped the front of the man's suit. "Paul! Paul!"

It shocked Jake to know she'd rather have a man who was obviously brutal to her. And by knocking her lover out, he'd most likely never gain her forgiveness for leaving without a word.

Jake glanced around, noticing the few stragglers on the street rushed around with their heads down, acting as if they hadn't seen anything. Removing his cell phone from his pocket, he knelt on the other side of the man and felt for a pulse. As he relayed the need for an ambulance, Emily tried to stop the bleeding and wake the man. Her attachment to him unnerved Jake.

After he ended the call, he reached out to her. "Em."

She turned on him, slapping his hand away. "How could you?" Tears rolled down her face, obscured by rain droplets sliding down from the top of her head, yet anger laced her voice. "You weren't supposed to knock him out! You were just supposed to help me with him. He has my daughter! She's in the hands of a stranger, and they'll kill her if this man doesn't return within the hour." She reached up and beat on his chest. "You've killed my daughter!"

Daughter? Shit! Was this man the father? Did he really have the little girl hidden? Why would he want the little girl dead? Jake thought he was saving Em, but it appeared that he'd royally fucked up.

Struggling to understand her words between sobs, he pulled her to him and slowly stood, stepping over the man's unconscious body to hold her snug in his arms. "Shh. The police will be here shortly. We can tell them about your daughter." He kissed her on the top of her head, wanting to comfort her, to find her daughter. "I'll help you find her."

The chilly rain stopped, and the warmth between them remained. Keeping her close, providing her comfort calmed him, his love growing, and his need for her never stronger. Due to the situation, the intimacy was wasted. She felt so perfect in his arms. He didn't want to let her go, let her get away from him.

Shoving against his chest, she screamed, "No! He said no police!" She dropped back down beside the man, catching herself with her hand as she slipped, and shook Paul in an attempt to revive him.

Jake watched her and realized he'd lost her before he'd had a chance. Because of him, her daughter was in danger. He would help her find her daughter without the police. He'd do whatever it took.

Knowing he had only one option, he pulled out his cell phone and made another phone call. One he wished he didn't have to make.

The line rang once before AJ answered. "We're already on our way. What's going on? Most of the conversation was muffled."

Quickly, in short, clipped words, Jake relayed what had happened since he'd come on the scene. While he spoke, the welcome sound of jet engines took some of the weight from his shoulders, the burden of possibly causing death to a little girl, Em's daughter, was more to bear than expected. "I'm not sure who he is, but he might be her daughter's father."

"Jake," AJ hesitated, then cleared his throat before he continued, "that's not possible."

A chill enveloped Jake's bones. Who the fuck was this man, and why had he kidnapped Em's daughter?

****

"How did you get here so fast?" Jake asked AJ as they exited the police station into the humid air left hanging oppressively over the city after the rain. He'd been brought there to "clear up a few things," the police officer had said.

A mysterious phone call to the police chief had been the only thing preventing him from being slapped with an assault charge. Nerves knotted in his stomach because he knew if Paul didn't survive, things could change very quickly for him.

"Em had the common sense to dial our family emergency line. We had grabbed our gear and were out the door before we even knew what exactly was happening. Jesse worked his magic, and when we arrived at the airport, a jet waited for us." Without breaking stride, AJ handed him a black wallet. "Here's your FBI badge. Arthur dropped it off before Em called. Your weapon is in my bag. What the fuck is going on with your status as an agent? He seemed hesitant to give them to me. Like he wanted to say something about it."

Rage snaked through his entire body, and Jake saw red, not at AJ, but at the situation. If he'd had his badge, he wouldn't have had to leave Em in the first place. Then again, he'd told Arthur to take the badge and shove it up his ass for forgetting about him for so fucking long. So why had the man given it to AJ then? Pissed that he didn't have the answer, he ground out his response, "I don't want to fucking talk about it right now."

They closed the doors to the rented BMW, out of earshot of eavesdropping police officers. "Did they find her?" Jake's breath hitched, and a small hand squeezed his heart. "Did they find Em's daughter?"

Leaving her to deal with the situation alone had torn at him. His urgency to return to her had made him impatient and argumentative with the police, nearly landing himself in a jail cell, which would've been no help to Em or her daughter.

She'd stood stoically, detached, refusing to say a word about the kidnapping while the police took their statements. He'd worried about her present state of mind, but couldn't do anything about it. Jake hadn't even met the little girl, and his heart felt as if it had been ripped out of his chest and shredded, knowing she was in danger, and he'd made it worse.

AJ started the car. "They're on their way there now."

"Let's go! I want to be there!" He punched the dashboard, guilt eating at his belly for how he'd fucked up. If what Paul had told them was true, he should've returned hours ago to the other kidnapper. "I may have gotten her killed."

"Jesse and the team have it well in hand. I need to be there for my sister."

Jake was torn. As much as he wanted to be a part of the rescue operation, he felt the urgent need to be there for Em, to comfort and hold her in his arms again. While his cock had twitched at the feeling of her soft body, his heart wanted to be the one she leaned on, the one she needed.

The car jerked to an abrupt stop, and Jake bounced forward, the seat belt cutting across his chest. "Christ, AJ, get us there alive!"

"I hate driving in this city." AJ scowled.

Jake snorted. "Last I remember, you drove like this in Baltimore." He swiped a hand down his face, hoping to wipe away the nightmare affecting his sprite. "Why did this happen? Why Em and her daughter Amber?" A sudden shard of ice stabbed through him. "Shit. Do you think this had to do with me? Arthur said a few terrorists had escaped the raid, but he also said my cover was fine." The possibility this was his fault made him want to retch.

"I'm not certain, but I do know it wasn't because of

you or terrorism, so you can stop worrying about that crap. She was a bit emotional and didn't make much sense. Dev remained at headquarters and tried to calm her over the phone while he located and tracked the vehicle he believed picked Amber up from daycare." He looked over his shoulder and crossed two lanes of traffic, cutting off a cab. "The man is a miracle worker. I don't know what the hell he did in the CIA, but he gains access to computers, cameras, or whatever without being caught in their systems. This time, I don't care what it took. He followed the vehicle throughout the city to get us a location."

"And?" Jake waved his hand, urging AJ to continue.

"The team separated at the airport. Most of the men went to rescue Amber, and the remainder went to Em's in case something new happened. The entire team wasn't present when she called, and we didn't wait for those who weren't available. I was headed to Em's when Dad called about you, so I immediately diverted to pick you up before you did something stupid."

"Fuck. Dad knows?" Jake grasped the door handle in time to catch himself from being tossed across the seat as they skidded around a corner significantly faster than the speed limit. "He must've been the mysterious caller to the police chief."

"More than likely. I'm sure Jesse called him. If everything goes right, Dad will meet us after this in Maryland. If not, he'll be here rather quickly." AJ slowly shook his head and sighed. "He's torn up about this, especially since Em didn't want the police involved. Our wives are visiting him and he's trying to keep it from them so they won't rush here and get in the way."

Swallowing around the lump in his throat, he'd expected to choke on his own blame in it. "Do they think she's still alive?" How would Em handle losing her daughter? It had to be the most painful thing for a woman. For any parent. Would she ever forgive him if that happened? Could he ever forgive himself? Christ. What had he done?

"Don't even think it. She's alive as far as we're concerned. It does them no good otherwise. They need leverage."

Growing up, positive thinking had been a trait Jake had most admired in AJ. Although, Jake had learned that trait had been put to a serious test when his brother met Megan, ran away from a drug lord and saved her life. Their lives.

"You'll fall in love with Amber the moment you meet her. Don't get me wrong, she's precocious and says inappropriate things, but she's a happy child. We miss having her around all the time. We miss them both."

"Why did you let her move away from the family, especially when it's just her and the baby?"

Shrugging, AJ glanced over his shoulder and then passed a quick look at Jake. "You know, Em. She has a mind of her own. She never said it, but we all figured it had to do with being away from the memories of you."

A bone crushing pain lit through his body. It was his fault she'd moved away from the security of her family. He closed his eyes, knowing if only he'd contacted her before he'd disappeared undercover, things would be different. Her daughter would be home with their family in Maryland. Safe.

He wondered if that was truly the reason she had left, or if it was for someone special. She did have a daughter. Clearly, there'd been at least one important relationship in her life. He cleared his throat. He needed to ask the question he'd been holding back since they'd rescued him because a part of him didn't believe he'd like the answer. "Is she married?"

AJ turned to look at him, his gaze solemn, almost painful before the car swerved.

"Dammit, AJ! Pay attention to the fucking road."

Steadying the car, his brother looked forward, his knuckles tightening on the leather steering wheel. "No. She never married."

AJ parked the car and rushed out before Jake could ask if there was someone special, who the little girl's father was, and if that man was still in her life. Jogging to catch up, he braved it and opened his mouth to ask. He needed to know before he spoke with Em about the two of them. He really should've asked those questions while he was recovering.

Without breaking his long strides, AJ looked down at his phone.

"What?" Jake asked impatiently as they passed Ken and Rob, two HIS team members protecting Em's house.

AJ blew out a heavy breath and smiled. "We have her."

"Is she okay?" God, he was scared to know the answer. What if they'd harmed her? Fuck, in the delay to her rescue, anything that happened to the little girl would be because of him.

"Jesse said she's fine."

Elated to be the first to share the news with Em,

Jake pushed into her home, searching for the petite blonde who held his heart. What he saw made his blood run cold. *Dammit! I can't catch a fucking break.*

To keep from doing or saying something he'd regret, Jake turned and walked back outside. He'd seen enough of Emily wrapped in Trent McKenzie—an old family friend, former FBI agent, HIS team member, and "God's gift to women's,"—arms with a look of sheer bliss on her face.

Chapter Five

The day had drained her, taken every ounce of strength she'd had, leaving her vulnerable and weak. With her daughter's capture, she'd been left terrified and feeling alone, even with her brothers presence. These unfamiliar emotions had sent her mind and body spinning, falling into a place where she'd had to fight hysteria. All because in her mind's eye, she'd been doing the right thing by reporting what she'd considered fraud.

How could she have been so stupid to think she could have handled this alone? To help return what little money was left to her boss's clients? Clients who had, more than likely, lost their entire life savings. This event assured her she was correct that her boss was assisting a wealth management company in running a Ponzi scheme.

It had to be a large operation for them to go to this much trouble. Would they come after her again until they had whatever it was they were seeking? Emily wouldn't risk Amber's life again.

Flashing images of her little girl in the hands of criminals wrenched Emily's gut, left her teetering between fear and anger, completely distraught.

Then, to add to her stress level, Jake had been perched on her doorstep when she'd arrived home. Elation had immediately filled her heart seeing him alive, and she'd wanted to rush into his arms. But quickly remembered their ending and anger rose to the forefront.

But their reunion hadn't been important; she'd needed him and could only pray he'd remember her signal and help her, without a chance of risking her daughter. *His* daughter.

How could he have hurt Paul so grievously? She'd thought he'd just subdue the man so she could find out where her daughter was. *Damn him.* She'd needed the man conscious. Her body and mind immediately went into turmoil. One hour.

Things happened in a flash. The police arrived and questioned them while an ambulance took Paul away. Crushed, knowing she'd failed to protect Amber; she'd listened to Jake's directive for her to stay home in case she received a phone call as the police had taken him to the station. She'd wanted, no, *needed* to go to the hospital in case Paul woke up, but she also knew he was right. They'd try to contact her again if they truly wanted the information.

The initial hour had passed, and she'd been alone—no phone calls, no one dropping off her daughter. Worse, the previously dialed number on Paul's phone led to a disconnected number. Yes, her brothers had taught her a thing or two, and Paul's phone had made it to her pocket before the police arrived. What could she say? Her daughter's life had been at stake.

Her brothers and a few members of their team had arrived less than two hours later to find her on the floor in a ball, nauseous, face and eyes red, completely cried out, fearful that her little girl was dead, and there was nothing she had done to save her. Worse, she'd caused this.

Having her brothers and the men of HIS around her, someone to help locate her daughter, had rejuvenated her spirit and gave her new hope. With this new resolve, her heart had beat only for Amber, sending every bit of motherly love her way, making sure she knew her uncles would save her.

She'd prayed her brothers were right, and Paul had been bluffing. She needed to believe it.

After changing into jeans and a blue blouse, she'd returned to her living room, filled with the controlled chaos of men with weapons, waiting for word on the rescue, ready to assist if needed, while quietly protecting her. When her twin brothers, Matt and Brad, stepped out of the room, a cell phone to Brad's ear, she panicked and tried to follow, but Trent stepped in to distract her. At least that was what she'd suspected he'd been doing. She couldn't imagine that he'd be hitting on her at a time like this. Then again, Trent hit on women every moment of the day.

The shouts from the team were all she'd needed to hear they'd been successful, that they had her daughter. Relief gushed through her, lightening her body and mind. She'd waited for her brothers to tell her about Amber's condition. Emily couldn't fully relax until she knew. Was her little girl hurt?

Matt walked back into the room. "They've got her, Em, and she's perfectly fine."

That was when her legs had collapsed, only to be caught by Trent before she hit the carpeted floor.

She recovered when she saw AJ walk toward her. "Pack a bag for both of you, Em. We're leaving now.

Amber will be waiting on the plane." He wore a grim expression on his face, and his body looked to be strung tight as a bow. Why wasn't he pleased they had Amber back? Something had to be wrong. Something he wasn't telling her.

It didn't matter at this point. She needed to see her daughter, to hold her, to ensure she was truly all right, both physically and emotionally. She couldn't believe her brothers had taken her to the airport instead of bringing Amber home first. She had to get there right now. She'd be damned if she'd take the time to pack.

"We already have stuff at Dad's. Let's get to Amber now!" She strode to the door, ready to depart, ready to be reunited with her daughter.

"We aren't going there."

"Then we'll buy whatever we need. Now, let's go."

Shaking his head, AJ followed, her other visitors having departed, and waited while she set the alarm. He then moved aside, letting her walk right into Jake.

After her initial thoughts of his sitting on her doorstep, her daughter was all that held her captive. Or, maybe she'd pushed the ones with him back, not wanting to deal with him now, not wanting to unleash her rage on him.

"Em." His pained, confused expression dwindled her anger at him. Her pulse raced at the sight of him. He was lean, too lean. His clothes hung on him. What had happened?

The man had been gone four years. *Four damn years without a word.* He just left, hadn't fought for the two of them. She'd kept up hope he'd return the first year. That he'd at least contact her.

She loved him, after all. She'd known he felt

something for her. It wasn't much longer after that when she'd closed herself off, her shattered heart never repairing itself, and she blamed him for it.

Knowing she'd have something to remind her of Jake had pushed her to create a wonderful life for their child and herself. One that allowed her independence from the family who'd tiptoed around his name.

Whenever Amber had asked about her father, Emily simply answered he'd had to go away. She'd only hoped he'd one day return to meet his daughter and give her the love only a father could. Now he was here, and she didn't know what to say to him.

Why was he here? What did he want from her? Oh no, did he know about Amber and want to take her away? *Over my dead body!*

Taking a deep breath, she willed her voice to sound normal, so he didn't hear the strain his return had imparted upon her.

Before she could speak, AJ halted her, no doubt saving her from replying and saying something she'd more than likely regret. "Let's go."

Two BMWs awaited them on the curb, parked illegally, but who cared since they were leaving. Climbing into the first car, she remembered something important to Amber, something she'd want with her.

"I need to grab Nemo. I'll only be a minute." She moved toward her home, only to be stopped by Jake. Looking up into his eyes, she melted, kicking herself for allowing her body to respond to him.

"I'll grab it. What is it?"

She froze. If he went into her home, he'd see the photos of Amber. She wasn't ready. She had to see her daughter first.

Matt walked by and took the keys from her. "I've got it."

Settled in the car with AJ driving, she rubbed her temples to ward away the pain not only in her head but also in her heart. "I need to see my daughter."

"Hang on."

She grabbed the handle over the window and closed her eyes. No wonder many referred to it as the "Oh-shit handle." If anyone could get them there quickly, it was her brother. However, with his driving, getting there alive was foremost on her mind.

****

"Mommy! Mommy!"

To Emily, that word had never sounded so sweet, so heart-warming, making her world perfect again. She'd never complain when Amber repeated it over and over in an attempt to gain her attention.

Entering the private jet, she knelt as her daughter raced on her short legs across the cabin, throwing herself into her mother's embrace. Euphoria rushed through Emily's body, relief coursing along with it.

The HIS team members on the stairs behind her, waiting to enter the aircraft, didn't say a word about their progress being halted by the reunion of mother and daughter. They were Amber's unofficial uncles.

Wrapping her arms around the little girl, tears rolled down Emily's face knowing she'd almost lost this moment, almost lost the most precious thing in her life. She closed her eyes, attempting to control her trembling, relieved as the crushing weight lifted from her shoulders.

"Too hard, Mommy." Amber wiggled, pushing back to escape the tight embrace.

Before releasing her, Emily sighed and placed a kiss on the little girl's soft cheek. "I love you." She hadn't wanted to let her daughter out of her arms, but apparently, she needed that hold on her more than Amber needed it.

Small hands held the sides of Emily's face, keeping her turned toward the toddler. "*Luh* you, Mommy." A quick kiss on the lips and she pulled back, tugging her mother's hand. "Come *tee*." She pointed at Jesse. "*Unca Jethe* let me *dribe plane*."

"Ah, little bit, that was our secret."

Amber giggled at her uncle's fake distress of tattling on him. "No *ecret wid* Mommy."

Jesse shook his head dramatically. "Now you tell me you don't keep secrets."

Regaining her feet, Emily smiled and allowed herself to be dragged off by the toddler, who seemed to have no lingering issues with what had happened to her. For that, Emily sent a prayer to her mother, thanking her for watching over her grandchild. Her mom had passed from cancer when Emily had been two years old, so she didn't remember her, but she knew that she'd be there when her daughter needed her most.

She followed along behind the exuberant child, becoming acquainted with every little spot or thing on board the jet, and now Emily knew why Jesse brought her daughter here first instead of to an emotional reunion with her mother. The child's interest had become diverted for the moment.

Amber demanded center stage and soon the men were participants of her audience, whether or not they chose to be. When she had no idea what something was on the airplane, she made up a name and what it did, keeping smiles throughout the group even though Emily knew they couldn't understand half of what her daughter said. This was a much welcome change from the grim expressions they'd worn at her home.

Once she'd situated Amber on a small sofa, the item her little girl had deemed the coolest thing on the plane, Emily threw her arms around her oldest brother. "Thank you, Jesse." She fought the tears of relief that wanted to continue to flow.

Holding her head against his chest, her brother bent down and kissed the top of her head. All of her brothers stood over her by about a foot. She wasn't by any means tall, but compared to her brothers, she felt significantly shorter than her five foot four inches.

"How are you?" Jesse rubbed her back in a soothing gesture, something he'd done whenever she'd hurt herself or been scared as a child. It wasn't that she couldn't go to her father. Although he traveled a great deal, whenever he was home, she preferred the safety of her big brother's arms.

Pulling back, she sniffed, looked around the cabin, and smiled. "Thanks to all of you, I'm fine." She swallowed with difficultly, her throat drier than the Sahara Desert. "I don't know what I would've done…."

"Shh." He pulled her back against him tightly and then separated from her, leading her to two seats facing each other. He looked at Amber and then back to her. "He doesn't know, does he?"

There was nothing like a stab to the heart to bring reality crashing back into her life. Her gaze left Jesse and rested on her daughter. "There wasn't time." Snapping her head back to her brother, her eyes narrowed, venom seeping into them. "How long have you known he was alive? How long have you kept this from me? And not to warn me? To let me be caught unprepared?"

He at least had the smarts to look apologetic. "It's a long story. Needless to say, we felt it best he face you first."

He'd said fighting words. "That is the problem! You all feel you know what's best for my daughter and me. Well, this time you were wrong." She slumped back into the leather seat, her anger abating. She knew what he would say, and he was right. She just refused to give him the satisfaction of admitting it.

"Em, if he hadn't been there, who knows what would've happened? Enough of this. What are you planning to do? He'll be here momentarily."

A wave of panic washed over her, and she snapped up in the seat. "Here? He's flying with us?" Why had she thought differently? Hell, he was in the second car with Matt and Brad. She just wasn't ready.

Jesse stood. "They're here. Go rescue Trent from Amber crawling all over him."

The smile was automatic. Every one of the men allowed Amber to do as she wished. Shaking her head, Emily walked to her daughter and sat down to join in the fun, hoping she looked engaged instead of keeping an eye on the cabin door with her heart lodged in her throat.

Trent leaned over Amber's head. "Do you want me to take her to the back of the plane and keep her occupied?"

Oh, how she'd love for them to be on another flight, but waiting at a commercial terminal when they had access to this plane wasn't on her list of things to do, hoping to avoid Jake. It had to happen sooner or later. Heck, maybe he wouldn't realize it. Men were typically clueless about a child's age. She covered her inner turmoil with a slight shake of her head.

Before she could respond, Amber bounced out of Trent's lap, pointing at the doorway. "*Who that*?"

Chapter Six

Fuck me! Am I to be punished for the entire flight watching her and Trent be all cozy?

"Keep moving," Brad growled.

Jake continued inside the cabin before his brother shoved him through it. The air crackled with tension. Had something happened since they'd parted at Em's house? He furrowed his brows at what appeared to be all of the attention focused on him. Were they worried he'd rip into Trent? *Fuck them!* They'd known she and Trent were an item, yet they'd failed to tell him. They'd let him make a fool of himself by coming here, hoping to be a part of her life, a permanent part.

Em jumped up, fear in her eyes. What the fuck had happened? He felt a tug on his pant leg and gazed down.

"Who are you?"

His heart skipped a beat at the sight of the little cherub-faced child with blonde pigtails looking up at him. She looked to be about three years old and had his unmistakable ice-blue eyes. AJ's words that she'd never married came back to him. Now Jake knew why the tension existed. They all fucking knew this, and no one thought to tell him. He'd never have done such a thing to any of them.

How was he to answer the child? He looked at Em, and the truth was embossed on her face.

He kneeled down, eye level with the little girl, taking in every detail while he considered how to respond. "I'm…." He cleared his throat nervously. This was completely unexpected. Why had no one warned him? An, "Oh, by the way, Jake, you have a daughter," would've been nice. *Fucking assholes.*

Amber scrunched up her face and tilted her head to the side. "*Aw,* you my *unca*? I have *alotsa uncas.*" She pointed a little finger at her chest, proudly. "I'm Amber, and I'm *free*." She held up one hand with three fingers showing. Her other hand held the other two digits down. Presumably satisfied with his seeing her holding the pose, she dropped both hands. "*Unca Jethe* let me *dribe plane.*"

What the hell had she just said? He'd only figured out uncle and plane. Based on the chuckling from the men in the cabin, they understood her words.

Jesse, whether sensing his distress or not, saved him from attempting some sort of reply. "Come on, little bit. Let's buckle in so we can take off. Are you ready?"

Bouncing on her heels, she pointed to the couch. "*Sit there?*"

Avoiding Jake's gaze, Em picked Amber up and toted her to a seat. "After we're in the air."

Frozen to the spot, he watched the woman who held his heart lead her daughter, no, *their* daughter, away. The possibility of a baby from his night with her had never crossed his mind. Hell, it had only been the one time, and he'd thought it had been a dream. Okay, the thinking it had been a dream was a copout excuse. All he knew for certain was that he'd left Em to raise their child alone and because of that, she'd moved here and had almost lost her daughter. *His* daughter.

A slap on the shoulder brought him out of his reverie. "Come on. Let's get you a stiff drink before we take off. I bet you could use it."

He wasn't sure how he felt about AJ for keeping this secret, but he couldn't argue about needing that drink.

Sitting as far from Em and Amber as possible, but where he had a clear line of sight to them, which wasn't easy in a small plane, he kept a low voice so no one would overhear his conversation with AJ.

"Why didn't anyone tell me about her? I've been back for over a week. Do you really think I would've waited if I'd known?"

His brother shifted in the seat. Good, he should feel uncomfortable. Why the hell had AJ, of all people, kept something of this magnitude from him?

"We felt it best for Em to tell you."

He could fucking understand, but he couldn't completely forgive his friend for withholding that information.

"And Trent? Were you planning to tell me about him as well?" He couldn't believe his family would allow another man to become a father to Jake's daughter. *Shit. They hadn't known I was alive.* But still.

AJ's lip quirked. "Nope. That's for her to say."

Fucking great. Now the mountain he needed to climb to earn her forgiveness and bring the two of them together was higher than he'd expected. He needed something lighter for his current thoughts. "Tell me all about my daughter."

While AJ entertained him with Amber's antics while growing up, he thought through the situation, his mind swirling around the fact he'd abandoned his child. It didn't matter that he hadn't known she'd existed, but if he hadn't left Em, things would be different. He wouldn't have been like his father.

No one could've punched him in the stomach harder than the pain he felt. He'd thought abandoning the family one thing, but this…this was exactly what he'd not wanted to turn into. He gulped down a healthy dose of the bourbon AJ had kept refilling, the burn down his throat unnoticeable.

It wasn't too late. He may have missed the first few years of his daughter's life, but he was here now. He'd make it up to her, do anything it took to be there, be the father he'd never had, so the little girl never ached like he had growing up thinking she'd done something wrong to have her father not want her.

Em had finally allowed Amber to move to the sofa where the little girl had curled up in her mother's lap, thumb in mouth, and was sound asleep with a seat belt wound around her small body. Em pulled her hair free from the hair clips and rubbed her hand lightly down the little girl's head, love emanating in the soft tune she hummed.

The sight choked him up, his heart swelling with happiness. She was his daughter, his flesh and blood. It didn't sound as scary as it had the first time he'd thought it. Em looked up, right at him with a mixture of grief and fear in her gaze. Neither spoke, gestured, or moved. Something passed between them. Something he wasn't sure he understood.

She may have changed, but he knew his feelings for her were right, solid. Love. Suddenly, he knew what he had to do.

After the jet landed at the private airport in Baltimore, Maryland, he stopped Em before she reached the cabin door. He'd never felt more confident about a decision that he'd made. This was right. This would make everything right. "We're getting married."

****

Dumbfounded, Emily stood in front of Jake. *That pushy, demanding son of a bitch! How dare he dictate to me? Especially something like that?* Had it been a few years ago, she'd have jumped at the chance to finally wed the man she'd loved all of her life. The father of her child. But not now. Not only had he left her, he'd done it without looking back. What a fool she'd been waiting for him to return to her.

Red-hot anger surged through her, attempting to wash away the happiness she felt at being with her daughter. Their daughter. So that was why he wanted to marry her. It had nothing to do with love. It was all about Amber. She had wanted her daughter to have Jake in her life, but she was no longer sure.

She was so damn confused. One moment her heart leaped at the chance to finally be his wife, for them to live happily ever after. The next, her heart remembered the crushing blow from him. How could she ever trust him not to leave her again? Where had he been? Why hadn't he contacted her?

No matter what her heart said, the defiance her brothers warned her would get her into trouble one day kicked in. "No, we aren't." She spun around and exited the airplane as quickly as she could, almost tripping down the stairs. Under her breath, she cursed Jake and all mankind for thinking women should bow to their whims.

Her daughter, racing back to her, broke the litany of unladylike curses, Amber's little arms raised for her mother to pick her up, tripping on her sandals and falling on the tarmac. It only took a moment for Emily to rush forward and pick up Amber, who now wailed loudly.

Without hesitation, she lifted the best thing in her life, remembering the smell of the little girl, baby lotion, and sunshine. Okay, sunshine didn't necessarily have a smell, but it was what Emily imagined it would smell like.

"Is she hurt?"

She jumped. Jake had startled the crap out of her. Focusing back on the hiccupping and sniffing bundle, the cries stilled at the sound of a man. She picked up a small hand and looked over the marks from where they'd met the pavement. "Does it hurt?"

Amber, clinging to her mother, gave a dramatic nod and poked out her lower lip, playing to her small audience. "It *hut* bad."

Softly holding the hand, Emily brought it to her lips and placed a light kiss on it. "How's that? Is your booboo better?"

Another dramatic nod. The little angel looked at Jake with wide eyes. "*You* ride *wid* me?"

A heart palpitation hit Emily. A heavy weight pushed on her ribs, making it hard to take a breath. There would be no running anytime soon. She'd have to face it, face Jake, and face her daughter with the truth. She just wasn't doing it now. Especially not after his directive. *Damn man!*

"Ready?" Jesse walked up to them, looked between the three, and reached for Amber. "Come here, little bit."

Handing her over, Emily had a thought. "Jesse, we don't have a car seat."

"Sure we do. Let's get out of here." He turned, leading them to a row of SUVs and the waiting men.

Looking over Jesse's shoulder, Amber sought out Jake. "*You* ride *wid* me?"

"Um." He looked at Emily, who quickly diverted her gaze.

Dammit. Of course, she'd like the man, not even knowing he was her father. "Sure he will." Her daughter had been through a lot today. If having Jake ride with her meant so much, Emily would swallow her hurt and embarrassment, and allow it. She'd move heaven and earth if that had been the girl's desire.

Settling in the backseat with her daughter, Emily stared at the back of Jake's head. Was now the time? No. She had to speak with him first before she told Amber who he was. She needed to know his motives for showing up now.

Oh, right. He expected her to marry him. She still had a lot to say to him about that. *But wouldn't it be great if we were a family? No.* She wanted a happy, loving family, not one based on only responsibility.

She tried to picture them together, but his thin frame, and the dark circles under his eyes, called out to her. He looked like he'd been through hell. Yet, she still craved him like when she was a teenager. He still turned her body into a raging inferno without a word.

Amber kicked the back of Jesse's seat. She gave her daughter what she expected to pass as her stern mother look. "Don't kick Uncle Jesse's seat while he's driving." The feet stilled, and no appearance of being chastised appeared on the girl's face.

"Jesse, how'd you manage the car seat? I thought Kate and Megan were visiting Dad."

"Mrs. Kessler. I called ahead, and she went shopping. There were still a few things you'd left at the house, but now you should have everything you need."

She'd forgotten about Mrs. Kessler, who'd been hired when Jesse was a widower, to help him take care of his daughter. Now that he'd married Kate, Mrs. Kessler seemed to keep the men in line more than anything else. She looked forward to seeing the older woman again. She'd been a great help with Amber when Emily had needed it.

Her little darling took over the conversation, peppering Jake with questions and telling him all about her fish, the animals at the zoo, her potty training and more. While nervous about what Jake might say, she couldn't hide the smile when he would look bewildered trying to understand what their daughter said. At three, she still couldn't pronounce many words, and it took a trained ear to figure out what she was saying when she talked really fast.

When she asked if he had kids, he glanced back at Emily, who held her breath.

"Look, Amber, we're almost there. Dottie will be happy to see you."

Thank you, Jesse, for once again saving me. Her daughter's attention diverted to talking about Reagan's pet.

Once they entered the house, Emily rushed Amber upstairs to rest. She knew it only postponed her and Jake's talk, but she needed to sort out her feelings.

Closing a bedroom door behind her, she heard AJ

speak. "What'd you do?"

She'd let Jake try to explain to her brothers his not-at-all proposal. His demand. They wouldn't appreciate it any more than she had. But, part of her wished....

Chapter Seven

The pain couldn't be any less than if he'd had a knife thrust through his chest, piercing his heart, ripping a jagged edge across it. Nothing had happened like Jake had hoped it would, dreamed it would, somewhat planned it would. Not a fucking thing.

He stared at the departing Emily and her luscious backside, bewildered at her avoidance, her cold shoulder. She obviously no longer loved him, and it appeared she didn't want him to know his own child. Bullshit. He'd know his little girl, a small, talkative, toddler who had already stolen his heart. He'd just have to make Emily love him after they married.

Fingers snapped in front of his face, bringing him out of his reverie. "Hey! Earth to Jake. What'd you do to my sister?"

Putting a hand on AJ's face, he pushed him away and thought back to everything he'd said and done since seeing Em. Coming up with nothing that would elicit that response, he lazily shrugged. "Unless she's holding me responsible for Amber being held longer, I have no clue. I said hello in New York and told her we were getting married on the plane."

An uncomfortable silence followed his answer. Eyebrows rose and his brothers, all five of them, broke out in laughter hard enough that tears formed in some of their eyes. He didn't see what was so damn funny, but his stomach became unsettled at the thought he must've missed something important. What did he forget to say? It was too early to tell her he loved her. Besides, these assholes didn't know that. "What?"

Devon, who'd met them at the door, slapped him on the back before wrapping his arm around Jake's shoulder in a familiar gesture he'd missed since seeing his brothers last. "Boy...did," he said between gulps of air and laughter, "we miss you."

Comfort and security were things freely given from this family, something he'd never received from his father. The man who'd beaten his mother regularly had reminded Jake daily how much he wished Jake had never been born, the man who'd left, only to return years later to murder his mother.

Nicole Cavanaugh had tried to give her son comfort and security, but when his father lived with them, he would rip it away the moment he felt there was something other than hatred and fear in the home. He couldn't really call it a home. Not after seeing the loving family he'd spent twelve years with. Twelve years without his mother. Twelve years of promising himself he would not be like his father.

Many a night he'd heard his mother crying after his father beat her. Once the man left to join friends at a bar, Jake would go to his mother and hold her as best he could. Each time he swore he'd do something about it, but he'd been too young...too weak...too fearful. Then his father had left them.

For years, it had been joyous even though there were nights when he went to bed hungry because there wasn't enough money left from his mother's waitressing job. It didn't matter. They were safe.

One night, he'd heard a loud argument from the living room. His father's voice. Jumping from his bed, he'd rushed to the door only to find it locked from the outside with the lock his father had placed there years ago when he'd punished Jake. His heart pounding, all he could do was bang on the door and scream, his body shaking with fear and anger. Fear for his mother and anger at his father. Father. Jake snorted. He was the man who'd planted his sperm inside his mother, not a father.

After what seemed like hours of his pounding on the door, pulling on the doorknob in hopes it would magically open, there was absolute silence. Jake hadn't been able to move. He'd held his breath for a moment, trembling at what he knew must've happened. His mother had been knocked unconscious before, but at that time, he was locked in his room and hadn't been able to treat her injuries or hold her until she woke.

He'd preferred feeling unloved and unwanted rather than his mother being harmed. He'd resumed his pounding on the door and screaming her name, threatening to kill his father.

"You think you can take me, boy?"

He'd doubted his father even knew his name. All he'd ever called him was "boy," which hurt just as bad as the crap load of emotional pain the man had happily inflicted.

"It's your turn now." The door had opened, and Jake hadn't hesitated. He'd flown through the doorway at his father, catching the man off balance, and knocking them to the floor. Jake had hit at his father's chest, pummeling with the little bit of strength he'd possessed at ten and a half years old. Something had changed in him this time. Jake had known it was time to stand up to the man with the only thing his father understood—fists and violence.

It hadn't taken long for his father to roll over with Jake beneath him. His weight almost doubled his son's, pinning him to the floor, his heavy legs preventing Jake from being able to free himself.

"You worthless piece of shit. I can't believe you're mine." His father had fastened his large hands around Jake's neck, squeezing his windpipe, slowly cutting off his air supply. When black spots floated before him and darkness rimmed his vision, slowly closing the tunnel, pulling in a breath was nearly impossible. It was then the door slammed open, hitting the wall with the force of it.

"Police! Let him go, Jim!"

Jake had forgotten a police officer lived downstairs. He'd thanked God. The man must've been at home and heard them. He'd wanted to kiss the man's feet for coming to their rescue.

James Michael Cavanaugh released his son, stood and snarled at Officer Patton. "Mind your own damn business."

Rolling over onto his knees, gasping for air, all Jake could think about was his mother. He crawled to her, crying her name, begging her to speak with him. Her ice-blue eyes had flickered open once, and she'd smiled at him before taking her last breath.

They'd been unable to revive her.

He swallowed hard and took a deep breath, calming the emotions rolling through him. The Hamilton family loved him like his mother had. He'd been a fool to leave them without a word. No matter what had happened.

"Come on." Matt led the group to the family room, large enough to entertain the family and the HIS team.

Dropping onto the black leather couch, Jake glared at the group sitting on the other furniture in the room. "What's so damn funny?" Their laughing at him for no reason irked him. He could probably handle it if he knew why.

A wide, playful grin spread across AJ's face, causing Jake to become wary of what his brother would profess. "Did you *ask* Em to marry you, or did you *tell* her?"

Furrowing his dark brows at the question, Jake leaned back and crossed his arms over his chest, then closed his eyes. Oh hell, he'd fucked up again. He opened his eyes and sheepishly responded with an answer he knew wouldn't be appreciated by this group of men, "I told her."

His brothers shook their heads, almost in unison, with low-volume chuckles.

Decking each of them came to the forefront of Jake's mind, but the thoughts of fists on flesh set a cold sweat sweeping over his skin.

If he'd asked Em, she might've said no, especially with Trent in the picture. There was no way someone else would be a father to his child while he was alive.

His adversary, in his tight jeans showing all of his junk, walked in with Ken, who was the field team leader of the HIS men. He'd heard his brothers joke and call Trent "God's gift to women." At that moment, the man's woman was Em, and that had to end. Trent had been a playboy when Jake had left, and he doubted he'd changed. He wouldn't remain faithful to her, and Jake wouldn't let her be hurt like that, especially when his child was involved.

Leaning against the marble fireplace, his elbow on top of it, Trent scanned the group and smiled. "What's so funny?"

AJ, still on his roll to embarrass Jake, pointed his thumb toward him. "This one told Em they were getting married." He raised his brows and laughed. "Told."

This was not that fucking funny. AJ was having too much damn fun at his expense. He'd be sure to remember that when the tables were turned.

"Our stubborn, headstrong Em?"

That son of a bitch! Not only did he also break down laughing, but he'd also called her *our* Em. He'd show him *our*. Jake had begun to rise before he'd realized it and only had then because Matt placed a hand on his arm to stay him.

Ken returned from the kitchen with a bottle of water in his hands, oblivious to what was happening, or so it appeared. Jake couldn't tell with the man. "The boys called in." He took a long swig of water. "By the time they arrived at Em's work, the office was fully engulfed. Arson is, of course, suspected."

A variety of expletives erupted from the men in the room.

"Was anything recoverable?"

"They pulled some computer shit for you, Dev." He shrugged. "Router, server, no idea. It's melted down quite a bit, but they wanted to bring it back to you, just in case."

"I'd been worried about something happening since Em had called the SEC in the morning. That gave her employer plenty of time to get the hell out of there.

How did they get it?"

A sly smile crept on Ken's face. "The fire department was surprised at how quickly ATF arrived on the scene. The men never confirmed that's who they were, just went along with the assumption. Thankfully, no one asked the boys for a badge. I'm sure they'll be even more surprised when real ATF agents arrive."

A few hearty chuckles bounced around the room, bringing a lift back to the group for a moment.

"I'll see what I can do with it. Depending on how badly it was damaged, I might be able to pull something."

Jesse stood and began to pace. Something Jake remembered he did when he contemplated things. "We still don't know everything."

Water dribbled down the front of Ken's black T-shirt as he guzzled the remainder of the beverage. "It gets even more intriguing. While the rest of the team waited at Em's home, a cab pulled to the curb. When Rob stepped forward, the driver sped off." His jaw tightened. "My men couldn't make out who was in the back seat."

More expletives exploded from the group.

AJ stood. "I'll get her."

"I hate to say it, but we need to speak with Amber about it too," Matt added.

"Are you fucking nuts? She's fine now, but what will happen when you bring it all back up? There's only so much a three-year-old can handle." The redness on AJ's face deepened with every word.

Matt leaned forward, his forearms on his thighs, his hands clasped. "I know. I don't want to upset her either, but we need to know if she heard anything that can help." He glared at Jesse. "If you'd kept her kidnapper alive, maybe we'd have something."

Devon surged to his feet. "Enough! Don't even start the bickering. Em and Amber need us as a united group. You all know Matt's right. Jesse, you're the only one used to dealing with kids that closely. You should ask the questions."

AJ shook his head. "Em won't go for it."

Jake had had enough. "I won't fucking go for it! Do *not* bring this back up with my child. You know, the daughter you all failed to tell me about."

AJ cleared his throat, cutting into the tension that had engulfed the room. "I'll get Em."

Disgusted with them, himself, hell the situation, he had to leave. Jake rose from the couch and stomped out the French doors that led to the back deck and was greeted by Jamaal, another member of HIS, who guarded the back entrance.

Jake nodded and stepped off the deck and into the yard. Between the high temperature and humidity, sweat beaded his skin almost immediately, dampening the dress shirt he'd worn to make a good first impression on Em. A dip in the pool sounded good to cool down his body and temper. He glanced at the fence placed around it to protect the children.

Children.

He was a father. He thought he had his head wrapped around it until it came to the need to question his little girl. The thought of upsetting her, bringing up possible bad memories, made him sick to his stomach. It would have done the same thing to him if it had been any other little girl, but it seemed ten times worse since it was his daughter.

He pushed through the gate, walked to a chaise lounge by the pool and collapsed on it, exhausted both mentally and physically. Gaining his physical strength back was taking longer than he'd expected, and he still tired easily. He ate plenty, making up for being nearly starved to death with one meal a day, if he'd been lucky.

Kicking back in the chair, he covered his eyes with his forearm, successfully blocking out the sun, but not the tumultuous thoughts running round and round his mind. He had no idea what to do from here. Arthur had placed him on an extended leave from the bureau so he could recover. The bureau he'd quit.

Dammit! The man had to have known Amber was his. He was the only one who knew the entire story—what had happened that night with Em, where Jake had been, and that he had a daughter. His brothers had expressed their anger at Arthur for not telling them where he'd been until Devon found him through some of his mysterious computer work. Then, he'd waited to tell them that the FBI had been out of contact with Jake far too long.

Yeah. He was also pissed at the man.

"You doing okay?"

Jake lifted his arm to spy Jesse standing behind him, looking around the area as if he hadn't a care in the world. He knew that was far from the truth. As the oldest brother, he'd try to remove the burdens from his siblings' shoulders and willingly place them on his.

He covered his eyes again. "I don't fucking know. Em's pissed at me and hasn't told me Amber is my daughter or told our child."

A heavy sigh reached his ears. "What'd you

expect? In her mind, you left her high and dry. You just came back into her life. She just needs a bit of time to figure things out."

Hearing the truth from Jesse didn't make it easier to swallow. He'd been stupid, but he couldn't undo it. He could only hope to make amends. "I'm also pissed at all of you for fucking hiding it from me. I'm pissed at Arthur for not pulling me out right away when he learned Em was pregnant. I'm pissed at myself for how I handled things after AJ kicked me out. Right now, I'm just fucking overall pissed."

"As much as we'd all love to, we can't undo what's already been done. It's all about how things are handled from here. Do you plan to carry this anger and the feeling of been wronged with it? Or, are you willing to step up and be the man I know you can be? The man Em and Amber need."

Wow. Jesse had delivered that pile driver to Jake's heart with minimal effort. His brother was right, which also pissed him off. But releasing all of that anger wasn't easy, or he'd have dropped it already. Wouldn't he?

He'd lost so much by asking Arthur to help him disappear. That was what angered him the most. His actions. If he would've waited for tempers to cool so he'd cleared things up, Em wouldn't have been in New York, and he'd have been there for her and his daughter.

Jake understood why his brothers hadn't told him. That hadn't meant he agreed. However, he couldn't stay mad at the men who risked their lives to save him.

So how did he tamp down the anger at himself? Irritated with himself or not, he needed to man up as

Jesse implied.

His brother left him alone, and Jake decided he'd best get inside and see what was happening.

Back in the family room, Amber had taken full stage again. In AJ's arms, she recounted the tale of how Nemo could do tricks. Several heads turned to look at the granite countertop bar that separated the kitchen and family room to see if the bowl that Matt had placed there held a floating fish. A blue fish staring at them with its fin swishing back and forth brought out quiet sighs of relief throughout the room.

The tension and worry that had settled in the room, worrying how Amber would be after her kidnapping, relaxed. Apparently, the criminal had been excellent with her but hadn't wanted to be taken into custody. Thankfully, he'd allowed them to take Amber before he'd begun his deadly gunfight with the team.

Jesse eyed him, raising an eyebrow, a question in there. Jake nodded, signaling that he had a clear level head and was ready for what was about to happen.

"Em, we need to talk." When Jesse spoke, a hush fell over the room.

Trent walked to AJ, holding out his arms for Amber. "I'll take her until you need her." Exiting the room, he blew kisses on the little girl's stomach, eliciting the cutest giggle Jake had ever heard.

A red haze filled his vision. It should be him taking care of his daughter, not Em's lover. He wanted to scream and reach out and snatch his daughter from the man. But, he needed to hear what was happening. What had put his family in jeopardy? Yes, he considered them a family. The three of them. And they would be soon.

Emily plopped down, with AJ settling himself on the arm of her chair. "Sit your butts down. I hate it when you loom over me."

"Well, if you weren't so damn short."

She narrowed her eyes at Brad. "Do we want to talk short?"

Her brother scowled. His little sprite still had the ability to put her big brothers in place. Pride filled him, making him want to puff out his chest and tell the world this was the woman he loved.

He may have been in love with the eighteen-year-old Em, but he knew that no matter how much she'd changed, he'd still love everything about her. She'd been in his heart since they'd met.

Jesse led the conversation. "What's going on, Em? Why did someone kidnap my niece?"

AJ reached down to hold one of her fidgeting hands. Christ. Jake could see her visibly shaking. He felt the urge to jump up and pull her into his arms, making the world safe for her and his daughter.

"I'm not quite sure exactly what's going on. When I overheard my boss speaking with someone and said something about their Ponzi scheme, I freaked. I decided to call the SEC, but somehow got Paul, a crooked agent. He had to be in cahoots with my boss."

Jake wiped his sweating palms on his jeans, remembering how he'd almost fucked up any chance of rescuing Amber alive by knocking the man out. It was pure luck the man who kidnapped her didn't listen to his instructions, or Paul had lied about having to return in one hour.

"When I met Paul, he told me they had Amber and wanted something I had. He said I'd downloaded files from my computer. I have no idea what he was talking about."

Devon leaned forward on the couch. "Did he say anything else about the download? When? What it was?"

Em shook her head. "No."

Every muscle in Jake tightened, his pulse pounding in his ears, knowing this wasn't over. If they thought Em had something important enough to kidnap her daughter, they wouldn't give up. By the serious looks on the men's faces, they knew it as well.

"This is important, Em. Think back. What files had you accessed recently? Maybe you inadvertently downloaded them."

"I have. The only thing I'd been working on was an audit of Mr. Mills's account. The only problem there was my coworker had misplaced some of his money." She shrugged, removing her hand from AJ's. "I just don't know."

Emily furrowed her eyebrows, her face appearing deep in thought before her eyebrows bolted high enough that they almost touched her hairline. "Wait. When I went back to my desk after I'd heard Mr. Wright, his assistant was in my work area. She never would've waited for me there. She always told us her time was too valuable to wait for anyone and that's why we had to come to her when she needed to speak with us."

"Teri Sheppard?" Ken asked.

"That's her. Did you talk to her?"

"No. The boys said it looked as if she'd packed a bag or two and left hurriedly."

By this time, Jake wanted to fly back to New York

City and beat the shit out of some people until he got the answers they needed. He'd remained out of the conversation until now. Sure, he wasn't part of the brothers' security company, but he was family. "What happened this morning?"

Her eyes met his for the first time since they'd been in the room and an electrical storm zipped between them, almost knocking him off-balance. Nothing that strong had passed between them before. He tried to hold on to it, but she cast her gaze away. *Fuck. She doesn't want to look at me.*

Em relayed what had transpired in her meeting with Paul and subsequent interaction with Jake.

No one looked his way or appeared to condemn him for what he'd done when he'd thought he was protecting her. He wiped his hand over his face, exhausted and frustrated. None of this helped them. "Shit. The two men we know were involved are not available to question."

A snort escaped Brad. "One of them permanently."

Jake caught the slight nod Jesse gave AJ. He held his breath, knowing the question his brother was about to ask.

AJ turned to Em, pulling her hand on his thigh and covering it tightly. "We have to talk with Amber."

He'd never seen someone stand so quickly. Her protectiveness made him want to smile. It meant she'd been a great mother, not that he'd really expected any different. She'd always mothered them.

"No way!"

AJ stood in front of her, reached out and held her by the shoulders. "Em, we don't want to do it, but we must. She might know something to help us."

Her eyes watering had Jake jumping to his feet. "I agree with her. Leave Amber alone." He fisted his hands at his sides, ready to swing at anyone who disagreed. He'd never felt so violent, especially against this group, until his daughter was involved.

"Look, we'll be easy with her."

"Jesse, please…."

"Trust me, Em." After she nodded, he turned to Jake, pointing a finger toward his chest. "And you, back off."

Jesse's eyes remained locked with his until he reluctantly consented with a short, sharp nod.

"Ken, get Trent and Amber."

The mention of the man's name made Jake's blood boil. He needed this shit to be over with so he could kick Trent to the curb and marry Em. Hell, nothing was stopping him from marrying her. If she fought him, he'd tie her up and carry her to the church. He didn't care if a shotgun wedding was what they had. He knew she still had to have some love for him. She was just hiding it for some reason.

Amber raced into the room, heading straight for Em. "Mommy, *Unca Twent thay* bad *woid*."

Another fucking bad mark against the man. That was it. He was talking to Em right after all this. She was dumping Trent, and the two of them were getting married. It shouldn't be a problem, as it was something she'd always wanted. Christ, he'd heard it enough growing up.

Trent shrugged sheepishly. "It just slipped out."

The little girl pointed at Jake. "*He nice.*"

His gaze snapped from Amber to Em to see what she would say…what she would do.

She looked from their daughter to him with uncertainty in her eyes.

His heart stopped for a brief moment, and his breath caught as if all the air was sucked from the room. Maybe Em would tell his daughter the truth. He wasn't sure he was ready. Hell, he could turn out like his father.

Jake's pulse raced. *Good God, what if I turn out like my dad? Amber deserves better than that.* But, he'd promised himself he'd never be like the man, and now was the time to keep that promise. He knew what not to do. Now he had to figure out what to do.

No one moved while Em walked toward him, Amber's hand in hers. He watched the hard swallow slip down Em's throat.

Nervousness skidded up his spine. She was going to do it.

"Amber, this…this is…your daddy."

The little girl's eyes widened, and Jake knelt when she walked to him. Reaching out her hands, she put them on his face and whispered, "Daddy?"

Jake couldn't bring any words forward to answer. He blinked rapidly to clear the tears that had formed in his eyes. Gaining control of his emotions, he nodded. "Yes, princess."

She squealed and launched herself into his embrace, her short arms hugging him so tight he almost choked. Snippets of hands wrapped around his throat, cutting off his breathing, squeezing the life out of him, flashed before him. He snagged the little girl and yanked her arms from around him.

A rapid heartbeat banged against his chest, and his breath came in short, jerky puffs. He blinked the little girl into focus. It wasn't a terrorist torturing him. It was only his daughter. His sweet daughter who looked at him with confusion in her eyes.

He had to get a grip. Standing, he pulled her back to him and held her in his arms. He closed his eyes and sighed in contentment.

He hoped no one noticed his reaction.

He looked back at the world around him. Tears slid down Em's face. With his hands full, he couldn't reach out and wipe them away for her. He did mouth the words, "Thank you," receiving a brief nod from her in reply.

Amber loosened her hold, leaned back, and looked at him. Jake shifted her to his arm like he'd seen Em do and smiled. It felt so natural to hold her.

"You came home like Mommy *thaid*."

"Yes, Daddy's come home." Home. It was where he'd remain—home. No matter what.

He was thankful she was too young to understand how long he'd been away from her. This child amazed him. She'd had a big day—kidnapped and then meeting her father for the first time—and she held up as if it were a normal day.

"Put me down."

He bent over to set the girl on her feet before she fell from his hold. When he stood, he noticed the room was vacant except for him, Em, and Amber. When the hell had that happened?

"I need to tell *uncas Daddy home*." Amber raced from the room.

"Em."

She turned from watching her daughter race away. "What, Jake?"

Was that hostility he detected in her voice? The men's joking came back to him. He hadn't asked her to marry him. Did he dare? He wouldn't allow any other answer than yes, and her current demeanor didn't emanate any semblance of a yes to anything he said, but he had to try.

Taking her hand in his, he pulled her a step closer to him. "Let's talk about getting married."

Before she could respond, a loud ruckus came from the front of the house as the rest of the family arrived. In a whirlwind of movement and noise, Em was out of his hold and hugging her father as they whispered to each other, a tear sliding down her face. Jake could've sworn Blake's eyes were also wet. When they finally broke apart, her sisters-in-law rushed to them, each pulling her into a tight embrace.

His hope to gain an answer from her disappeared. He was truly happy to see the rest of the family; he only wished they'd arrived at a different time. Smiling, he allowed himself to be drawn into the chaos that now reigned around him with adults, children, and pets greeting each other.

Reagan skipped behind Amber. The cousins stopped in front of him, and his daughter pointed. "*That my* daddy."

Joy swirled within him. One of the best things possible had turned in his favor. His daughter had happily accepted him.

Chapter Eight

Emily's sisters-in-law herded her into a guest room on the pretense of Megan needing rest after the flight. Although dragging her and Kate along wasn't questioned by anyone. She remembered getting away with anything with her brothers when she'd been pregnant. She'd found the one thing the men feared: a pregnant woman.

"Wait. I don't want to leave Amber." After the events of the day, she didn't want to let her child out of her sight. Those few minutes, when she'd been in another room with Trent, had been pure torture. She trusted her family, but her daughter could get lost in the mix, and someone could snatch her with no one noticing.

Kate touched her arm, empathy in her eyes. "It's okay. You know your brothers won't allow anything to happen to her while she's with them. Besides, I imagine Devon and AJ have two girls and a dog tackling them."

Devon had somehow become Reagan's favorite uncle, and AJ had become Amber's. The men would roll around on the floor playing with the little girls, acting a fool and not caring.

Megan collapsed on the bed and rubbed her hand over her swollen belly. "Well? Did you tell him?"

Emily sat on the chest that still held some of Jesse's childhood toys and sighed heavily. She had expected this question would be the first thing from the women. Although she'd never told them that Jake was the father, her brothers, who couldn't keep their mouths closed with their wives, had spilled the beans. "I told them both."

Kate took a seat next to Megan on the bed. "And?"

"I couldn't help it. He stood up so protectively of her with my brothers. Then Amber singled him out. It felt right to tell them." She looked down. "I cried. For a moment, I thought he was going to as well." He hadn't tried to disguise the wetness behind his eyelids.

She'd wanted to see her daughter with Jake for so long, and it was more beautiful than she'd imagined. Although his initial reaction to Amber's hug confused her. He'd jerked her away like he'd been frightened of her. But, then he'd pulled her back close.

She had a decision to make. Emily didn't think he'd give up on the marriage thing. Why wasn't she jumping for joy? It had been her dream for as long as she could remember. She couldn't forget the embarrassment of his leaving her. "He told me we were getting married."

Kate's brows raised and a ghost of a smile touched her lips. "Told you?"

She nodded and chuckled. It hadn't been funny at the time, but the more she thought about it, the more it became one of those shake-your-head moments. "Yep, told."

Megan gasped and covered her mouth. "He didn't!"

"He sounds like one of the Hamilton men," Kate added.

Emily smiled. They truly didn't know how to ask

for things.

"What happened this morning? All I caught was Jesse rushing off the phone and telling me to grab a flight home," Kate said. "It hadn't made sense since he and AJ had planned to meet us in DC before we flew to Oxford next week for Jason's birthday surprise."

"I hadn't heard of this. What's the surprise?" She couldn't believe they'd not shared this with her before now.

Kate leaned back on her elbows. "You know how he is about football."

Emily nodded. The entire family knew about it. After they'd found his leukemia in remission, Jason had tried out for quarterback at his junior high school. It had been all he'd talked about when he'd been in the hospital before Jesse and Kate had adopted him. They'd all worked with him, improving his strength, stamina, and arm. Wanting him to have a fighting chance, Jesse had hired a trainer to help him perfect his aim and understand how to run the team on the field.

It had worked. He was now the starting quarterback, and the high school coach was already talking with him.

"Since your dad goes every year, he decided to take Jason to Ole Miss's opening game. He somehow finagled a suite from someone and locker room passes for Jesse and Jason."

"That is perfect for him. Wait. Why didn't anyone tell me about it?"

The two women on the bed glanced at each other.

"What?" Emily asked in a strained voice.

Megan seemed to muster the courage to spill the beans and reveal the secret to her. "Well, the men knew you would say no, so your dad had planned to call your boss, and AJ was to show up and take you and Amber along."

She surged to her feet, blood barreled through her veins, spiking her temper. "They what?" She was going to kill them. How dare they think to manhandle her into doing something she didn't want to do? Actually, she would've said yes if they'd asked her. What the hell made them think she'd say no? It wasn't like they'd expected Jake to be here.

Kate snorted laughter. "Yeah. We told them it was a bad idea."

Waving her hand in the air, Megan shook her head. "Who cares about that right now? What are you going to do about Jake?"

What was she going to do? It was the focus of her thoughts. It was too much to process, though. "I don't know. It's been a trying day, and I don't want to think about it."

Kate furrowed her eyebrows. "What happened today? We only got bits and pieces."

The last thing she wanted to do was recount the story again. Each time, knowing her little girl had been in danger and in the hands of a criminal, she choked up, and her heart sped up to an uncomfortable level.

But this was her family, so Emily told her story again to her captive audience. "It started when…."

****

"EM, can we talk?"

Dammit. Jake cornered her as she left Reagan's bedroom where Amber slept in the second twin bed. The little girl had been exhausted and had fallen asleep quickly. Emily had kissed her goodnight, worrying what their future held. Apparently, it was time to discuss it.

She swallowed hard, determined to find her voice and speak without letting her anger show. "Sure."

"Is she asleep?"

"Yes."

"May I…may I see her?"

Emily almost gaped at him. Was the man choked up? Or was he nervous? Either way, it wasn't the Jake she'd known. He'd been fearless and smiled all the time, and while he'd become emotional when times warranted, she'd never seen him like this.

His curiosity about their daughter pleased her. She hadn't wanted him to run again once he'd learned about Amber. Questions still remained. Where had he been, why had he left her, and why was he back? She expected she'd learn soon enough. Somehow, she doubted her brothers would allow him to get away without an explanation. Hell, she wouldn't allow him to get away without one. "Come on."

Relief and joy emanated from him, and her heart leaped for her daughter. It soared for herself also despite how she tried to brush the emotions away. She placed her finger on her lip to signal quiet.

A look of pure love bled from him as he watched his daughter sleep. At one time, Emily had always hoped for that much love from him. But she no longer knew what she wanted.

She lightly touched his arm, ignoring the heat shooting through her hand to guide him out of the room. Closing the door, she turned to him. He was such a handsome man. Tall, like her brothers, he hovered over her by a full head. Now that she took a good look at him, he wasn't as thin as she'd thought. His broad shoulders stood strong, and his arm muscles bulged beneath his shirt. However, he was leaner than he'd been when he'd left. Maybe times had been tough for him and food hadn't been a priority. But, then he surely would have come home sooner.

"We have to talk, Em."

She nodded and led him downstairs, then passed between the family room and kitchen to the patio. Without looking back, assuming he followed, she chose a set of chairs at the far end of the deck.

"Les, can you give us a bit of space?" Jake said.

Emily snapped her head around. She'd been so focused on her path and tamping down her anger enough to speak calmly, that she hadn't noticed Les, their resident cowboy on the HIS team, patrolling nearby. Did her brothers think it necessary to have this protection? She didn't recall them ever having it when she'd visited before. Sure, the men had been around, but not in this protective mode.

Both of them settled on the brown, cushioned chairs; their gazes focused on the well-lit backyard, and the sound of crickets breached the silence. Even after dark, the heat and humidity were stifling, and beads of sweat formed on her skin almost immediately. Grasping the neckline of her blouse, she waved it to pull air inside and cool herself.

Jake reached behind him and flipped the switch to turn on the ceiling fan with hands that distracted her. She'd remembered his large hands running over her body when she'd become a woman.

Did he regret it? He must've to stay away for so long. Her mind reeled. What was he planning to say?

She didn't want to hear about him marrying her again.

His chair creaked as he turned his body to her, heat rising as she felt him observing her. Heat from his gaze. Heat from her fury. She loved him with an intensity that hadn't scared her when she was younger, but now, terrified her. He'd rejected her, abandoned her, leaving her devastated.

Tears stung her eyes, but this was finally the moment of truth.

"It's a beautiful night, isn't it?"

Ignoring his question, she turned to him. "Why, Jake? Why did you abandon me?" She threw up her hands, her voice rising in volume. Watching him cringe at exactly what she'd said took the wind out of her sails. When she'd been twelve, she'd heard him and AJ talking about how his father had abandoned him and how much he hated the word. Shit. She hadn't meant to be such a bitch. Well, maybe a bit, but not like that.

"Em, it's not…." Jake cleared his throat and took a shaky breath. "Em, I'm sorry."

The tremor in his voice had her emotions regrouping on their own, pushing her to allow him to explain, to give him a chance to say the right things. Whatever they might be.

"That's four years too late." The anguish plastered on his face cooled her blood, making her heart ache for him. Then she kicked herself. He deserved to feel like that. How did he think she'd felt all these years? If this was difficult for him, then so be it.

"I know. I know. I shouldn't have handled things the way I did. If I could go back and do it again, things would've been different."

Emily wanted to ask how they'd be different, but

107

she was afraid of his answer. What if that difference didn't include the two of them together? Once he found out she was pregnant, he'd have married her, out of obligation, not out of love, which was the only way she wanted him.

As she wrestled with the indecision of what to ask, how to handle the rest of their conversation, Dottie, Kate's pregnant Dalmatian, bounded out of her doggie door and bee-lined straight for her. Their bomb-sniffing dogs, Daisy and Bomber, didn't have the run of the place like the Dal. Rubbing behind the dog's ears, sending white fur flying, she decided to jump in with both feet, giving him that chance, hoping her heart wasn't about to shatter again with his answer, that he wouldn't make her feel any smaller than she did by seducing him when he hadn't wanted it. "What happened? Where were you? Why didn't you stay and fight for me, for us?"

He let out a deep, exasperated sigh and hung his head low. He looked so vulnerable that she wanted to hug him to her breast and assure him everything was okay. But, it wasn't, so why pretend? Capturing her gaze with a tortured look in his eyes almost made her want to take back her questions. But she had to know.

Breaking eye contact, he looked over the yard again and chuckled lightly. "That's quite a few questions at once, but I wouldn't expect less from you, sprite."

When he called her by the name only he'd been allowed to use when she was growing up, her heart did a little flip-flop. As a girl, she considered it his endearment to her. His expression of love. She'd been so wrong, so very wrong.

"It's a long story."

"Let's start with why you left and didn't call me or anyone else? We thought you were dead. Do you know how that made me feel, knowing I'd have to tell our daughter that?" She had to stop before he caught how choked up she'd become.

"I really don't know what to say that can make it right. As for leaving," he began and turned back to her, "I was in shock when AJ woke me." He paused. "You see, I wasn't…." A lump visibly slid down his throat. "Em, I wasn't awake."

Closing her eyes to the tears that quickly formed, she turned away. She'd known in her heart he'd never completely woken up, but she'd hoped and prayed that he had. When his eyes had slid open for those few moments, she'd thought he'd realized it was her. Was this his cop out?

"You called out my name," she whispered, turning back to him.

"I didn't realize." He rubbed his forehead and then wiped his hand gradually down his face. "I thought I had an erotic dream with you in it. At the time, I didn't realize it was truly happening."

It took her a moment to understand his response. He'd actually dreamed about having sex with her? That would explain it. And deep down, she'd known. "I'm sorry. I knew you were drunk. I shouldn't have—"

"You have nothing to apologize for." Jake flashed a sexy smile. "It was an amazing night."

"Then why did you leave?"

"I didn't know what to think. There wasn't really time to process everything before AJ tossed me out."

She crossed her arms over her chest. "You know he

would've cooled off after a day or two."

"Well, that's where the story gets long. It was too late."

Once she'd learned of his trip to Arthur, the undercover assignment, and his captivity, every bit of anger and disappointment with him evaporated. Her heart contracted with compassion, leaving her feeling lighter. Yet, it still stuck with her that he'd run instead of turning around, fighting for them, and the lividness slowly returned, seeping back into her blood.

"I was stupid, Em. I know I should've come back. You deserved that. I was a coward. I didn't want to face your father or brothers. What I did was wrong."

Oh God. Did he mean having sex with her had been wrong? Was that how he really felt?

"I won't leave you again. You or Amber." Regret dominated the tone of his voice. "Will you tell me about her?"

Had he not run away, she wouldn't have to tell him about his own daughter. Dammit. She couldn't let it go; even knowing she needed to for her daughter's sake. Emily wouldn't make a fool of herself again. He didn't love her, and she wouldn't allow herself to love him that deeply again and have her heart ripped out. Again.

With a palpable, undeniable strain on their relationship, she regaled him with the years he'd missed in Amber's life, sure she'd caught his eyes shimmering with unshed tears.

Chapter Nine

An uncomfortable silence permeated the air between them. Jake had planned the picnic by the pond well. The women watched Amber so she and Jake could be alone, and he'd had Mrs. Kessler make a small feast of Emily's favorites that he'd spread out on a soft blanket. She snacked without a word except in direct response to a question.

Had he thought that after explaining himself, she would fall into his arms and declare her love and willingness to marry him? She'd sat up the night before, unable to sleep, thinking about all that he'd told her. He'd made a mistake by taking the assignment with the FBI, but he'd still left. She couldn't resolve herself to forgive him for that. Not yet.

To top it off, finding out he was a father, he suddenly wanted to be a family. Even though he said differently, it had to be because of Amber. No way would he appear after all of these years and just want to marry her. While she wanted that to be the case, she wasn't that gullible.

Casting a glance in his direction, she almost drooled as he leaned back on his arms and dropped his head back to soak up the sun. Her gaze ran the length of his body. Thin or not, he still had a presence that drew her to him. That had not changed.

Her heat level rose, and she knew it had nothing to

do with the sun beating down on them. She'd been cool enough in her shorts and tank top. This heat blended through her veins and made her mouth water for a taste of him.

If she reached over and touched him, this time, they could make love while he was awake. She craved his hands sliding down her body, shooting desire through every nerve ending. Her nipples hardened at the thought. Oh, it would be so easy to climb over to him, slip his T-shirt over his head and run her hands over his chest before sliding herself down on his hard shaft with a heady sigh.

But no. She wouldn't give in to her baser instinct. Then he'd think all was well between them, and she'd acquiesce and marry him, being the good wife to make him feel like a responsible adult. It wouldn't work like that with her. If he wanted her, he had to win her heart back. That would be a tough feat since she'd locked it away from him and hidden the key.

Romancing her today with this time together, and his catering to her, did knock at the door of the vault. She ignored the attempted intrusion. Instead, she smiled at him. "Thank you, Jake."

He turned his head to her with an uncertain smile. He'd been nervous the entire time. In truth, it was their first date, so maybe he had a good reason. "I'm glad you enjoyed it."

Emily wiped her hands on a napkin and scanned the pond, looking everywhere but at him. The vulnerability she caught in his eyes hit her gut with a punch. He wasn't sure how to handle the day, either.

"We can go for a swim if you'd like," he offered.

She did need cooling off, but she feared even the

pond wouldn't be enough. Looking at him, the sweat that trickled down the side of his face called to her to wipe it for him and then maybe kiss the area. She mentally shook her head. She'd been without sex for far too long, if that turned her to putty. "No. I'm not wearing a suit." Although swimming without suits did hold its merits.

With a crook of his brow and a wicked grin, he responded in a challenging voice, "Who said anything about suits?"

A shiver of delight slipped down her spine. She couldn't break the connection between their gaze. The flame of desire in his eyes grew with each moment. Surely hers did the same, but he couldn't know she wanted him, though. He had to work for it.

Emily cleared her throat and looked away. "No. But I'd like to walk along the edge."

Jake sprang to his feet and reached out a hand to help her stand. She hesitated a moment and prepared herself for the electric contact before taking it. Standing beside each other, he stared at her for a moment before dropping her hand.

Releasing a pent-up breath, she followed his lead and kicked off her shoes before turning to the pond. They'd only taken a couple of steps before he clasped her hand back in his. She stiffened, not ready for the intimacy, but wanting it more than anything. She forced a calm to cascade through her body.

Dipping her toe into the cool water, she peeked up at him. Holding his hand, touching him—he'd always been the one.

He tugged on their hold. "We talked about Amber last night. Thank you for that. Now, I want to know what you've been doing."

She took a deep breath. "There's not much to tell. I went to school and raised our daughter."

His jaw tightened, and he squeezed her hand. "Let's go sit on the dock."

She spied it on the other side of the pond, closest to the house. The walk would do them good, maybe put some distance between them physically so she could think straight. "Okay."

Turning, he didn't release her hand as she'd expected. Truthfully, she wanted to keep holding it, keep feeling the warmth of his touch.

"Did you enjoy college?"

Had she? It had been a means to an end. While her friends went to frat parties and dated, she'd had a child at home who depended on her, and her free thoughts had been of only one man. The man beside her now.

The late nights of studying. The days of leaving her baby in someone else's care. It hadn't been easy. Thinking back, she wouldn't change any of it because it gave her and her daughter independence. Of course, she'd have preferred Jake beside her during it all.

"It was fine." She raised and dropped her shoulders. "It was school."

He shook his head and laughed. "College was never fine. What course did you dislike the most?"

"Biology." Cutting up small animals just to see their insides turned her stomach. If she hadn't needed the credits in science, she'd have boycotted the class.

"Did you take Professor Donaldson?"

Jerking her head in his direction, she gasped. "Yes. Did you have him too?"

With a gentle tug, her brought her a little closer,

their hands swinging in perfect harmony with their steps. "Yep. Hated the old geezer. He gave the most god-awful homework." He shuddered.

A laugh bubbled up from her chest and escaped. This was what they needed to break through the tension. Common ground. "I almost failed the class."

He stopped and stared at her with a surprised expression. "Are you kidding me?"

She pulled his hand to keep him moving. "Yeah. I've always hated science classes." Give her math any day, and she'd be tickled pink. Thank goodness, they only had to have a few science courses to graduate.

"I remember."

Those two words wrapped themselves around her in comfort. He'd paid attention to her when they were growing up together. She wanted to drill him for everything he could remember, to see how much he paid attention to her. But that could also be disappointing. "Well, it's over. If Amber ever needs help with her science classes, she'll have to have a tutor."

His thumb slipped between their hands and stroked her palm. Goose bumps ran up her arm, and sexual awareness tingled in its descent to her core. She closed her eyes. Damn the man.

"I'll tutor her. I may have disliked the classes, but I did well." He turned to her with a crooked smile. "Eventually."

Sure he could tutor. She wouldn't dream of denying their daughter her father. He just wouldn't be there all the time because they wouldn't be married. Not until he wanted to marry her because he loved her.

They stood at the tip of the pier, the silence

comfortable this time. They'd grown up with a pond at her father's house and a pier similar to the one they occupied. So many times she'd followed Jake and AJ out when they'd snuck away to swim. In fact, he'd only just moved in with them, but he'd been the one to spend the most time teaching her to swim.

That was probably when she first fell in love with him. At six, what did she know? Infatuation. Love. It was all the same thing to a child. But she never forgot all those moments.

Next thing she knew, an arm wrapped around her waist and another grabbed under her knees. Knowing what he planned, she kicked and squealed but to no avail. He pulled her close to his chest before he launched them into the air.

Her nose burned as water rushed up it. *Damn him!* She surfaced, sputtering and coughing. "Jake Cavanaugh!"

He kept one hand on her waist, holding her an arm's length from him as they tread water. "Yes, sprite?" His loving, playful tone prompted her laughter. This she'd missed.

She swatted at his chest, eager to move away yet desperate to move closer. "That wasn't funny."

"I beg to differ." He inched closer, then with the hand at her waist, he released her to rub a thumb down her cheek ever so tenderly, his eyes turning dark as desire took over.

A tremor built deep within her and the breath rushed from between her lips. Did he plan to kiss her? Oh how she wanted it badly. She remembered the warmth of his lips and the stroke of his tongue. Plenty of nights were spent dreaming of them. Would he kiss her with such fervor while awake?

She swam closer. "I don't know about this."

"I do." His voice, a husky murmur, brought her to her senses. She would not just jump into bed with him.

Emily pushed away and floated on her back, ignoring the rapid beating of her traitorous heart. The push and pull of her libido, the battle raging within, drove her to the steps of the pier. She pulled herself up the ladder, water sloshing from her clothes, and studiously ignored Jake calling her. Instead, she walked back to their picnic. She needed space. Otherwise, she might fall into him and beg him to take her.

He caught up to her after she'd disposed of everything on the blanket to pick it up and wrap it around herself like a safety blanket.

"Em, look at me." The pleading in his voice drew her gaze. He reached out, grasped the top edges of the blanket, and moved her closer to him. She couldn't fight him. His lips met her forehead in a tender kiss. "I'll wait until you're ready."

Did he realize that could be an awfully long wait? She might want him with every fiber of her being, but she might never be ready again.

****

Jake couldn't decide if his new sisters-in-law were a godsend or the Devil's spawn. Kate and Megan had read him the riot act on how he'd best treat Em. He'd never been dressed down so expertly in his life. They reminded him of how much she had been hurt, and they needed to ensure he was serious. No way was he toying with his true love's emotions as the women had worried.

Only after they felt comfortable with his pursuing

Em did they agree to keep everyone out of the way so he could romance to his heart's content. The problem was he didn't really know romance. He'd never had to work to get a woman in college. Of course, he'd never wanted one to love him either.

Megan's idea of a picnic the day before had worked. Em's resistance had cooled, and she seemed open to him. He'd also seen her watching him with heat in her eyes. God, he wanted to make the leap in their relationship to physical. He needed to touch her. But, he held strong, barely, needing her to be sure about her feelings for him first.

Now what, though? He didn't want to go to the women and ask what else he should do to win Em's heart. He couldn't take her to a nice romantic dinner because they were still keeping her out of the public eye.

He'd spent half of the night worrying about this thing with Em's work. He worried more about Amber. But, not her safety with the Ponzi scheme issue. It was her safety with him. That initial hug and his reaction—almost freaking out—still bothered him. Sure nothing had happened since, but was he capable of being the loving father his daughter deserved? Or, would he freak out on her, haunted by his nightmare?

"Do you want to play Scrabble?" Em stood from the couch and walked to the shelf holding board games and pulled one out before he responded. Her tight backside in green capri pants filled his vision, ripping his worrisome thought from his mind. A bolt of heat shot to his groin.

He'd only had his hand for a companion since the night he'd left the Hamilton house all those years ago.

Em had been his fantasy woman during that time. Since returning, whenever he saw her, he fought whisking her in his arms and carrying her to bed.

Looking at her tight rear, he wanted to walk up behind her, yank down her pants and plunge deep inside her until his cock was covered in her sweet juices. This waiting for her to be ready was hell.

She turned, a hopeful smile on her face. It hadn't been what he'd wanted to do to romance her, but he had no idea what else to do at the moment that didn't involve tossing her to the ground. So, Scrabble it was.

He slid his chair over to the coffee table, across from the seat she'd vacated, and rubbed his hands together. Time alone was time alone. He'd take advantage. "Bring it on."

Laughing, she returned to her spot and pulled out the board and pieces. "I remember playing with everyone when we were growing up. I don't think you ever won."

"Ha-ha. Very funny. I will have you know that I did win one time." Although she hadn't been playing, or he probably wouldn't have won then. She had no idea that in the beginning, the brothers would throw the game so she could win. Then she challenged them so much they couldn't find a way to beat her.

She shook the bag of letters and then opened it, holding it out to him. "Draw."

Their hands brushed, and heat worked its way up his arm. Their gazes locked and he could tell by the fire starting in her eyes that she'd felt the connection. He hesitated for a moment, wanting to pull her close, but instead, he reached in and pulled out a game piece to see who went first. His mind focused more on shifting to get comfortable than on the actual letter in his hand.

She reached into the bag, played around with the game pieces, and then pulled one out. "A." She beamed proudly.

Jake shook his head and chuckled. It had already started with her luck in letters. "Okay, sprite. Do your best."

Em narrowed her eyes and scrunched up her face. His chuckle cut off any words she might have said. Instead, she turned her focus to her game pieces.

Three turns later, and she was already kicking his ass with her double-word scores. He didn't pay attention to potential words on his rack. Instead, he leaned forward, his forearms on his knees, and silently observed her.

Em stared down at her letters, extreme concentration on her face. He had the urge to reach out and smooth the deep groove that had formed between her brow. He feared if he touched her, he might not stop.

"Covered." She laid the tiles on the board in their respective boxes. "Double-word score and all seven letters."

He jerked his attention back to the game. Son of a bitch. He hadn't cared if he won the game or not; he'd just wanted the time with her, but to have his ass kicked this badly? No way. "Lucky."

She smirked and played around in the bag to refill her letter holder. "Be jealous all you want." Damn if she didn't smile broader when she saw her new letters.

This game with his fun-loving Em had been a great idea. Seeing her laugh and not worry about anything lightened his spirit. They would have plenty of fun family nights to enjoy each other. And for her to kick his ass at board games.

Reaching down, he shuffled his letters around, hoping to find more than a measly three-letter word worth three whole points.

"How long do you think they'll keep us here?"

He stilled his hand at the fear in her voice. Oh, how he wanted to pull her on his lap and hold her, assuring her he would keep them safe. "It's only been a few days." He looked at her and shrugged, hoping to convince her there was no danger to her and their daughter while here. "They just need a bit of time."

"I know. I just wish…." She trailed off in a wistful voice.

That was it. The men had to work harder. She deserved to be free to do as she wished without worrying about her daughter being kidnapped or worse. He had to push them to resolve this. It rankled him that he couldn't do more than be there for his family. While a couple of men from HIS were in New York City, the team depended heavily on Devon to dig into anything electronic that he could find to tell them who might be responsible.

On a much-needed break between assignments, her brothers and the team hadn't grumbled a word or blinked an eye when it came to protecting Emily and Amber. They didn't plan to relax their security of the place even though it already had one of the best security systems available. No one would breach the property. If they did, Jake might take him down bare-handed himself. The asshole had been responsible for taking his daughter and for causing pain and heartache to his Em.

If only he'd allowed them to tell Em he'd been

Sheila Kell

alive, she might've been visiting them with Amber instead of being alone in New York City. He'd been selfish about how she saw him for the first time, and his daughter had paid the price.

Of course, if he'd never left in the first place, none of this would have happened. He needed a mental slap for thinking of that again. Those thoughts had no place. He couldn't change them. He could only move forward and be the man he was. The man who loved her and Amber with everything he was.

She cocked her head. "I think I'll help Devon."

"I think he's counting on it. Let him do the digging first." Jake gave her what he hoped was his most charming smile before he looked down at the game board. He rubbed his hands together. "First, let me whoop some ass at Scrabble."

Hearing her chuckle set his mind at ease. Somewhat. He didn't want her to fret about it. That was his job. And, he'd been doing it every second since everything had happened. She didn't need to know that. She needed to think him calm and confident so the situation would resolve itself quickly.

He still had to think it through. If Devon didn't find a clue, how long did they keep Em and Amber under wraps? He planned to protect them for the rest of his life, but to live like this wasn't in the plan. Being around the family was great, but being around the family meant little time without them being involved in their lives.

No matter what, he would help find the person responsible for creating the upheaval in her life. They would pay for having his daughter kidnapped. Yet, even in the midst of his need to see her safe, he couldn't stop

122

wondering what happened after this? If they found out who was responsible too soon, he might not have won her heart back, and she might push to be on her own, without him.

Yet, he couldn't fathom it taking long. He just wanted his little family living together, alone and, most importantly, safe. He wanted to curl up every night next to the woman he loved after kissing their daughter goodnight.

They would be together. There were no ifs, ands, or buts about it. He wouldn't rest until she was in his arms forever. As for being a good father, he'd have to figure it out as he went along.

"Quip with the letter q on a double-letter spot." Spending time with her like this was a good start. She only had to get comfortable with him again. He was sure of it.

She laughed in that sweet voice that tugged at his heartstrings. "You're going to have to do better than that to catch me, Jake."

"Oh, I plan to," he murmured in answer, knowing they had different interpretations of her statement.

Chapter Ten

Jake glared at Emily. "Please do the smart thing and stay on the airplane."

She clenched her fists and wanted to sock him in the nose. This wasn't the romancing Jake she'd been dealing with lately. This was the alpha with his arms crossed over his chest screaming, "You'd better listen to me," Jake. Although he pissed her off like that, he was damn sexy. A delicious shiver jumped through her veins. She mentally shook her head and relaxed. It was not the time.

"No, I'm not staying on the plane. It's not your landlord who called and said your home had been broken into and tossed." She jammed her thumb in her chest. "It's mine, and I'm going to see if anything was taken."

"Dammit, Em. You shouldn't even be here. It's not safe."

She raised her eyebrows in question. "How can I not be safe? I have my own armed guard with me."

He looked around the small plane on its way to New York City. Her brothers napped or chatted quietly. Turning back to Emily, Jake sighed in resignation. "Will you at least wait until they clear things?"

Good grief. She wasn't so stupid as to run right into her home, not after her last experience in her hometown. She smiled. Let him think he'd convinced her to wait. Based on how her brothers reacted to their wives doing the same thing, it was a magic balm to their ego. "Of course."

He nodded and then looked at the window, leaving her alone with her thoughts.

Even though the police officer who'd contacted her had told her otherwise, Emily knew this wasn't a random home invasion, and she suspected nothing would be missing. She didn't have what they were looking for, and she couldn't tell any officer she met what she suspected. HIS wanted first crack at it since it affected family. But, that didn't keep her from demanding her brothers take her with them. She'd been pleased that Jake insisted on coming along also. Having him near calmed her nervousness and fear. Yes, she remained afraid about what could happen, but she trusted her family to protect her. And, she trusted the men from HIS who'd stayed back to keep her precious daughter safe.

This incident told her they, whomever they were, wouldn't stop until they got what they wanted or until HIS caught them. God, she hoped it was soon. She and Amber had a life to live that didn't require hiding out with her family. Yet, the time with Jake….

"Em, snap out of it," Jesse said.

She looked up at her older brother, who stood beside her. "Sorry. What?" Surely pink tinged her cheeks. She was that embarrassed at where her thoughts had been about to take a turn.

He grinned knowingly and then sat beside her. "Brad and Matt are going to go to your old boss and coworkers' places again. We'll have you call them from your home while we're there."

Emily missed being able to use her cell phone, but Jesse had demanded she turn it off until this was over. She drew her brows together in thought. "So, you think Teri is the one who downloaded the information?" It made perfect sense. No one had said it aloud before, but she could see it happening. The woman had been alone near Emily's computer. And, thinking about it, there had been a file open on her desktop that she hadn't opened when she'd rushed to shut it down in her escape.

Jesse waited until after the pilot informed them they were landing before he spoke. "I can't be sure, but it's a possibility. The big question is whether they are together or not." He patted her leg before buckling his seat belt.

The landing and deplaning had gone well, as had the trip to her house and her waiting for the men to secure the area. Then, she walked into her home. Jake stood beside her. She'd barely registered him holding her hand and squeezing it. Someone had destroyed almost everything.

The sofa had been sliced open and stuffing tossed across the room. Books from her bookshelf were strewn on the floor. DVDs had been pulled from their spot and opened. She sniffed. Some were broken. Actually, many things were broken as the burglars had either knocked items out of the way or broken them on purpose. Probably to see if she'd hidden anything inside.

And, that was just the living room. She wasn't sure she wanted to see the rest of the house. She wasn't sure she was strong enough.

She found herself wrapped in Jake's arms, his

hands rubbing her back soothingly. With her head against his chest, a soft sob escaped her.

"Shh," he whispered. "It'll be okay."

Emily allowed herself to absorb his strength. She would not allow this to get her down. So they'd destroyed some of her belongings. She and her daughter were alive. That was what mattered. She stepped back from Jake's arms and stiffened her spine. "Actually, I'm pissed off. I can't believe they did this." She reached down and picked up a broken DVD. She shook her head and held back a snort. At least now she didn't have to watch that DVD of *The Backyardigans* again.

Jake stared at a white pearl photo frame with broken glass. He smiled and showed it to her. "Was this her first time in Santa's lap?"

Her heart ached for him at the missed moment. But, he'd have a chance to see the photos of Amber growing up. A chance to get closer to his daughter without her even being around.

Remembering the photo session put a smile on Emily's face and forced a small chuckle. "Yes. She was afraid of him." She looked around and moved forward, reached down, and picked up another picture. "This is her first birthday."

And so the day went. The sharing of Amber's childhood in photography as they straightened her home.

Deciding to pack up a few of her daughter's things, Emily sifted through the mess in Amber's bedroom. She paused when she heard a feminine voice. Curious, she poked her head into the living room and smiled. Jesse chatted with Sofia Strickland.

Emily and Sofia had been friends for as long as she

could remember. Bill Strickland, Sofia's father, and her father were old college buddies and attended the first game of the season at Ole Miss each year. The kids always stayed home and played. That was how the siblings had come to know Sofia. Over the years, the two women had become somewhat close, speaking a couple times a month. But, they hadn't seen each other the last couple of years since Emily had forgone the games with her family.

A squeal and a big hug later, the two broke apart. "Emily Hamilton, you look magnificent. Motherhood wears well on you."

Embarrassed, and possibly beet red, she took it in even though she knew her friend was full of false flattery. "Me? You look fabulous."

"Of course I do. It's the European spa treatments. They're all the rage." Sofia laughed. She turned to Jake. "Oh, my God. Is that Jake?"

Emily jumped, and her hackles raised a bit. *Damn jealousy.*

Jake moved closer to Emily and smiled. "Hi, Sofia. I think you've caught us at a bad time for a social call."

Sofia's eyes widened. "I know. I can't believe it. Jesse and I were just talking about it. It's a good thing no one was home."

Emily cleared her throat. That thought hadn't occurred to her. Thank goodness her brothers had rushed her off. "Maybe we can get together another time."

Her friend heaved a dramatic sigh. "Well, I only stopped by because I can't get through to you on the phone. I wanted to share the good news that I've moved here and now we can hang out." She scanned the room.

"I hope I don't have this to look forward to." She shuddered.

"Are you going to the game this year?" Emily had to steer the conversation away before Sofia asked questions that shouldn't be answered. Like where Emily was staying and why the armed men were outside.

"Yes." She smiled. "Please tell me you'll be there this year. It's not the same without another woman my age."

Although doubtful that she'd attend, she knew saying yes would buy her time with her next visit with Sofia since it wouldn't be easy to just pop down the street for coffee when she was in Maryland. "Yes." She ignored Jake's glare.

The door opened, and her twin brothers entered.

Brad narrowed his eyes. "Sofia, what the hell are you doing here?"

Sofia cocked her head at him and smiled flirtatiously. She had always had a thing for the twin. "I'm here to see Emily."

"Well, she's leaving, so you may as well go too."

Emily's eyes widened at her brother's rudeness. Sure he'd been annoyed at Sofia always throwing herself at him when they'd been younger, but now?

Her friend huffed. "Fine." She circled back to Emily. "I'll see you in a couple of weeks in Oxford. Give me a call before then and we'll grab coffee and catch up. There's much to tell."

They hugged and the woman left.

Emily narrowed her eyes at Brad. "That was uncalled for."

He shrugged. "Got her to leave though, didn't I?"

Her mouth dropped open.

"Anything?" Jesse asked.

"No sign of them." Matt looked at her then back at her oldest brother. "Their places were tossed too."

Jesse faced her, his muscles bunched up and his jaw tight, frustration bleeding from his features. "You almost ready to leave? I'll have someone clean this up."

No Teri. No Michael. Without them, they had only a piece of burned-up computer. They needed her boss or coworker. Were the two in on this? That didn't make sense, though, if Teri was the one who'd downloaded the information.

"Let me grab a couple of things for Amber." If she could collect her daughter's favorite stuffed animal, at least the trip wouldn't be a total waste.

****

Amber giggled as she climbed the steps out of the pool, stopping to the side, on the edge with her arms held out, air-filled plastic triangles eating up most of her short arms. "*Again*, Daddy."

With nothing new to go on to remove the threat to Em and Amber, Jake stood in the water, ready to catch his daughter when she fearlessly launched herself at him. She'd shied away from the pool at the beginning, but Reagan had coaxed her to finally get in the water and then she was jumping in like her cousin. He discovered she was okay with it as long as her head didn't go underwater. And he was okay with it. So far. He prayed she didn't decide on a death grip around his neck.

Spending the last few days with Em, he'd heard all that he'd missed in his daughter's life. One of the most enjoyable stories was when Amber had tried to ride Dottie. Most importantly, he'd learned more about his grown-up sprite and how her life had been without him. He hated she'd had to sacrifice so much because he'd left. He vowed to make it up to her, determined to go to any lengths necessary.

Each day, he witnessed the anger he'd initially felt from her melt and heat spark, making it difficult to keep his hands off her. He needed to feel her body against his while he was awake. Not like it had been all of those years ago.

They'd avoided the topics of Amber's conception and of marriage. Both conversations silently hung in the background after her initial reaction to his proposal. Speaking of the two subjects before they'd become close again would be a disaster. He'd lose any ground he'd gained.

Showing he would be a good father to Amber and a loving man to Em had been important. The question residing in his mind was whether he'd push so hard and so fast if they didn't have a daughter. Showing her what existed between them—yes. Get married right away— probably not. He'd have let her pick the timeline for marriage. But, they *would* get married.

It no longer mattered what his thoughts were. He did have a daughter, and he would be a father to her and not one who saw her every other weekend. They'd be a loving family.

Maybe by showing Em what was still between them, reigniting the passion he'd felt in his dream would pull them closer together and open her heart.

In a pool chair beside Kate and Megan, he caught Em's gaze. He could've sworn a flash of desire crossed her pupils as she looked him over. Thankfully, the cold water helped him not embarrass himself with how much she affected him.

"Daddy, *again!*"

Accepting him without question, his daughter had attached herself to his side, and since Em kept her daughter close, he spent more time with her as well. He hoped that she felt the bond forming between them, that they were becoming a family.

Water splashed at him as a little water nymph landed in his arms, sputtering as her face caught wet splashes.

"Lunch is ready," Brad announced before turning back to the grill. The smell of chicken, burgers and hot dogs floated his way, and Jake's stomach growled.

Standing at the shallow end, he pulled his daughter against him. "Are you hungry, princess?"

A loud wail sounded in his ears, frightening him for a moment.

"No! *Wanna* jump!"

He turned to step back to his spot in the pool.

Em walked to them wearing a stern expression. "Amber, it's time to eat. No more pool."

Afraid to set his daughter down for fear she'd jump in the pool without an adult, he exited the water and handed her to her mother amidst the struggle to be released from their arms. Watching Em handle Amber, convincing her a hot dog would be good right now and then the pool later and drying up the child's tears, amazed him. He wanted to be able to do the same thing. He was too much of a pussy and gave in to her tears.

"You two sit. I'll grab your plates. What do you want, sprite?"

Em started, electricity shooting between them. "Chicken with potato salad. Get Amber a hot dog, no bun, no sides, please."

Sitting down with two plates, one for his daughter and one for Em, he took the time to slice Amber's hot dog as he'd witnessed Em do before. With their lunch plates prepared, he returned to the grill for his own.

"Smooth move."

He looked at Devon curiously. "What?"

His brother nodded toward his daughter and Em, who had been joined by Blake, gushing over his granddaughter. "Cutting that for Amber. You could tell Em liked that."

Gazing at the two most important people in his life eating their meals, a smile touched his lips, and his heart beat with love for the both of them. Em stood, leaving Amber with her grandfather, and slipped into the house in the short covering she wore over her yellow bikini. It only took a moment to decide to follow her. Setting down his plate, he slowly strode in her wake.

Welcoming the cool air, he closed the door behind him and sought Em. Before she could close the bathroom door behind her, Jake snuck into the room and locked the door.

"Jake," she whispered, her voice nervous, "what are you doing?"

He wrapped his arms around her and pulled her snug against his body, groaning at the bolts of lightning zipping their way through every nerve ending in his body, from head to toe, sending blood rushing to his groin. Her shiver at his touch made him want her even more.

"Showing you there is something between us." His mouth swooped down on hers, claiming her lips before his tongue invaded her mouth, tasting her sweetness, while his arousal grew and his swim trunks began to tent.

The kiss was just as he remembered in his dream and somehow, he knew sliding back into her body and watching her face as she came apart would be just as blissful. Thinking those things vanquished his self-restraint, and his kiss turned fierce as he devoured her mouth, suckling on her swollen lips and tongue, demanding more from her with each passing moment.

Before he realized his actions, he'd picked Em up, situated her on the vanity, and slid between her legs. Her heat burned through her shorts to his stiff member as his hands grasped her buttocks and rocked his hips against hers until she could feel how hard she made him.

A low mewling sound escaped her, enticing him further as he reached for her shirt to strip it over her head to allow him to worship the body beneath it before he exploded like a teenager on his first time with a woman. Pushing aside her bathing suit top, he closed his hand over the full swell of her breast and feral desire ripped through him, increasing his urgency to have her, to show her that she was his and only his.

A knock on the door broke through the haze clouding his mind when a small voice followed it. "Mommy, I *gotta* potty!"

****

Emily pushed Jake back, her hands burning on his naked chest, and slid from the vanity and corrected her clothing before reaching for the door. It took several tries to unlock it with her trembling hand. Using her other hand on Jake's forearm, she shoved him out the door, past her daughter, who hopped around doing the potty dance. It was time to move Amber from pull-up diapers to panties. She was growing too quickly that it almost saddened Emily to move her to the next stage of her little life.

"Come in and potty." She kissed her daughter on the head. "I'm so proud of you."

While they'd been residing here, she'd had quite a few people interrupting and saving her from making mistakes with Jake that she knew she'd regret, but she'd never expected one of her saviors to be her daughter. His magic touch tossed her will to keep a distance between them out the window, leaving her weak and wanting. Hell, she'd been ready to fuck him right there in the bathroom.

They may be close again, but she hadn't been ready to make that jump from friends to lovers. Yet, resisting him was near impossible. Knowing he wanted her as badly as she wanted him left her breathless, and her heart did a pitter-patter when they were near each other.

Amber scooted the little stool so she could use the regular toilet and then fought to pull her wet swimsuit off. "Mommy, *hep* me."

The frantic cry told Emily they only had a few moments before this potty trip failed. Deftly stripping the little girl down, she picked the child up and sat her on the toilet.

Looking up, Emily saw Jake in the doorway, watching their interaction with a strange expression on his face. She reached under the counter and removed a pull-up to give herself a moment to settle the chaotic beating of her heart from their sensual encounter.

Damn, he was handsome. He'd begun to put on a little weight, and he looked rested for a change. She wished she could say she'd felt rested. The entire situation had kept her tossing and turning most nights, unsure what her next steps should be or what Jake would do.

His throat clearing, deep and sexy, had her raising her eyebrows at him in question.

"How long does she do that?"

Embarrassment at almost being caught like they had been by her daughter temporarily forgotten, she fought the smile trying to explode on her face. "Do what? Go to the bathroom?"

"No." A slight redness crept up his neck. "Still need those diaper things. She didn't wear one today, and she seemed okay on her own."

Glancing over, she witnessed her daughter pulling enough toilet paper to clog the commode for days. Dropping the diaper, Emily reached over, tore off a piece, and handed it to Amber. "She is close to being on her own. She's had only one accident this week. As for today, they'd only weigh her down, so I decided to chance it." She picked up the article and placed it back under the counter. "I'm not putting that on her. It was habit to grab it."

The flushing of the toilet turned Jake's focus on his daughter, watching her with wide eyes filled with wonder.

Emily's lips still felt the tingling from his kiss, the heat running through her body from his touch. Shit. She could barely remember her reasons for pulling back from him.

Amber bumped into her foot when she scooted her

stool to the sink. "*I torry,* Mommy. *You hut*?"

Emily shook her head, and the little girl continued, stretching to reach the cold faucet, pumping some colorful bottled child's foamy soap in her hands. Finished, she jumped down and pushed her stool out of the way. After she helped her daughter back into her swimsuit, Emily was forgotten.

"Daddy, I *wanna* jump."

Jake held his hand out, and a small one slipped in it. "Let's get those float things back on your arms and check out the pool."

As they moved to the back door, she heard him ask, "Do you think there are sharks in the pool?"

Her daughter giggled, a joyous sound that always made her smile. "No, *thilwy.* There's just *Unca Jethe* and Rea-Rea."

The door to the patio closed, leaving Emily alone. She leaned against the vanity and looked at herself in the mirror. "What the hell did you just let happen?"

"What indeed?"

She spun around to Trent, leaning lazily against the doorjamb, wearing a sly grin on his face.

"Nothing." She slipped past him and tightened her jaw at his hearty chuckle.

Chapter Eleven

Cozy evenings with the family while watching a movie, usually an action one with a badass hero, was another thing Jake had missed, but he'd never expected the next time he'd experience it that the feature film would be a children's animated movie. With Amber and Reagan sitting on the floor hypnotized by the cartoon, no adult complained about the change in genre. Glancing around, he noticed the men's eyes were glued to the TV. Amazing.

Focusing on the talking animals on the screen became an impossible task for Jake. His thoughts kept flashing to the feel of Em's soft body in his hands, her sidled up next to him, the friction as their groins rubbed against each other, only separated by thin bathing suits, which had been beyond the memory of his dreams these past few years. It also had his cock twitching.

Earlier, he'd stalked outside after the heated encounter in the bathroom. Strutted was more like it. He'd just had a taste of Em. Amber had run off toward Reagan, leaving him with his thoughts. He couldn't wash the feel of Em's body next to his from his mind. Damn if he hadn't been imagining taking her to bed and doing everything to her he'd dreamed.

Then he'd been caught off-guard with a splash of cold water that drenched him, cooling down his fevered body, returning his mind to what was happening around him.

"There are children out here. Get yourself under control."

Realizing what Matt meant, he'd placed his hands in front of his crotch and hastily made his way to the pool, diving in before the kids noticed how his swimsuit had tented and asked about it. He couldn't believe Amber hadn't said something with that ardent curiosity of hers.

If the water hadn't cooled down his growing desire, Em's expression and actions when she'd returned to the family would have. He'd expected a smile, something to encourage him, but she'd gone out of her way to avoid him, always having a sister-in-law or Trent close by to intervene when he neared her so he'd watched helplessly as her anger returned, closing her off from him. He couldn't wrap his mind around why. Her passionate response proved she'd wanted the same thing. Hell, they could've set the bathroom ablaze with the intensity of their kisses alone.

Jake's heart clenched painfully. It'd been too soon to make a move, but damn if being near her without touching her, holding her, caressing her, didn't push him almost past the point of insanity. When she'd been younger, her age had always frozen his lust. Now, there was nothing holding him back from having her. Except her acquiescence. And fucking Trent. He'd yet to discuss her leaving the man behind, and her brothers wouldn't give him any hints about how long she'd been with the man. They just smirked and shrugged when he asked them anything about the two.

Earning her trust back and rekindling her love for him was the course he had to continue to take to make her believe he loved her and would not leave her again. And, it didn't mean seducing her every time he could get her alone.

A smile automatically grew on his face as his mind returned to the present when his baby girl climbed into his lap. She leaned back against him and stuck her thumb in her mouth, fighting to keep her eyes open. Looking across the room, he captured Em's gaze, and he could've sworn her eyes were damp, holding back tears ready to spill.

Wanting an opportunity to apologize for earlier, he'd refused to hand Amber over to her mother when the movie ended. He'd kept the sleeping girl in his arms and followed Em instead. After a light kiss on his daughter's head, he turned to the woman he loved, only to find she wasn't in the room.

His heart thudded heavily in his chest. She was pushing him away, giving up on the desire that drew them together, not giving them a chance to make a life as a family. Wanting to chase her, but knowing he needed to give her time to come to grips with where their relationship was moving, he sought his own bed. Alone.

Which turned out to be the right thing since he'd woken in the night, twisted in his sheets and swinging his arms, from another nightmare of his captivity.

****

Over another of Mrs. Kessler's wonderful breakfasts, the Hamilton brothers held an impromptu meeting. Jake wondered how often they held the meetings when he hadn't been invited. He hadn't been invited this morning, yet here he was and he damn well would participate. His Em and princess's safety were too important.

"What do you mean you've got nothing, Dev?" Jesse demanded, angrier than Jake had ever seen him.

Devon shrugged. "Just what I said. Nothing. The piece of equipment was beyond salvageable."

Matt took a bite of pancake, chewed, and swallowed. "Well, that fucking sucks." He returned his attention to his plate.

Anger at the loss of a lead and fear for the people Jake loved ran through him. His appetite squashed. "What about her boss and coworker? What if we find them?"

The eldest Hamilton brother cocked his head at him. "We've been looking for them."

Surprised, he just stared. They *had* been having meetings where he hadn't been privileged enough to attend. "When did this happen?" he croaked.

"As soon as everything happened and the two disappeared." Jesse stood and carried his plate to the buffet. "No real luck yet."

Forks clanked on plates, and men gulped their beverages. They acted like nothing was wrong. He'd think they cared more about their sister and niece's safety than to act so nonchalant about the investigation. Dammit. If he was in charge, he'd... he'd... just what the hell would he do? The Ponzi scheme was a crime committed entirely on paper. And, her boss's records were all destroyed.

Okay, maybe they weren't nonchalant. Maybe they realized the same thing.

But... "Were you able to track the kidnappers back to anyone?" Jake thought aloud.

Nodding, Jesse retook his seat. "Yeah. Back to her

boss, Michael Wright."

"Then you'd better damn well find him." Maybe he should go out and search for the man. No. He wanted to be here beside Em and Amber. He'd have to trust her brothers. "What now?"

Devon set his coffee cup down. "Em gave me some of her boss's clients to research. It'll take time for me to successfully grab the information we need."

"Why not bring the SEC in on it?" Hell, Paul was out of the way.

"Not yet," Devon responded. "We need to find out how deep this thing is first. This doesn't sound like a small operation. If we get the wrong person, we've exposed her."

Jesse looked pointedly at him and cocked one eyebrow. "Don't worry. We will when the time is right. In the meantime, they're safe here. As you see, we have someone tracking down her boss and coworker, and Devon is pulling more information. Does this meet with your approval?" His lip twitched.

Cocky son of a bitch. Jake stood and tossed his napkin on his plate. "Yeah. Just keep me in the loop." He turned and walked away before someone could make another comment. They had the investigation handled. For now.

****

Pulling off his gray T-shirt, Jake used it to wipe the sweat streaming down his face and neck while walking to the huddle with Jesse, Kate, Matt and Les. In their game of touch football, his team was ahead by two touchdowns. It would've been three, but he'd allowed Em to pass him to score for her team. His team wouldn't let him forget it or cover her again.

The brothers had always been competitive, and with the addition of Kate and a couple of the HIS team members, the game had turned into a rivalry that mimicked dirty warfare where sometimes touch became tackle, and they were gunning for him.

"Who's winning now?" Blake shouted across the yard, long tongs in his hand, smoke from the grill floating up behind him and disappearing, but not before it sent a tantalizing smell of beef, chicken, and pork toward their makeshift football field.

Raising her hands over her head, Kate grinned widely. "We are! Woot woot!"

Laughing, Jesse ran to his wife and grabbed her close for a kiss.

Her right hand on her hip, Megan turned from her game with the children and raised a light-colored eyebrow. She looked cool with the fan blowing on her, swishing the skirt of her flowery sundress around her legs. "AJ Hamilton, are you really letting them beat you?"

Before her husband could respond, Les, who'd been named temporary field team leader when Ken had been called home on a family emergency, mocked AJ, garnering deep laughs from everyone except the man himself who didn't seem to appreciate his wife laughing along with the group.

"Let's just get back to the game," AJ growled. "It's our ball."

"I want Trent," Jake said to his team. The bastard had given Em a friendly, sporty swat to the butt, and he hadn't liked it one bit. The intensity of his jealousy almost suffocated him as his mind whirled around scenarios of Em and Trent in scenes that only boiled his blood. A wave of newfound energy, probably that green-eyed monster, flowed through his exhausted limbs. Being on defense was the perfect opportunity to let the playboy know how Jake felt about his actions.

Jesse narrowed his eyes at him as if assessing him, then nodded.

Four shirtless men and one woman in a drenched tank top, lined up on each side of the football and an imaginary scrimmage line, facing their opponents, spouting bullshit in an attempt to rile them.

Devon hiked the ball to AJ, who stepped back, watching his team race down the field, attempting to find an open player. AJ looked up, and his eyes widened at Matt pushing Brad, so he rushed a pass to his closest teammate, Trent, who Jake had left open.

Charging, Jake tackled Trent, hitting the ground hard, the impact knocking the wind from the man, the ball dropping to the ground. Kate and Em raced over while Trent worked to suck oxygen into his lungs.

"What the fuck?" AJ shouted.

Jake wasn't sure who chastised his brother first for his language with the children around—his wife, his father, his sister-in-law or even his brothers. He thought he even heard Reagan yell to her mother that Uncle AJ said a bad word.

Looking at Trent as he stood, Jake smirked. "I tripped."

While the women babied their injured player, everyone took the opportunity for a water break, chased the girls around or looked over Blake's shoulder at the grill, giving him instruction.

"Do you feel better now?" At least Jesse hadn't lectured him or given him shit about it.

Jake moved the bottle of water to his lips and nodded before he chugged it.

His brother wiped sweat from his brow. "How're you holding up? Tired?"

Hell yeah, he was tired. There was no way he'd sit down like a pussy while the women still had the energy to play. He'd never live it down. "I'm good."

Jesse crossed his arms over his sweaty chest; his expression belied disbelief of Jake's answer. "Okay. I'm putting you back on Em then. Let her have another touchdown, and I'll beat your ass myself. And don't you dare fucking tackle her."

Chuckling, he reached for a towel and wiped his face before running it across his upper body. His eyes strayed to Em and Amber petting Dottie. The sight made him smile, but it was missing one thing… him. "Gotcha." Taking a step toward his daughter, his brother's hand on his shoulder halted his progress.

"Break's over. Let's go, boys and girls!" Jesse yelled.

Standing across from Em, her tank top stuck to her body, outlining her breasts and small waist, set his blood afire. She turned her head away from him after he winked at her. His patience of waiting for her was at an end, but how to change it without angering her more still eluded him.

With the entire family here, doing that and having just the three of them alone was not easy. Asking the family to go somewhere wasn't possible. Without knowing who the leader of the scheme was, or where her boss happened to be, left the requirement to keep Em and Amber protected.

That thought sent a shiver snaking through him,

rubbing its scaly cover everywhere, bringing his desire down a notch. This game had been a break for everyone since they'd hit a few roadblocks. A chance to blow off a little steam and kick out some of their anger at not solving it yet. Glancing over at Devon, he knew the only way they'd pulled him outside, into the game, was because his computer was compiling the information he spoke of at breakfast. Jake prayed they'd find something useful.

Em darted past him before he realized AJ had the ball ready to pass. She stopped and turned with her arms up.

Yes! They planned to throw it to her, expecting him to allow her to score again.

Jogging in her direction, he left space so AJ could see she was still open. After she caught the ball, he grabbed her around the waist before she could turn and then pulled her close, spinning her around as the football dropped to the ground.

Stopping, he watched her eyes darken, and she didn't look away like she had been doing. The world slipped away, and it was just the two of them, locked in a heated embrace, a current of desire flowing between them, melting them together. Her breath hitched when his dick began growing against her belly.

He had the urge to kiss her, and based on her reaction to being in his arms again, there was no mistaking that she wanted the same. Memories of her kisses… the sweetness… the passion… the urgency had his pulse speeding through his body faster than AJ's driving.

What the hell? AJ? Why did he come to mind?

Slowly, an awareness of everything other than Em

returned to him. Fuck!

"Enough you two," the unwelcome invader of his thoughts said before slapping him on the shoulder. AJ was damn lucky Em was in his arms, or Jake would have connected his fist with the man's jaw.

Letting her down, he slid her close to his body, giving her a promise with his gaze. Or at least that was what he hoped she got from it.

"Daddy, *fudball.*"

Looking down, he watched Amber struggle to pick up the football with her small hands. Figuring it out, she held the ball close to her chest, smiling up at him, looking proud of her accomplishment.

His lust for Em gushed away, and parental pride replaced it. Kneeling a couple of feet from his daughter, he opened his arms. "Throw it here, princess."

No one laughed at her attempt to toss the ball when it fell from her hands to the ground. She leaned over to pick it up again, fumbling, but determined.

Reaching forward, Jake grabbed her and stood, swinging her around, her legs flying through the air. He couldn't get enough of that giggle, even when it included hiccups like it did now. Dizzy himself, he stopped and set her on her feet. She tried to step and fell down. The laughing never stopped.

After recovering, she stood with her arms open up to him. "*Again*, Daddy."

Scooping her up, he strode toward the family by the picnic tables. "Daddy can't do that again, or he'll fall like you." He poked her in the belly, and she reached up and grabbed his finger. "What has my little girl been doing?"

"*I pet* Dottie. *Thee gonna* have baby dogs."

Finally, he could understand her words. He'd worried she was behind or had a speech impediment, but he'd been assured by Em, Jesse, and Blake that it was normal at that age. Smiling, he kissed her on the cheek. "You know now that she's going to have puppies, you can't ride her?"

Amber nodded, almost butting him in the nose. "I *not* ride Dottie 'cause *I too bid*." She turned to him. "Can I *hab* a pony?"

Chuckling, Jake wondered if every kid asked for one. He remembered the day he'd asked his mother for one, promising to keep him in his room and brush him every day. She'd held a smile behind her serious voice telling him that ponies weren't allowed where they lived. He'd huffed off when she wouldn't agree to move so he could have one.

He'd been on his bed, arms tight across his chest, his head down and lip poked out when she'd come to the room to tell him dinner was ready. He grumbled that he wasn't hungry, yet his stomach rumbled, making a liar out of him. She'd played dirty and cooked his favorite—macaroni and cheese with hot dogs cut up in it.

"Mommy *tay* no pony in New *Ork*."

Stopping beside Em with a twinkle in his eye, he smiled at her. "Mommy's right. You can't have a pony there."

Amber wiggled out of his arms and ran to Reagan. They dropped down on the bench beside a sleeping cat. Megan's cat, Bob, stretched and yawned when the girls petted him. Amber needed something bigger than a fish. Maybe one of Dottie's puppies. He wondered if Em's landlord would allow it.

Mentally shaking his head, he knew that Em and his daughter couldn't return to New York. She no longer had a job there, and he lived here. Plus, the family was here. They should live near the family so Amber could grow up around everyone.

He had no idea what she wanted. His jaw tightened. She might want to move back there. Jesse had hired someone to put her home back to rights.

She'd mentioned her career as an accountant was over, but he couldn't believe that. Why would any firm hold what she'd done against her? She'd reported a criminal.

Her love for numbers growing up had helped him and AJ on more than one occasion. Even though she had been four years behind them in school, she could figure out almost any problem they had in their high school math courses. They might not have passed if it hadn't been for her tutoring them and refusing to do their homework but agreeing to check it.

There was no need to waste his time considering her move. They'd be married and live in Baltimore. He worked here and couldn't just up and move to New York for her to have a job there. *Shit.* He didn't have a job any longer. He'd quit the FBI and didn't want to go back. He needed a job before he proposed again. That could be remedied easily.

As for being a family, his heart felt light since he hadn't had an episode with his daughter, or anyone else. No flashbacks, no terror-filled moments. It must've been temporary. Now, nothing held him back.

"She looks just like you," he told Em with his gaze fastened on their daughter.

"She has your eyes." Her breathless response

caught his attention.

Looking down at her, he saw desire still swimming around in her eyes. He wanted her to be the one to come to him, but she'd been the one to do that the first time, so he figured she wanted him to take the step this time. Leaning down to whisper in her ear, he rasped, "Tonight."

Her breath hitched.

"Food's ready!"

Dammit! They had to get somewhere alone. He loved the family, but they kept interrupting at the wrong times.

****

Nervously pacing her bedroom, Emily brought her hand to her mouth to bite on her fingernail. Realizing what she'd been about to do, she yanked her arm back to her side. That had been a bad habit she'd fought to end in college after she'd bitten them down to the cuticle and had drawn blood during a history final exam. She'd passed the class, barely, and after tasting the jalapeño juice she'd placed on her thumb to halt her from chewing on it again, she'd decided she couldn't stomach the little, hot pepper ever again, even mixed in food.

Pushing aside her thoughts she'd used to divert her attention from the issue at hand, she dropped onto the bed; the mattress bounced in response. Would Jake really come to her room? After the demonstration in the bathroom, she'd say he would. But, was he using her desire for him to drive her to agree to marry him for her daughter's sake, or did he truly want her?

The man had gone his whole life pushing her away like a petulant child and now, suddenly, he wanted to be with her and be her husband. Funny how telling a man he was a father would do that. How was she to truly know? If she asked him and he said it was only for his daughter, Emily would be crushed. She couldn't do it.

Memory of their one night together, the two of them naked and sweaty in each other's arms, elicited a warmth to spread across her flesh at the thought of the pleasure of his touch. She closed her eyes to will away the need driving through her, puckering her nipples, leaving her breasts tender and a pulsing between her thighs.

Maybe it would've worked if she hadn't been in his arms earlier, absorbing the electricity that zapped to her from the arms that held her tight against his hard body. His working out to rebuild the muscles in his body left her drooling whenever he returned with her brothers from the basement gym. He typically wore a sleeveless T-shirt that was wet and stuck to his body, and she admired the returning definition of his muscles. A sight she didn't want any other woman to see.

She jerked her head to the door when Jake slipped in wearing shorts, and *only* shorts. *Holy crap.*

He silently walked to her, slid his hand behind her head, and angled his head down. With his lips barely touching her, in a hoarse voice, he said, "My sweet Em."

Loving the sound of it, she didn't argue when he reached his other arm around her, pulled her against his body, and claimed her mouth with a slow, sensual kiss. The swirl of heat enveloped her, taking her breath away.

It had been too many years since she'd known passion that lit her need to be touched. She'd waited for the only man who could complete her.

She slowly slid her arms around him and pulled herself closer. The feel of his body, the touch of his lips, and his arms around her brought only the two of them into focus. The world around them melted away. Moving her hand higher, she ran her fingers through his short, dark hair.

She opened her mouth, and their tongues danced for several moments before the kiss changed to searing and then hungry, demanding. She moaned, and a delicious shudder rolled through her being, leaving tingles in its wake.

Raising his mouth from hers, heat coalesced between them as he searched her eyes. "Before we go any further, I need to know you'll leave Trent and be mine. Only mine."

Only his? She'd waited almost her whole life to hear that. What the hell did he mean by her leaving Trent? At that moment she didn't care; she wanted him to kiss her again. "I'm only yours, Jake."

His lips curved into a sexy smile that melted her insides. It was like all those years ago, except her dream was coming true, that this time she knew he was awake.

Leaning in, he brushed a tantalizing kiss in the hollow of her neck, weakening her knees. Then gently working his way up her neck to her ear, he nibbled on her earlobe. His warm breath created a heated shiver that moved through her, snaking through her veins with erotic pleasure that left an excited tremble in its wake.

"What is that delicious smelling perfume?"

"Hmm?" A sliver of coherence slipped into her mind. "Oh, Live Color Fully by Kate Spade."

"I'll have to thank Kate. But first, let me help you

out of these clothes."

Unwinding her arms, she stepped back, eager for him to touch her body, to make her feel what he had once before.

The next moment she was topless, and his hand slowly massaged her breast before he squeezed her taut, sensitive nipple. "God, Em. I need you." His gaze held hers as intimately as his hand did. There was more than just sex in his eyes.

She dropped her head back and held a moan in. Lethal hands. That was what he had. His simple touch sent currents of ecstasy flying straight to her lower belly. If she allowed him to continue to fondle her, they might not make it to the bed. She had it that bad for him. But she wanted more. She wanted all of him.

She took a deep breath, opened her eyes, and looked back at him, her gaze unwavering. God, the lust burned brightly in his eyes. He didn't appear to want to stand around and play either.

He reached for the boxer shorts she slept in and put his hands under the waistband. Slowly sliding them down, his hands caressed her hips and her ass before he shoved them down and did the same with his own. Stepping out of them, his magnificent erection jutted out, and his blazing gaze never left hers. "Are you sure?"

She nodded, and he caught one arm around her waist and moved her to the bed, and then poised himself over her. Excitement rippled through her every nerve, and heat blasted her body. At last, he was going to make love to her.

His right palm cupped her face and stroked her jaw with his thumb. "I can't wait."

"Please, Jake," she said breathlessly, "kiss me."

Chapter Twelve

Heat slammed into him, and with a groan he reclaimed her mouth and slid one leg between hers, settling himself between her thighs. He ran his hand over the curve of her silky breast and then slowly down her body to between her creamy thighs. "You're so wet."

He hadn't planned to take her right away, but he couldn't fucking wait when she was so ready for him. Adjusting his hips, the thick head of his cock nudged her slick entrance. "Good God, you're tight."

She shifted restlessly below him. "There's been no one but you, Jake."

Oh, hell yes! Her words lit something in him that made him want to stand, climb the highest tower and pound his chest in victory. He was her only lover. She'd waited for him. She was truly his woman.

Slowly sliding into her, he thrust deeper and deeper into seventh heaven. She opened her legs and wrapped them around his waist, hooking her ankles just above his ass, and took all of him. He halted when she gasped, her eyes wide and her fingers digging into his shoulders. Afraid he'd hurt her, he stopped moving and watched until her expression changed to molten heat.

"Relax," he said breathlessly.

He needed to accept that advice. Being buried deep in the velvety wetness of the woman who held his heart captive jolted his system, and his balls drew tight. He closed his eyes, his neck muscles straining to hold back and wait for her. He'd fantasized about being inside her, connecting and experiencing pleasure on a level he'd never wanted with any other. He had to make it last. He would not go before her. He wanted to give her the pleasure he'd denied her before. Or at least the pleasure he remembered giving her.

He leaned down and his lips nuzzled the sensitive skin beneath her ear and nipped at her throat with his teeth. He smiled and licked at the goose bumps that followed in the wake of his ministrations.

A hand stroked its way up and down his back, and a ripple of electricity shocked his nerve endings. He lifted his head, and his gaze connected with hers. He couldn't break the contact as he moved, slowly pumping in and out of her, stroking deep into her heat, gritting his teeth against the mind-numbing pleasure. Quivering around him, her velvety friction sucked him deeper; every withdrawal made him want to grab her hips so he could keep driving in farther.

And it had everything to do with him finally being with Em. His sprite. He inhaled her scent, one that had stayed with him, and he'd imagined surrounded him on many cold nights.

Her chest rose and fell in quick succession, pushing her succulent breasts toward him, begging him to touch them. He leaned down and laved one with his tongue and then suckled on it, smiling at her rapid breathing and flushed skin. It hadn't taken much to bring her close with him.

He tugged on her nipple with his lips, flicking the tip with his tongue. She tossed her head back and moaned.

"Jake," she whimpered. "Jake."

He fought hard not to shoot his load. Hearing Em speak his name for the first time in ecstasy was something he'd never forget. With his heart thundering in his chest, he swooped down and took her mouth in his, devouring it, taking all she would give. And he wanted it all. All the fire. All the passion. All the love. She was his life.

Then the importance of it all slammed into him, knocking him off-balance, and he broke the kiss. This was their true first time together. The new beginning of everything for them.

"Em, you're beautiful."

"Hmm." Her hand glided up his chest and snaked around his neck, pulling him down to kiss her again.

Urgency filled him. Amid their sweaty tangled limbs, he moved a hand to her hip and thrust deeper, grinding the root of his cock over her swollen clit, hoping to give her what she needed to meet him as he couldn't last much longer. Moving together, she met him thrust for thrust, and every little noise she made, every move, burned in his memory.

How he'd missed so much their first time. Her responsiveness set his body ablaze. They would be perfect together. Forever.

Suddenly her breath came in shudders, and her fingers dug into his back. He looked at her, and the sheer look of ecstasy on her face undid him. He'd been a fool to walk away from her.

"Jake," she said in a breathless whimper.

"I can't hold out, sprite."

She cried out, and she clutched him like a fist,

milking him until he lost control.

He finally surrendered, groaning as the orgasm ripped through him, his release so staggeringly intense that his world tilted for a moment with a force that frightened him. He could try to blame it on not having sex in four years, but he knew it was because he'd finally welcomed Em where she belonged.

Still breathing heavily, Jake roused himself and raised his forehead from Em's. Brushing her lips lightly with his, exhilaration rocketed through him at the look of pure bliss on her face. He rolled off her, reached to pull her next to him, and kissed the top of her head. "You're mine, Em."

****

Arms wrapped around him, and his breath hitched as the dreaded fear returned. Fear for his life. Those arms had spent many hours squeezing his body painfully. The hands at the ends of them had pummeled him until he was black and blue. They were a threat.

Too many times he'd had to stand there and take it. He'd always been bound in some way. They gave him no chance to fight back. He wasn't surprised after he'd attacked his guard whenever he'd had the chance. He would escape.

Realizing his hands were free and he could gain the upper hand for once, Jake flipped his body and wrapped his hands around his torturer's neck. "Die, asshole," he growled.

Suddenly, something seemed wrong. His attacker flailed beneath him, but the neck was small and soft.

Jerking awake, Jake released his hands and leaned back, looking into Em's wide, fearful eyes. "Good God." He looked at his hands and then reached out to touch her cheek. She flinched. "Em, I'm so sorry." He leaped from the bed, disgusted with himself.

She sat up with her hand touching the red area around her throat.

Christ! He'd hurt her. He kneeled beside the bed. "Em, please forgive me. I was dreaming." He swallowed hard. "I'd never hurt you." *Fucking liar. You just did. Wasn't this your concern that something might one day happen? Well, it sure as hell did.* How the hell did he fix it?

"What happened?" she said softly. The look in her eyes was a combination of fear and concern.

He ran his hand through his hair and slid to sitting. "I dreamed I was back there." He was back in his small prison, trying to find yet another way to survive. "If I'd been awake, this wouldn't have happened. I know the difference. I mean, when Amber…." He caught himself before he said more than he should.

Em straightened, and her voice turned to steel. "When Amber what?"

His shoulders sank. With a deep sigh, he prepared himself for her to send him on his way as unfit. But, he wouldn't keep secrets from her. "When Amber squeezes my neck, it triggers memories. But, I know it's her. I just have to get her arms from around my throat."

She appeared in thought for a moment as she assessed him. What the hell was she thinking? He couldn't help but fidget while waiting for her judgment.

"The first time she threw her arms around you. When I told her you were her daddy?"

He nodded. He had hoped she hadn't noticed. Em wouldn't ever trust him with his daughter. Hell, maybe she'd be right. Just because so far he'd realized it was Amber when the panic and fear took hold, who was to say he might not notice it was her in the future? That was not the type of father she needed.

Then there was what had just happened. What about sleeping with Em? Hell, her life would be in danger.

Jake stood and dressed. "I should go." He reached out to the door and stopped. "I'm sorry."

"Don't go."

At her request, he released the doorknob and turned slowly.

"I'm not a doctor, but I think you have PTSD."

Yeah. He'd thought the same thing, but had hoped it'd been a passing residual effect of his experience. But, to admit to it was another thing…. He wasn't weak. "It's just nightmares."

She shook her head. "I might agree with you except for your reaction to Amber's arms around your neck."

"Are you"—he gulped— "are you afraid of my being around her?" *Please say no. Dear God, please say no.*

She wrapped the sheet tight around her chest. "I'd be lying if I said I wasn't."

His heart sank to his gut. It was all over. All of his dreams of their being a happy family.

"But, only until you figure out how deep your PTSD goes."

"Are you going to ban me from seeing her?" Emptiness tried to dwell inside him at the loss.

"No. But I want us to be together when you are. And, we can talk with Amber about squeezing you so tightly. She might forget from time to time when she gets excited, but you've seen how bright she is. She'll follow along."

Relief, pure and simple, slipped through his bloodstream. It didn't matter if he couldn't see his daughter alone. He preferred for it to be the three of them. Well, except when he wanted to be alone with Em. Speaking of which. "I don't think I should sleep here."

A sigh escaped her. "I want you to stay, but I agree." She cocked her head and studied him. "For now. Sleep where you need until you're ready to come back. I want you to sleep through the night, not stay awake worrying about me."

He nodded and turned away.

"Jake, we'll get through this together."

Sweeter words were never spoken.

****

The deliciously smelling spread of scrambled eggs, bacon, sausage, hash browns, biscuits, French toast, and bowls of diced fruits, roused Jake. The meal, enough to feed a small army, would be more than enough to fill his hunger for food, but filling his hunger for Em would not be so easy. Last night had been magnificent, but not nearly enough.

Christ, I could have killed her. I'll do whatever it takes to ensure that doesn't happen again. I'll break down and get whatever help is needed. I love her and Amber too much to put them at risk, or lose a chance with them.

After they'd talked, he'd snuck back to his room and finally drifted off for a couple of hours of sleep.

He'd checked in on her that morning, but she was

still asleep. Leaving her alone in bed to join the family for breakfast had been difficult. Finally having her where he'd wanted her, waking her to show her how much he truly loved and missed her had to wait. Figuring she was sore, and might be a bit nervous around him, kept him from attempting to be selfish. Plus, needing to speak with her brothers about her safety pushed him to escape before she'd woken. His cock had a mind of its own when his mind remembered the erotic picture she'd made, partially wrapped in a sheet, stretched out with her breasts calling to him to play before he pleasured her.

Damn. Walking into the dining room, he realized that he shouldn't have worn loose-fitting shorts.

"What's this? High school? Can't you control that thing? We know who you're thinking of, and it's not something we want to know about, so get it together," Brad growled before he turned away to fill his plate at the breakfast buffet.

Masculine laughter came from not only his brothers but also men from the team, men he barely knew. If the heat that flowed up his neck was any indication, he'd turned red, which is probably why they laughed harder. Did they know he'd been in Em's room, or that he was just thinking about it?

He grinned while lightheartedness seeped into his entire being. They could laugh all they wanted. He knew what had happened and damn if he'd be ashamed of it. At least not the sex part.

He willed his cock down and roguishly swaggered to the buffet laid out on the counter to piss Brad off even more. He didn't know why he wanted to fuck with the man, but watching him angrily slam things around because of him kept the smile on his face.

Men from the team continued arriving as if a beacon had been sent out that Mrs. Kessler had made breakfast. Then again, the smell of bacon never went unanswered, no matter the time of the day.

Jake hoped they knew what a gem they had in the older woman. Of course, he hadn't necessarily thought that when she'd been almost force-feeding him while he'd been recovering. Her motherly instinct and take-charge attitude with the men hadn't gone unnoticed by him.

Entering the room, Mrs. Kessler's eyes searched the dining area, an odd look on her face. "Jesse, you'd best go to the family room. Chief Reynolds is here."

Everyone halted. Conversation and laughter disappeared while forks froze midway to mouths. Jaws stopped chewing. Then the clink of forks clattering on plates and the scraping of chairs on ceramic tile preceded the mass bolting to the living room.

Jake stared at the action, bewildered. Hadn't she said Jesse? Everyone joining Jesse sent a sense of foreboding creeping through him since he hadn't stopped the men from following.

Mrs. Kessler wiped her hands on her apron. "You'd best go too, Jake."

Knowing not to argue and being extremely curious, he stepped into the next room where the tension pulsing around did nothing to ease his nerves. It definitely wasn't a social call.

A man standing next to Senator Hamilton caught his interest. "You must be the long-lost brother."

Stepping forward, he reached out his hand to the older man, who was a bit soft in the belly but held sharpness in his gaze. "I am. Jake Cavanaugh, sir."

"Chief of Police John Reynolds. I wish I was meeting you for a different reason." Releasing Jake's hand and stepping back, the man turned back to Blake. "We've got a big problem."

Men shifted as Kate sauntered into the room, her eyes narrowed at them before she flashed a warm smile that didn't quite reach her keen gaze. "Good morning, Chief." She walked to the man and kissed him on the cheek.

"You're looking as lovely as ever, Kate." He winked at her as she pulled back. "When are you going to finally leave this man and spend the rest of your life with me?"

Kate's laughter overrode Jesse's growl, barely. "John, what would your wife say?"

His sly grin made Jake realize this was obviously standard banter between them. "She'd tell me I was the luckiest damn man alive."

Kate raised her eyebrows.

"Then she'd kick my ass."

Short, tight chuckles sounded.

"As would I." Jesse snaked his arm out and pulled Kate close, possessively.

The police chief became serious again and cleared his throat. "Well, as I said, we've got a problem."

A nod from Blake prompted him to continue.

"Is Emily here by chance?"

Fuck. Was she in more danger or trouble? He glanced up the stairs even though he couldn't see her or his daughter's rooms. Protecting them, no matter what, was his number one priority. He wouldn't lose them now that he had them in his life. Hell, they were his life.

The senator narrowed his eyes. "Why?"

Chief Reynolds nodded as if his question about Em had just been answered. And it probably had been. "The post office received a letter for her, addressed to here."

Someone knew she was here. Jake's heart rate jumped. The police chief could've told them that in a phone call. A sinking fear dropped to his gut.

Team members slipped silently from the room. Kate almost tripped as she ran up the stairs, and he wanted to follow her to check on Em and Amber, but he needed to know more before he acted. His mind already raced through where he'd take them to hide.

He could ask Arthur to set up something for them without anyone knowing. The man would do it even though Jake no longer worked for him because he loved Em so much. Plus, he wanted Jake back. If he had to return to the FBI to assure his family's safety, then that was what he'd do.

"You got any coffee?" their visitor asked.

Mrs. Kessler, carrying a cup to the chief, saved Jake from grabbing the chief's uniform front and shaking him to keep the man speaking. When he did speak, Jake raced for the stairs before he heard everything. It didn't matter. There was no time to waste. He almost bowled over Megan in the hallway. Both of his hands on her waist, he steadied her and moved to the side to pass her.

"I've got Emily." She pointed down the hallway. "You go help Kate with the girls."

He didn't think twice about rushing to the one who needed his help the most. Em was tough. She could handle getting ready. His daughter couldn't do it alone.

Hastily shoving clothes in a bag, Kate glanced over her shoulder and tossed some of the clothes at him when he entered the room. "Get them dressed."

Two sets of sleepy eyes looked at him, and his panic morphed into the calmness and the fatherly voice he didn't realize he had but needed. "Come on, you two sleepyheads. We're going on a trip. Let's see how fast we can get dressed and beat your uncles back downstairs." In an attempt to push excitement through them so they'd hurry, he added, "They said girls couldn't beat them."

Reagan jumped up and had her clothes on before he'd had Amber stripped out of her nightclothes. Handing him the pull-up and then his daughter's clothes, Reagan urged, "Hurry, Uncle Jake."

Kate grabbed the girls' attention before they bolted from the room. "All right, you two, get two toys each to take with you. Hurry. I bet your uncles are planning on winning." With the children rummaging in their toy chest, she turned to him and whispered, "What happened?"

His eyes remained riveted to his daughter. "Anthrax in a letter. The post office caught it, but not before a few people were exposed."

"Christ."

"I planned to grab Em and my daughter and get the hell out of here, but it looks like you're a step ahead of me."

After zipping the two bags, she turned back to him, and her demeanor reminded him she was a strong member of the team and a former FBI agent. "Go pack a bag. We'll leave immediately."

"I'm not letting Amber out of my sight."

Em rushed into the room, picked up her daughter, and held her tight. Her eyes widened when she saw Jake. What emotion lurked in there was unreadable, but he could sense the fear rolling off her in waves.

Reagan jumped up and down. "Mommy, hurry. We need to beat Uncle Brad and Uncle Matt downstairs."

Em raised her brow at Jake, who shrugged in an innocent gesture.

"Great idea. I bet we'll beat them and still have time for breakfast." Kate reached out to stop Reagan from racing from the room. "You, young lady, stay with me."

Following the group out of the room, not willing to leave them out of his sight, he grumbled to no one in particular when Kate turned around and told him, again, to go pack. Only after seeing Jesse meet them at the top of the stairs, did he obey her.

Things had been so calm that the danger had almost been forgotten. Almost. Someone out there still wanted something from her. Something she didn't have. This danger had to fucking end. He would not lose them. *Anthrax. Christ!*

Chapter Thirteen

On the large private airplane Jesse had hired or borrowed, who the fuck cared at this point, the family gave the appearance of cliques in high school with three groups huddled together separated from each other. Observing the group with the women and children brought a smile to Jake's face, regardless of their reason for fleeing. At that moment, they were safe.

The two little girls chatted non-stop about how they'd showed the boys that girls were faster, the cupcakes Mrs. Kessler had given them for the trip, and their plans when they reached their new destination. The kids didn't even know where they were headed. A child's imagination was wonderful.

His eyes strayed to Em's, wishing they sat together, her on his lap, and then joining the mile-high club. A smile crept on his face but immediately disappeared when she glanced at him and quickly looked away. She said they'd do this together so he wouldn't let her take them a step back. Fighting the pull between them was futile, and she'd soon realize it.

As for the other, he would see someone in Oxford. Someone who could help him heal, if that was what he needed. He wouldn't harm his family, even accidentally.

Dragging his gaze to the second group, Brad and Les pointed to spots on the house plans Jake knew they were reviewing with the team. While the men had military, law enforcement or a government alphabet job behind them, Brad's secret service experience had enhanced the group's tactics and planning in situations such as this.

Matt's question brought his focus back to his group. "Jesse, are you sure going to Oxford is smart? It's not a safe house."

"I've had enhancements to security installed this past year," Devon said. "It's just as secure."

"And they can't find it attached to us in public records because it's in a dummy corporation." Questioning eyebrows rose at Blake's statement. "I wanted a place I could stay where people didn't know it was mine. You see how people are driving around to see Grisham's house. I wanted you kids to have peace and quiet."

"But, don't you come here for ballgames regularly?" At least Jake remembered them doing it while he'd grown up in the Hamilton household.

The senator nodded. "I do, but not regularly. But remember, there are quite a few prominent people who attend these games. Quite a few. So I'm not necessarily a big deal."

Jake still didn't like it. They'd be too exposed. "Yes, but don't you attend the first football game every year? Wouldn't someone expect that at least?"

Jesse smiled. "But, they're not after Dad, and that's why this location is perfect. They know we're hiding Em and wouldn't expect us to bring her near Dad and somewhere so public."

Outrage rushed forward in Jake's mind. "Are you fucking nuts? Are you really thinking of bringing her to the game?"

From behind him, a hand rested on his shoulder. "Don't worry, Jake." Brad continued around him and sat. "We've got this covered. You don't truly think we'd put our sister in danger, do you?"

"It sure as hell sounds like it." Did they not hear themselves? Bringing her to a place where people knew the senator would be didn't sound like keeping her out of danger to him. He should've taken off with her and Amber before anyone had been the wiser.

Jesse heaved a heavy sigh. "Jake, trust us. It's not like we'll be flaunting her all over town."

Blake stood. "My boy, this isn't the first time I've allowed my sons to hide a client there. It's secluded, and they've got it down pat." He walked to his daughter.

Turning back to the men, Jake faced numerous stern faces. He raised his hands in a surrender gesture. "Okay. I'll trust you. But, if even a hint of danger rears its ugly head, I'm getting them the hell out of there."

AJ chuckled and leaned back in the leather seat, moved his hands behind his head, and closed his eyes as if he hadn't a care in the world. "You'd have to catch up to us first."

A giggling toddler raced across the cabin and launched herself onto AJ's lap.

"Oomph." AJ's eyes flew open, and his hands grasped Amber's waist, a smile stretched across his face. "Is that my little doodle-bug?"

The volume of her giggling increased as her little hands scratched at her uncle's chest in an attempt to tickle him, only to end up squirming when he returned the favor.

The playful laughter and antics of his daughter and AJ sent an unwanted slice of jealousy carving its way through his heart. Not that he begrudged Amber loving her uncles and playing with them, but he envied the close relationship she and her Uncle AJ had, a closer one than he'd developed with her so far.

Giving himself the mental kick in the ass he deserved, he had to remember to be thankful that AJ had been there for Em and Amber when he hadn't.

Jake had wanted to wring Jesse's neck when he'd learned about the danger when they had been possible targets in a deadly game a psychopath played with Jesse and Kate. All had turned out well, but it only reinforced his thoughts to the fact they were once again in danger. Whereas before it was just a possibility, this time, they were the targets.

Amber climbed onto Jake's lap, leaning against him, her thumb in her mouth. Pulling his tired daughter against him, his heart still ached about her being in the hands of a kidnapper. Thank God that man had treated her well, as if it was an afternoon of fun with a family friend. Hugging her tightly, never wanting to let her go, Jake kissed her soft hair on the crown of her head.

Although early for a nap, he'd already learned to take advantage when he could to let her sleep. Reclining in his chair as AJ had, the love any father should have for his daughter flooded his veins. Snuggling her, he closed his eyes and washed away the jealousy he'd felt with her and AJ. He'd take her trusting him to keep her loved and safe any day.

He just had to live up to that.

"Em, we need to go through the information I pulled."

"Sure, Dev. Jake?"

Opening his eyes, he drank in the sight of Em, still in awe of the womanly figure she'd grown into. Without her makeup and hair all fixed up, she reminded him of his little sprite. How had it taken him so long to realize how deep his feelings for her ran? He'd definitely been an idiot. "Yeah?"

"Will you keep Amber occupied for me?"

Part of him wanted to scream, "Hell, no," because he wanted to know everything that Devon had pulled. The other part of him mentally leaped for joy at the fact she'd asked him, trusting him after what they'd discussed. The sucking noise from his daughter's sleeping form made the decision for him. He nodded. Devon would update him later. This was what he needed to be doing.

****

Keeping her eyes focused on the financial documents her brother had handed her proved difficult for Emily because she kept gazing at the loving picture of Jake and their daughter sleeping.

Damn Jake, and damn her body's intense craving for him that had taken over her actions last night and allowed him into her bed. The warmth of his lips slanting over hers, his tongue making love to her mouth, and his hand fondling her breast brought back the erotic events on her eighteenth birthday and the beautiful love they'd made.

This time, he'd been awake and oh, how she'd enjoyed it, enjoyed touching him, knowing his responses were real. It had been something she'd craved for so long, but she no longer knew what to do. The painful memories of rejection and humiliation returned and warned her to let it go, let last night be what it was—sex.

Her hand moved to her neck. And then there'd been that.

"Are you going to give him a chance?"

Snapping back to the present at Dev's question, she wondered how long he'd been talking to her while her mind had been elsewhere. She bounced the edge of the stack of papers on her thigh in a half-hearted attempt to straighten them. Focusing on the printouts as best as she could with her mind being a traitor and returning her to last night and the pleasure she'd experienced. "Did you get these from the burned piece of equipment from the office?"

His silence made her almost blurt it all out... her feelings... her fears.

A heavy sigh reached her ears. "Okay. I'll leave it for now. But, give him a chance. I believe he's sincere."

Looking up, her gaze fell on Jake and Amber again. Give him a chance? She somewhat had by spending time getting to know each other again and by rolling in the sheets with him. Maybe she needed to go with it and see where it took her. Besides, she had promised to help him. And she had to do that to ensure she and Amber were safe around him. And so he didn't look so pained. She hated seeing that despair in him the previous night.

"In answer to your question, no, I didn't get these from the burned piece of equipment. These are from where I dug into the financial companies you told us about."

Flipping through the few pages, she furrowed her brow in confusion and then looked up at her brother.

"Dev, there are only two companies here. I gave you a dozen."

"You did. These are the only two that had the red flags you told me to look for. Both Strickland and Randall have had problems with the SEC that mysteriously disappeared. I'm pretty confident Strickland is clean, but wanted you to take a look."

"Oh, no," she whispered in disbelief. "These are Dad's friends."

Nodding, Dev's gaze landed on their father. "We'll have to tell him, but I want you to do that forensic accounting stuff you do. Maybe I'm wrong and overlooked something with another company, but we need to eliminate these two. Unfortunately, my gut tells me it's Randall."

"I hope not, but these are the two wealth management companies we dealt with the most."

"I know this isn't all you'll need, but I hoped you might notice something from here before we pulled more data. These companies have security the likes of the CIA. I don't dare stay in too long and tip our hand too early."

Flipping through the pages, absorbed in reading through numbers, doing quick recalculations in her head, she ignored any further comments from her brother. Math, her favorite subject in school, came naturally, and after taking a class in accounting in high school, she'd found her calling. The potential loss of her career in accounting wouldn't discourage her from finding the man who had swindled people, stealing their investments and, for some, their life savings. And who had kidnapped her daughter.

She wanted to quickly rule out her father's college

buddies, the men who generally went to the first Ole Miss game of the season with him, especially since that was where they were headed. But she refused to rush.

Setting aside Strickland's financials, she glanced up at the still sleeping Jake and Amber. The picture of them set a flip-flop in her stomach. She prayed he didn't have a nightmare. That thought almost had her out of her chair and reaching for her daughter. Then she took a deep breath. Trust. Plus, there were plenty of people nearby; it wasn't that big of an airplane, in case something happened. Mind somewhat settled, she turned back to the task at hand. "When are you calling in the SEC?"

"Soon."

Tearing her gaze from the paperwork, she looked at her brother and furrowed her brow. "Why not now?"

He chuckled. "You're as bad as Jake."

Her eyes automatically snapped to the man in question. He'd been asking her brothers about her problem. She shouldn't be surprised at how protective he was.

"You know why we're not calling yet, Em. We don't know if it was only Paul. Plus, we don't wish to implicate Dad's friends without cause."

Nodding absently, she searched through Randall Wealth Management's file, her finger sliding across the page as she read. Halting her finger, she moved it back. "Pull up Randall and any trades he did for Warren Mills earlier this year."

Dev plucked away at his keyboard. "Any particular reason?"

"It's the trade prices on February fourteenth. They seem off."

He stilled his hands, looked at her, and raised his dark brows. "I know you have somewhat of a photographic memory when it comes to numbers, but that was a long time ago, Em."

Looking away, deep in concentration, she stared at a stained spot on the dark blue carpeting, recalling the Mills's account financials. "His was the most recent account I audited, and I went through it three times. His numbers stick out."

Her brother spun the laptop around on the small table between them, so it faced her. "Here you go."

Flipping between Randall's reporting of Mr. Mills's account and the archived trading on the stock exchange, she stopped and looked up, and then started when she noticed Jesse sitting in a seat facing her. When the hell had he come over?

She nodded at Dev.

He spun the laptop around and pushed some buttons before looking expectantly at her.

"I think it's him. Mr. Randall. I remember specifically how the accounts seemed off on that particular date. It's because there are different stock prices listed on the accounts between Randall and my boss. The other lines seem to match, but I didn't review his entire account, just a snapshot."

"If they were running a scheme, they'd have a separate set of accounting files with the actuals before Randall shuffled the money around and sent the statements with the doctored amounts to his clients." Jesse waved Kate over. "If they didn't cover their tracks one day, they're bound to have screwed up again."

Emily's sister-in-law settled in the seat beside her.

"Dev, tear through everything you can find on

them." Jesse turned to her. "Em, I want you going through what he finds."

Kate cocked her head to the side. "What did you need me to do?"

A sly grin stretched across her oldest brother's face, and he winked at his wife. "Nothing. I just wanted to look at you up close."

She tossed him a saucy look. "I'm glad you're in a good mood. Tomorrow, we're taking the Graceland trip we'd planned."

"Dammit, Kate. You know better."

Stabbing her index finger on the table, she snapped back at Jesse, "Tomorrow is the perfect time, *and* your sister is coming if she wants to."

Emily's gaze bounced back and forth between her brother and his wife, watching their silent standoff. Kate knew she wasn't going with them, so this must be a war of wills. The dynamic between these two always surprised her.

Dev broke the uncomfortable silence. "Jesse, if it's Randall, we need to move Em. He goes to the first game with Dad every year. Him and Strickland."

Shaking his head, Jesse pursed his mouth. "Randall canceled his trip. I sent a couple of the men to watch both of them for us when you gave me their names. I'll call back the ones on Strickland, which will give us more men for things like"—he glared at his wife—"the Graceland trip."

"See, it's all settled. We're going." Kate's confident nod brought a smile to Emily's lips. She loved how her sister-in-law typically got her way with her controlling brother.

Reaching across the table, he threaded his fingers

through his wife's hand. "Sweetheart…."

Jake cleared his throat and gazed down at Emily. "She wants you to take her to potty."

Chapter Fourteen

Requiring the direction from a six-year-old in the proper buckling of his daughter's car seat embarrassed Jake, and he imagined Em was observing and silently laughing. Pulling here, clicking there, and inserting an arm through a hole confused the hell out of him. He'd never figure out how to get Amber out of the torture device.

Bags were tossed in the cars and van at the small Oxford private airstrip. One day he wanted the pull Jesse had. A couple of phone calls and they had the private jet for the trip and vehicles waiting for them in the otherwise deserted parking lot.

When he triumphantly stood, a round of clapping from the men heated his blood. Turning around, he responded with his middle finger. He caught himself before he twisted back to the car. *Shit.* He'd have to remember to act more mature with his daughter around. His brothers were going to test him. He just knew it.

The drive to the farm, as they liked to call it, went uneventfully. The large magnolia trees lining the side of the road, hiding the property, were a glorious sight. The nostalgia of it choked him up as he remembered when he'd climbed them, when he was younger to hide from Em and when he was older to spy on her.

The convoy of vehicles turned down the asphalt drive before stopping in front of the pale blue wood house with white columns and a full porch across the front. He'd always wondered why they decided to call it a farm when it was nothing more than a Southern mansion on a whole lot of land.

Kelly Jones, the live-in housekeeper, met them at the door, beaming as each of the men wrapped the older woman in a bear hug before they filed into the house and drifted toward the tantalizing smells within. Since he could remember, she'd greeted them with homemade chocolate chip cookies.

Bringing up the rear, Jake groaned at the news that with the addition of the team, the men had to bunk together and in shifts. Since they'd used the house for HIS business before, most rooms had been outfitted with two full-size beds that were, thankfully, extended length. He'd hoped since AJ had married, he'd have their old room to himself. Now, it looked like he'd not only have to share again, but someone might use it during the day to rest. It was important to have them all here for Em's security, but he'd have no privacy.

He smiled when he heard Em was able to use her old room, where she would sleep alone. Or so everyone thought.

****

Sitting on the back porch with his brothers and friends, drinking beer and listening to stories, was another part of putting Jake's life back to rights. One of the things he'd missed over the years. There had been so many nights they'd sit outside, and the older brothers would give him and AJ beer when they weren't old enough to legally drink. They'd always treated him as one of them, never as the straggler they'd picked up to care for until he was old enough to be on his own.

A greater family couldn't be found. He thought back to what had happened and realized how stupid he had been at jumping the gun on things. These men would've listened. He almost snorted aloud. Once they took a month or so to calm down. And maybe took a bit of it out on his hide.

He shifted and twirled the neck of the bottle in his fingers. He would've screwed things up with Em and then they'd have eventually married because she was pregnant and there would have been resentment. Damn. He wasn't sure things would've worked out right because he hadn't realized how much he loved her at the time.

A round of laughter returned his mind back to the conversation. Last he'd heard they were talking about when Brad and Matt had fought on the fishing boat and tipped it in the middle of the pond. That wasn't unusual, so there must've been something unique about this time that made it so funny.

"Les, you should bring us on another trail ride." AJ held his side from laughter, catching his breath. "I loved watching Brad and Dev try to ride."

The group chuckled.

Brad grumbled instead. "I rode just fine. I couldn't help it if my horse was fucked-up."

"You were thrown." Trent howled with laughter.

"Fuck you."

Les removed his cowboy hat and wiped the sweat from his forehead with his forearm. "Well, you were, Brad," he drawled. "Maybe I should've given you a pony."

Brad's face turned red. "Fuck you, too."

Even Jake laughed with the men this time. He

hadn't been there, but he could imagine Brad getting tossed over the head of a horse, and he could picture him trying to ride his big ass on a pony.

Les had grown up in the area but had left and joined the DEA after his parents passed. Jake hadn't heard how he had hooked up with Jesse to become a member of HIS. All he knew was when they came here, generally with the senator for the first game of football season. Les typically took charge since it was his old stomping grounds. He also led the activities, and the trail ride appeared to have been a hit. For some of them.

Devon cleared his throat. "You can go without me. I can do without riding one of those beasts."

Another fit of laughter. Jake must've missed something good on their last trip. He couldn't wait for more adventures with them again. To have fun. To make new memories.

The cowboy shook his head. "It wasn't that bad. You did fine for a greenhorn." Les flashed a fun smile. "I'll just put you on a gentler horse next time. You don't need a pony like dipshit there." He pointed his thumb toward Brad.

Brad, of course, jumped up toward Les, who had a broader chest than the twin.

"Sit the fuck down, Brad. Christ, I'm getting tired of saying that." Jesse shook his head.

Jake took a sip of beer. He had a serious subject to broach; he was apprehensive, but he couldn't wait. His brothers were together, and it didn't matter if Trent and Les were there. They seemed to be with the group most of the time.

Jesse had made him an offer when he'd returned, and he hoped it still stood. He had a child and a soon-to-be wife to provide for and no job. Sure, Arthur would take him back, but that wasn't what he wanted. At one time, it had been all he'd wanted as a career; he'd wanted nothing more than to stop terrorism, but he'd changed. He wasn't sure how. Maybe it had been the assignment, maybe it was his life, maybe it was just him. Whatever the reason, he knew he wanted something broader, and he wanted to be part of this family again.

The brothers owned and ran HIS. They decided which assignments to accept, and one of the brothers led the mission while Ken, or in this case, Les, led the field team that was made up of ten men. His brothers typically worked closely with their client and the logistics, except Jesse, being a sharpshooter, joined the field team quite frequently.

When Jesse had asked him to join them, he'd never said specifically in what capacity. Jake wondered if they'd bring him in as a brother or put him on the field team. Either way was fine with him. No, what he really needed was their acceptance. Full acceptance. Sure, he wasn't a blood brother, but he'd been their brother since he was ten and a half years old. Bringing him into the family business as an equal would show him they approved of him as one of them. It would show Em they approved of him.

During a lull in the conversation, he decided it was time to bite the bullet. "I have something to talk about with you."

When each man gave Jake his attention. He cleared his throat before speaking. "You once offered me a position with HIS. Now that Em and I are to be married, I need a job. If it's still open, I'd like it."

He glanced around the group that remained stoic and gained nothing from their facial expressions. The smiling and laughter were gone. His gaze halted at Jesse, who seemed to be the decision maker.

His brother furrowed his eyebrows. "Are you doing this only for Em?"

"No. I want to be a part of this family again. I like what you've put together. I want to be part of HIS." He swallowed hard. Had he misjudged the offer?

His heart pounded loudly, waiting for a response.

Finally, Jesse reached out his hand. "Congratulations. Your name is on the business as a partner."

He shook everyone's hand, and they toasted his addition to the team before going back to stories of their adventures.

Relief coursed through him, and a massive weight lifted from his shoulders. He was thankful for this group of men in his life. He and Em were staying with the family. Surely she'd be happy with that.

Chapter Fifteen

Denied the ability to make love to Em the night prior by his daughter's need to sleep with her mother, he was at least comforted that he finally had time alone with his family. The few people who'd remained at the house kept to themselves. In comfy cargo shorts and a T-shirt, he lay on his side, propped on his elbow, on the floor beside Em and Amber. Both sat Indian style as the little one worked with the learning toy her mother had insisted she play with. Since he had no idea what games a three-year-old was capable of comprehending, he went along, but later he'd find fun toys for his daughter. However, she did look adorable concentrating, but he also loved to hear her giggle.

Watching mother and daughter interact awakened something inside him that he hadn't known existed. The protectiveness of being a father had already consumed him, but this feeling…he couldn't comprehend it himself. Was this how a father felt when his family was complete? If so, he'd take that feeling any day.

And the two of them together, in almost matching khaki shorts and olive green tank tops, were more than he'd ever thought he'd have in his life. He expected that as the son of a murderer, the son of a man who beat his wife to death, no woman would marry him. Yet, he'd forgotten all that when he'd decided that he'd marry Em. He'd forgotten that she might reject him because of it. Okay, he'd remembered it a time or two, and his resolve had wavered, but his love for her had been so great, he'd moved forward.

He swallowed hard. He would not lose them. He'd made a call earlier to set up an appointment with a psychiatrist for a diagnosis. Em had offered to go with him, but he needed to do this himself. Knowing she stood by him would be enough. And he wouldn't wait until they returned to Baltimore. His family needed protection from him now. He needed a good night's sleep without reliving the beatings and torture.

"If you want to go to Graceland, I'll take you once this is over."

Even though she hadn't given her reason for turning down going on the trip, and he loved the family for not pressing her for one, he knew she did it for her safety, to keep from fighting with her brothers and to keep from leaving their daughter. He admired her for it because he knew that her stubbornness could get her in trouble if she allowed it.

She'd promised not to do anything to compromise her or their daughter's safety and, by her easily staying home, she showed him she was serious. He just hoped she was as set on staying home when the big game came around. There would be a lot of excitement around that one event. He'd have to trust her.

Em shrugged and then reached over and helped Amber turn the wooden puzzle piece to fit correctly in the triangle shape on the board.

His daughter's squeal and clapping at getting the shape in place brought genuine laughter rumbling through his chest. The little squirt might pitch some hellacious fits when she wanted to get her way, but damn if she wasn't the cutest child ever when she was happy.

Emily handed the little girl another puzzle piece without glancing at him. "I've seen it before."

He smiled at her serious, motherly look while giving a lesson. Damn if it wasn't sexy. Pulse pounding, heat rode out in his veins, and he fought running his fingers through her glorious golden hair. Demonstrating he wanted her in public didn't bother him, but he knew it would not sit well with her, and he had no idea what to do, or not do, in front of children. He'd have to watch Kate and Jesse and see how they behaved in front of Reagan. Granted, Reagan was older. Thinking of Jesse reminded him that he and Em hadn't spoken of where they'd live.

Hell, they hadn't spoken of getting married again. He didn't really know how to broach that subject, but he planned to do so today. Mrs. Kessler agreed to watch Amber later so he could have time alone with Em. The older woman didn't know why, but he suspected she knew something by the sly smile on her face when he'd asked.

The advice from the men about how to propose made him want to laugh aloud again. The one thing that did hold true in their bullshit words was they loved their sister and wanted Jake to do right by her, and that meant asking her and not telling her. Taking their suggestion to heart, he decided to spend quality time with her, hoping it would help her regain her trust in him again. But, dammit, he was tired of waiting.

"I decided to work with your brothers."

"They're your brothers too."

It sounded so seedy when she said it that way. He

didn't want to add blood and not-blood brother into everything. That would get, well, annoying. "How about we just call it working with the guys?"

A light, feminine trickle of laughter floated to him as she turned to flash him a smile and sparkle in her eyes, and a jolt of lust sheared through his gut.

He waited until she finished helping Amber with a puzzle piece and then cleared his throat. Once she turned her head and he felt he had her undivided attention, he reached up and swiftly pulled her head down and stole a kiss before their daughter noticed the move.

Leaving Em wide-eyed, he released her and focused on the toddler who furrowed her brows, concentrating on matching a square to a square on the puzzle board. Wanting to help, he pointed to the correct spot.

Now glaring at him with a humorous glint, Em swatted his hand away.

He raised his brows and chuckled at her playfulness. "What? You helped."

The more time he spent with his family, watching them smile, laugh and play, the larger his heart grew with love for them. Almost to bursting. How could it possibly survive a lifetime?

Not long ago, he'd had absolutely no hope for his life. In fact, he'd been ready to greet his mother. Now, he was full of hope and some of that hope was that his mother was looking down on her granddaughter with approval.

Bob decided to make his appearance and walked across the board, rubbing against a giggling Amber, who proceeded to wrap her arms around the furry animal in an attempt to pick up the large cat that probably weighed close to his daughter's weight. Okay, not close, but still too heavy for his child to lift. Even he could tell that.

Emily reached out. "Don't pick him up. He's too heavy. Besides, he likes you to pet him more."

The little girl unwound her arms, and she slid one of her hands back and forth over the fluffball's head. "Okay, Mommy."

Jake and Em's eyes snapped to each other in surprise, and then they smiled in unison. Their daughter's speech was coming along. The letter k was a good start.

Before either could speak, Brad walked into the room. The serious look on his face wiped the smile from Jake's. He immediately went into defensive mode. He'd convinced Em to pack a small bag for her and Amber just in case they had to run at a moment's notice like before. She hadn't wanted to do it because it brought it too close to home, but she'd seen the need. It was important Amber have some familiar things wherever they went. Those bags were in the front closet for whoever was there for them to grab. Of course, he knew he'd always be one of those with them.

They hurriedly stood.

"Megan's in labor."

Em gasped, and Jake thought he might have to check her into the emergency room with how quickly the blood drained from her face. "Oh God. It's too early."

****

Jake couldn't stop Em from rushing into the hospital, unconcerned if he or Brad were by her side.

She raced to the family in the waiting room. "Is she okay?"

Kate grimaced. "We don't know yet. We hope it's false labor since she's not due for almost three months."

A wave of sadness and fear washed across Em's face, and he reached his arm around her shoulders, pulling her to him for comfort. She laid her head sideways on top of his shoulder and closed her eyes for a moment.

His throat tightened, making it difficult to swallow around the self-reproach he held. Thinking of not being there for Em during childbirth sent a perverse sadness creeping into his body. He'd missed this with her and their daughter. She'd suffered through it all without him by her side, supporting her, comforting her, loving her. Anything could've gone wrong, and he hadn't been there.

Jake leaned his head to the top of hers and inhaled the fruity scent she wore. He couldn't keep beating himself up for his decision. It was done and over with, but he couldn't stop the guilt that riddled his heart. It would probably never fully depart.

He thought of their daughter, safe at the house with a small team. "Did you have false labor with Amber?"

Jarring his head, she moved hers in some semblance of a nod, her hair rubbing softly against his cheek, reminding him of how the silky mass had slid through his hands. "Yes, but not this early."

"Was it painful?" He gulped. "Having our daughter?"

She jerked her head away and looked at him as if he'd lost his mind. "No. It was a piece of cake. What the hell do you think?"

He chuckled at her sarcasm. "Okay, stupid question. Was it an easy delivery is what I meant?"

She sighed softly. "I was in labor for nearly twenty hours."

His body jerked, and his eyes widened. "Shit!"

"And I cussed at you so loudly. I'm surprised you didn't hear me where you were." A twinkle sparkled in her eyes. "I'm sure Megan is doing the same to AJ right now, false labor or not."

"Well, I'm sure he deserves it." He playfully winked at her and was rewarded with a bright smile on lips he wanted to kiss again, taste again.

"Was anyone in the delivery room with you? You know, like AJ is?" He wanted to punch himself in the face for that question. *Great way to remind her of fucking abandoning her.*

Em snorted. "Believe it or not, AJ."

"What?" Even though he was her brother, jealously swamped him. "He saw you naked?" Jake gestured over her body. "All of you?" He didn't appreciate her laughter at his question. Did he really sound that foolish?

"I think he kept his eyes on mine or closed until she was born. Then they were only for Amber." She laughed softly. "I thought he might faint for a while when he accidentally looked down and saw the afterbirth."

Still in awe that AJ would go to such lengths for Em, Jake settled back in his chair. He swallowed hard, the sudden dryness of his throat made it difficult to speak. Growing up, he and AJ would've done anything for each other. Had AJ done this not just for Em but also for him? No matter. It was done. He owed the man a huge debt of gratitude. One he could never repay. He'd taken Jake's place at one of the most important times of his life. At one of the most important times in Em's life. When she'd needed Jake most. That was more than any man could ask of a friend. "I'm sorry. I'm glad someone was there."

Snuggling her close again, he kept an eye on the door, watching to make sure his friend had a chance at a child that was every bit as wonderful as the one he'd already helped bring into the world. The man who'd stood in his place deserved all the happiness a person could handle.

Settled in a corner of the emergency room waiting area, the men chatted about the upcoming football season. The group bolted from their seats when the youngest Hamilton brother walked out the ER door.

"It's false labor," AJ said in obvious relief. "But, they want her to remain here a while to keep an eye on her and Alexander."

Both AJ and the senator were named Alexander, but neither used it, so AJ and Megan had decided they'd name their child Alexander and actually call him by the name. Jake was curious how long it'd be before everyone shortened his name to Alex or, just to frustrate AJ, called him by his middle name, which Jake had no idea what it was.

Kate hugged her old partner. "Thank goodness. We'll be right here."

Stepping back, he looked over the group and shook his head. "You don't need to stay. There's nothing you can do. We'll be fine." Reaching out, he grasped and released Jesse's shoulder, and then he spun around to return to his wife.

Matt stepped forward, watching his baby brother push through the doors. "Does he really think we're leaving?"

Jesse shook his head. "No. He's just not thinking straight."

They all retook the seats they'd vacated. Chatter continued rattling through the group though the layer of tension that hung in the air had lightened, with many eyes periodically eyeing the door where AJ had disappeared.

Seeing a chance to be alone with Em, Jake reached out for her hand. "Can we get a coffee or something and talk?"

Without looking at him, she nodded. "Sure."

They followed the signs to the cafeteria, all the time he knew they had a shadow of at least two team members, if not her brothers. As long as they gave him and Em privacy, he didn't care how many followed. He had a question to ask.

****

Following Jake through the corridors of the hospital hand-in-hand comforted Emily, even if her brothers were behind them. She had an inkling he was ready to get back to the marriage question since they'd avoided any conversations dealing with a relationship. Although he had referred to her as *his* when they were in bed.

She'd enjoyed the time they'd spent getting to know each other once again, and he'd soaked up the stories she'd shared about Amber and had seemed lost while looking at photos. She'd watched him tracing one of them as if to memorize the moment he'd missed, which made her wish she could turn back time to allow him to spend time with his daughter.

Purchasing a large cup of sweet tea for each of them since the coffee was old, Jake led her to a secluded spot in the corner of the almost empty cafeteria. After sitting in the hard plastic seat he'd pulled out for her, she searched for their shadow, relieved to see the twins plant themselves far enough away from them for their conversation to remain private.

"Did you drop Trent?"

While prepared for almost anything, Jake's first question threw her for a loop. She'd forgotten about his statement when they'd been together. "What are you talking about? Trent and I aren't together."

Looking at her, he appeared to be mulling something over, maybe deciding if she'd told the truth. He heaved a deep sigh. "I'm sorry. I guess I misunderstood the situation."

"Hell yes, you did. Tell me where this came from." That explained the looks she'd witnessed him giving Trent, especially when the man was near her or Amber. While she should be angry at his assumption, his jealousy pushed her heart into a pitter-patter.

Taking a sip of tea and scrunching up his face at the taste, he scanned the room before seeking her gaze again. "It's not important." He cleared his throat. "Is there anyone else?"

Shaking her head, she frowned at the fact she hadn't had anyone special in her life. He knew that she'd waited for him and then devoted her entire life to her daughter, school, and then work. It kept her mind off her failed attempt at a relationship with him. "No." No one had compared to Jake. No one could take his place in her heart. And that had angered her in itself.

Reaching across the table, he clasped her hand, lacing his fingers with hers. The warmth flowed through her, the feel so welcoming, like she was home. "I know I messed up before not asking you to marry me, so I'm asking now. Will you marry me?" He grinned. "I'd get down on one knee, but your brothers may string me up by the ears before I hear your answer."

There it was, the question that had kept her up at night, affected her appetite and the myriad of emotions that jostled through her, constantly changing her answer. Jake had never pursued her when they'd lived in the same household. This new experience, his wanting to be with her, should've pleased her. And, it did, somewhat. Unfortunately, she worried the novelty would wear off like it always did with women in his past, that he'd stay because of his daughter, not because he loved her.

"You can't deny there's not something between us. You are all that I thought about while we were separated. If only I'd known…." He trailed off, leaving her wanting to knock him over the head for him to finish the thought.

Sliding her hand from his, she wrapped it around her cup and took a sip before returning the over-sweetened beverage to the table. What would it be like to wake in his arms each morning? To be taken into his embrace on a regular basis? "You don't need to do this for Amber. We can work something out."

His hand slammed on the table. "Dammit, Em. This is not about our daughter, and you damn well know it. This is about us."

"There is no us, Jake. You demonstrated that a long time ago." She had to drop this poison over the past, but the hurt had embedded itself too deep inside her heart, dug in deep over the years he'd been missing. How many times had she not wondered if she'd been the one to blame for everything? She had initiated the sex. No. He'd left and hadn't come back... until now.

Rubbing his hand on the back of his neck, he closed his eyes and exhaled loudly. When he opened them, the vulnerability shining within their brilliant blue took her back. "I'm sorry. I'm here now, and I want us to be together like we should've been. We should be a family, Em."

"What I don't get is that you never seemed this intent to be with me before. Why now?"

"You know why. You were too young." He flopped back in his chair. "Christ, Em, you were just becoming a woman. How were you to know what you truly felt for me was more than infatuation? Besides, I was an idiot and didn't realize how much I felt for you until it was too late."

Finally getting everything out in the open didn't heal her heart, but it made a big stride toward it as it betrayed her by slowly rekindling her love for him. Being a family would be a perfect scenario for her and Amber, but what happened when years down the road Jake regretted marrying her? Would he leave her again? She wouldn't be able to stand the easy dismissal from his life a second time.

He wanted an answer and the wrong one could ruin her and her daughter's lives. But whether being together or sharing custody was correct for Amber, she couldn't decide. Of course, their daughter absolutely adored him so being a family would please her, but would the heat burn out with her and Jake and bring bitterness into their marriage that would affect the little girl's world?

Now there was his possible PTSD to deal with. She promised to be by his side, but was she enough to help him? Waking up with his hands around her throat again wasn't something she wanted to happen.

"I need to think about it, Jake. This is a big decision that affects three lives." She'd taken his first proposal to heart after she'd let her anger at his demand they marry lift. Otherwise, she might not have taken that step. She wouldn't have risked the heartache again.

"There's nothing to think about. We both love our daughter and each other, with heat between us that is hotter than any I've ever known. Say yes and we'll get married tomorrow."

Did he just say he loved her? No. Not really. Not an, "I love you, Em," statement. It was tossed in with their daughter. It wasn't the love she craved from him. She couldn't get her hopes up that he was in love with her, but that would change everything. Love and not lust filled his gaze, and her heart attempted to pound out of her chest, seeking to be one with his. Her subconscious shoved the answer forward without the typical argument she'd been fighting. Yet, she didn't listen to it. Instead, she said, "I…I still need to think about it."

Chapter Sixteen

The sudden movement of the bed startled Emily awake.

"Mommy, *wake* up."

Pulling the pillow over her face, she grumbled, "Amber, how many times have I told you not to jump on the bed, especially when Mommy is sleeping?" She felt like such a hypocrite knowing she'd jumped on her brothers' beds many times when she'd been young.

What the hell? She tossed her pillow to the floor and moved to her knees, bouncing up and down on the bed with her daughter, holding hands with the little girl.

A moment later, Reagan climbed up with them, bouncing around the two of them.

"What's going on in here?" The stern voice from the doorway stopped them.

"Poppy, jump *wid* me and Rea-Rea."

Emily looked at her father, ready to stop Amber from saying anything more until she saw the smile he fought.

He rubbed his smooth chin as if giving his granddaughter's request considerable thought. "I think I might break the bed if I jumped on it."

Two giggling girls hopped off the bed and reached for their grandfather, tugging on his hands, and dragging him to the bed. Emily slipped off it, enjoying the relaxed look on her father's face as he pretended to resist the children.

He surprised them all by grabbing both of the girls and falling on the bed backward, allowing the two little ones to lie on top of him. His attempt at tickling them turned into a squirming session where each girl giggled and then squealed before moving out of his reach and then trying to slip back unnoticed to tickle him.

Before she realized what was happening, AJ and Jesse arrived and piled on the bed, taking turns being tortured by the little girls.

Laughing harder than she could remember, Emily grabbed her phone to take photos of a wonderful way to wake in the morning. It was days like this that she questioned her move away from the family.

Jesse extricated himself with his hands holding Reagan's waist, keeping her out of her arms' reach so she wouldn't torture him any longer. "Em, after you're dressed, we'll be waiting for you downstairs." He smiled at his daughter. "And now for my pumpkin." Leaning forward, he gave his daughter a noisy kiss. "I believe Mrs. Kessler has a special treat for you in the kitchen."

Amber stopped. "*Tweat?*" It was amazing the selective hearing of children.

Blake stood. "That's what I came to tell you before you captured me." He swung the little girl in his arms. "Come on, let's see if we can beat your Uncle AJ downstairs so he doesn't eat them all."

AJ followed. "What kind of treat?"

Emily laughed until her room cleared out. She had a moment to think. Actually, she'd done a great deal of that last night, tossing and turning in bed. She should've told Jake, "Yes." Heck, she should have shouted it out since it'd made her so happy.

She scanned the contents of her closet, glad she kept a few clothes here. And, thank goodness that she still fit in them. Well, most of them. She selected a tank top and shorts, dressed, and left her room. A shiver sliced up her spine. She halted her step. Damn, she was nervous about seeing Jake.

She had no idea what she needed to see or hear to tell him she'd marry him. Being around him would help her figure it out. That decided, she continued down the stairs and sat with her brothers in the family room. Unfortunately, Jake wasn't in sight.

Les stepped into the room. "Trent, Rob and Nef are having a picnic breakfast with the girls." After a few snorts from the group, he laughed. "I wouldn't discount babysitting duty today. Mrs. Kessler gave them the rest of the cookies."

Scrutinizing him, AJ's eyes widened then narrowed. "Are those crumbs on your shirt?"

"Yep. Temporary team leader privilege." Les pulled a cookie from behind his back and bit into it, taunting AJ.

Flying over the couch, she'd thought her brother was going to tackle Les, but instead, he arrived in time to watch the cookie disappear into the man's mouth.

Breaking through the laughter, Kate's voice stopped the youngest Hamilton brother from sprinting out the door. "Leave it, AJ. Do you want me to wake your wife and tell her you were on your way to steal the girls' cookies?"

"How is Megan?" Emily scooted to the spot her brother had vacated on the couch and sat.

"She's doing okay. The doctor told her to take it

easy for a few days." He collapsed in an empty chair, stretched and yawned. "Which means I may need to tie her to the bed."

"Brad can give you some rope if you need it." Matt shook his head as if in disgust.

Emily snapped her head to Brad. She didn't put anything past AJ and Megan's bedroom antics. She'd heard they were into Kama Sutra, but hearing this about Brad made her queasy.

With a thumb pointed to the front of the house, Brad raised and lowered his eyebrows. "I've got some in the truck if you need it." The sly smile on this face had bile rising in her throat.

"You are one sick fuck." Jesse shook his head.

Brad's smile widened. "Gotta be prepared." Hell, he'd prepared for while they were here? Good grief.

"I'm gonna puke if we don't change the subject." She wasn't lying either. This was too much information. They were a close family, but some things were best kept to themselves. Their sex lives were one of them.

Kate stood, walked over and punched Brad on the shoulder. "I think you forget there are women around now. Mind your fucking manners." She walked to the kitchen.

Emily wanted to laugh at Brad's stunned face and his rubbing his shoulder. It hadn't taken long for her sister-in-law to begin reining in the behavior of her brothers. Sure, a display or two got out of hand, but Kate always seemed to bring them back under control.

A thought suddenly occurred to her. "Jesse, what happened with Paul? Has he woken yet?" She immediately felt like an idiot asking. If he'd been awake, her brothers would've told her along with anything they'd learned.

Jesse cleared his throat. "He didn't make it."

She gasped and moved her hand to cover her mouth. "No. What about Jake? What will happen to him?" The thought of him going to jail for protecting her left her fighting the bile that once again attempted to rise in her throat. He'd never forgive her, and Amber would not see her father again for a long time.

"The case has been closed as it should be. Self-defense." Blake looked around the group. "Where is Jake?"

Kate walked back into the room and handed her a cup of coffee. "I forgot to pack Amber's swimsuit so he ran into town to pick one up for her." She gave Emily a small nod. Kate knew Jake had his appointment today with the psychiatrist. She'd given him cover.

"From the data I did find, Em and I were able to narrow it down to the investment firm we believe is involved." Devon turned his attention to his father. "Dad, we have to warn you that it's Randall."

Shaking his head, their father's face reddened. "You've known him all your lives. Does he seem like the type to swindle people?"

"Dad," —Jesse paused until he had this father's attention— "whoever this is, kidnapped Amber. We can't afford to pass anyone by, no matter how close they are to us."

"You're right." Blake ran his fingers through his hair. "Thank God, Charles canceled his trip."

Emily closed her eyes and willed her mind to clear and think back to the annual family trips. She focused on the room again. "It wasn't his voice that I heard."

At some point, Kate had slid down beside her. "Are you sure? How long has it been since you've heard him speak?"

"It's been a while, but I know his voice, and it wasn't him." The racing of her heart slowly normalized as she grew more confident in her brothers' abilities to keep her and her daughter safe with her brothers.

"Even so, it could be someone who works for Charles." Matt stretched out his leg, closed his eyes, and sighed. "What about Brian?"

"Who's Brian?" Kate asked.

Emily had forgotten about him. Charles's son had always kept to himself, staying in the background. She strained to remember his voice and then shook her head. "It's not him either."

"I can't see him being part of it," Jesse added. "He's as ethical as they come." He looked at his father. "Dad, when was the last time Brian visited for a game?"

"Hmm. Probably about the same time as you all stopped coming. Right after he finished college."

Emily brightened. "What if we talk with him? He wouldn't stand for his father doing this. He can't possibly realize it."

"If we do and he's involved or decides his loyalty is to his father, Charles will know we're investigating him," AJ stated.

Jesse nodded and compressed his lips into a thin smile. "It's definitely an idea worth pursuing."

"What about Bill? Do you want me to call and cancel his trip here? He won't like it, but I can come up with a good reason if necessary so we can keep Em being here a secret."

Shaking his head, Jesse looked thoughtful. "No, Dad, we've discussed it. We can handle Bill."

"If you're wrong, then bringing him here puts my daughter and granddaughter at risk. I won't have it."

A cocky grin burst forth on AJ's face. "You don't think we wouldn't have a plan, do you?"

Squirming, Emily was curious of this plan as well. Maybe she and Amber needed to leave and have her brothers watch them somewhere away from all of this.

"Let's hear it. If I don't like it, I'm not allowing anyone to set foot near this family."

Jesse offered his hand to help Kate stand, sat and pulled her onto his lap. "First thing is that Bill and his family can't use the guest house. They must go to a hotel. Tell him it's for the newlyweds or whatever you wish. Even though we're able to easily secure this place, two people will protect Em and Amber at all times. I'm not talking about watching over her from across the room. I mean glued to her." He looked at Emily. "That means you stick with Kate and one of us at all times. She even accompanies you to the bathroom."

Emily wrinkled her nose in disbelief. "Even here?"

"When we're here, without any company, you'll have more space, but someone will still be near you at all times."

"What if Amber and I just hide out? No one knows we're here."

Brad stood and pursed his lips. "Bill's daughter will be here and she's expecting you."

She wanted to slap herself on the forehead. She'd set herself up for that one. "Then maybe we should leave." She knew her brothers would keep her safe, but she couldn't understand why they didn't just let her and her daughter move somewhere else.

"No, Em. We're not worried about you here, and know we're going overboard with so much protection, but you're our baby sister, and we won't chance anything. Besides, we have a team on Charles." Jesse raised his eyebrows at her, his look stern. "As long as you do as you're told, things will be fine." He raised his eyebrows. "And, I'm serious about you not going to the game unless it's safe. Jason will understand." He took her hand. "Do you trust us?"

She always had and nothing had changed. "Of course."

"Then trust us now. But you're still stuck here. You go nowhere unless necessary and only with a group of us protecting you." Jesse looked at his phone and then answered it.

"Maybe I should stay back from the game."

Kate smiled. "It's Jason's birthday party, and we'd like you there, but don't worry, if things aren't safe, you don't get to go. Whether you want to or not. It's as simple as that."

Shaking her head, she still wasn't sure. It seemed it'd be smartest to stash her and her daughter somewhere else, but this is what her family did. They protected people and investigated things. If she left, her chance with Jake would fly out the window.

"Besides," Kate said amidst grumbling from her brothers, "Arthur will be here with his friend who happens to be the director of the SEC."

So, they did have some kind of secret plan.

Jesse ended his call and smiled. "The boys are bringing Teri in." Then he turned to Emily. "You're to remain hidden until we figure her out."

Emily shrugged. She'd already figured the woman out. The word bitch fit her well. She hoped Teri was useful.

Chapter Seventeen

Emily raised her eyebrows and then laughed. Jake returned from purchasing their daughter a swimsuit with probably a dozen bags of clothes and toys. He'd even picked up a couple of things for Reagan so she didn't feel left out. She loved this man.

The kids cared nothing for the cute outfits he displayed. His smile of pride showed. They tore into the toys.

With a serious look on his face, he took a moment and clasped her hand and squeezed. She took that as his silent reassurance that his appointment went well. She was so proud of him for seeking treatment and not waiting. Of course, she knew he did it for her and Amber.

Emily had fretted enough about her old boss's assistant. On one hand, she was immensely relieved they'd found the woman because they'd have the evidence they needed to end all this. But, on the other hand, the woman had always treated Emily like she was beneath her. Maybe Teri would try to implicate her. She wouldn't put it past her.

They walked silently down the stairs and into the family room and came up short. Emily had been so lost in her own thoughts that she hadn't paid attention or heard the voices. In front of them, Teri stood, taking center stage, flirting with Emily's brothers.

It was too late for Emily to hide. Teri had seen her. Worse, she'd seen Jake and by the way she dramatically licked her lips, Emily would say she found him more than appealing. Emily's hackles raised.

Teri floated to her, and in her haughtier attitude greeted Emily. "Oh, Emily, it's so good to see you." She didn't wait for Emily to respond before she turned her gaze to Jake, stepping closer to him. If she moved much more, she'd be plastered to her man. And, dammit if Jake hadn't moved back. Did he find the gorgeous blonde sexy? Of course he did. All men did. The woman used her looks to get whatever she wanted in life. It looked like she wanted Jake.

"Emily, I need something to drink. It was a long trip here." Teri's eyes never left Jake when she spoke. "Would you be a dear and get me something?"

She'd get her something all right. A slap across the face sounded like a good beginning. But, Emily reasoned with herself, they needed this woman, and she was only flirting. Surely Jake wouldn't fall for it.

Why did she have to pick Jake? All her brothers and most of the HIS men were handsome. Why did she zero in on her man? *Because she knows it'll get to you. That's why.*

Jesse tilted his head to the kitchen and Emily took his hint. "I'll go find Mrs. Kessler." She stomped from the room.

It took a few minutes to find Jesse's housekeeper. She and Kelly had been making beds and hadn't heard they had a visitor. Mrs. Kessler rushed off to prepare refreshments while Emily drew in a deep breath on her walk back to her brothers—and Teri. She had to calm down.

Unsure what made her do it, Emily stopped outside the room where she couldn't be seen.

"When's the last time you saw your boss?" Jesse's voice boomed. Maybe he had seen her. Otherwise, she doubted he'd speak that loudly, nor leave the door open.

"The same day as the fire. I came into work and saw Michael pouring something that I guess was gasoline on the computer systems, and he told me to go, to leave town and stay away because I'd be in danger. So, I did and haven't heard from anyone except your men since."

"Why did you take the information?" Matt probed.

"I'd rather not say. I'm waiting to speak with the FBI." She paused. "Your man, Danny, assured me that I'd get to talk with them. I want a deal before I speak about any of it."

Obviously unperturbed by her statements, Jesse pushed on. "Why did you pull the information from Em's computer instead of your own?"

A female huff sounded. "Because if it was found out by my boss, he'd blame her." Emily could visualize her shrugging without a care.

"They did blame her. They kidnapped her daughter!" Brad all but screamed.

"But, she's okay, so no harm done."

That bitch! Emily wanted to wring Teri's neck. How dare she! Emily peeked into the room, ready to reveal herself when she noticed Jesse give her a slight shake of his head. So he had known she was there. She remained hidden even though her feet wanted to propel her to wherever Teri sat and bitch-slap her. They had told her to stay out of sight. Although she was pretty sure they meant altogether. Too late for that.

"Tell me why we should allow you to stay with us instead of turning you over to the police?" Jesse's tone put a bit of fear in her.

"Because," Teri said softly, "I need the protection from your big men." Her voice turned seductive. "Like this one."

Emily stiffened. Oh hell no. Ignoring Jesse's subtle directive to remain hidden, she edged into the room. That bitch sat beside Jake on the couch and had her hand on his thigh. She narrowed her eyes. It took him entirely too long to remove it. And why hadn't he slid further away from her?

Her gut clenched. It was like when she'd been seventeen and thought she'd had his attention only to have him turn that attention to the closest willing woman. Betrayal.

She slipped back out of the room without notice, a tear sliding down her face.

Staying out of sight was best. Besides, she couldn't stand watching Teri throw herself at Jake. Nor would she watch Jake fall for it.

She had a lot to think about. And Jake's proposal was one of them. Since he hadn't pushed away from Teri, did he wish to rescind it? No. He'd want to be a father. Responsibility. That was what it was all about.

Her head spun. She only had to get through the day and then Teri would be gone. She climbed the stairs to her daughter's room. New toys awaited.

****

Mentally exhausted, Jake dropped onto the bed naked, his hair still damp from a shower. It had been one of the longest days of his life, and that was saying a lot considering what he'd recently lived through. Yet Teri and her cloying scent unnerved him. She didn't get the hint he was with Em.

His day had begun with his mental health appointment. Dr. Santos agreed it was PTSD and spoke with him about ways to help him deal with it. A support group met in town he could visit while he was here. The psychiatrist also mentioned drugs, but Jake declined any. That would be his last resort. But, he felt good about the appointment and was optimistic about his success in controlling it.

He'd also taken the opportunity to stop at a jeweler and purchase Em an engagement ring. That was after he had a chance to buy stuff to spoil his little girl. There had been so many cute outfits that fit Amber, he'd had a hard time deciding and ended up purchasing more than she'd need for a while. Or cared about. It was all about the toys. The stuffed dog with learning functions had captured her attention immediately. Although he noticed when it came time for bed, she had pulled out her stuffed frog and snuggled it close.

As for Em and the ring, he'd devise a plan to make the proposal special. Surely she'd say yes this time. He didn't want to wait any longer to be with her. He'd missed her today. After she'd left the meeting with Teri, he hadn't seen her again for the remainder of the day. Then again, he'd been fending off Teri's advances so it was best she hadn't seen him.

Light suddenly spilling across his room alerted him to someone slipping through the doorway. He grasped the gun he'd taped to the back of the nightstand, out of reach of the children, before the nauseating scent of Teri's perfume burned his nostrils. He glanced over and noticed his roommate's bed was empty. Of all the fucking time for Les to have security duty.

"What the hell are you doing here?" He pulled the sheet around his midsection, a shot of fury racing through him at her boldness.

She sashayed toward him in a short robe, nearly sheer and open to the belt that was tied loosely around her small waist, providing him a view of her goods. Goods that turned him off.

He only wanted Em. That was a big flashing sign that he loved her more than he'd imagined.

"I could tell that you wanted me today but held back because of everyone being around. I'm here now." She untied her belt, opened the robe completely, and then rubbed her hand up and down her body in a sensual manner.

The woman had lost her fucking mind if she thought he'd wanted her in any manner during the day. Hell, he'd done everything he could to separate himself from her. Yanking the sheet to pull it from where it'd been tucked at the bottom of the bed, he sprung up and haphazardly tied the sheet around his waist. "Teri, get the fuck out of here. This is not going to happen."

Reaching out to touch his chest, she scooted closer. "Oh, Jake, don't be afraid. Everyone is asleep. No one needs to know."

He snorted at what he suspected was a lie. He didn't have a high opinion of her, and she'd gone out of her way to make Em feel uncomfortable earlier. He bet she'd itch to tell Em that she'd been in his bed.

Grasping both of her wrists, he turned her toward the door, shuffling her in that direction. "No, Teri. Go back to your room."

Once she was outside his bedroom, he dropped her wrists. She turned her head down the hall and then looked back at him, reaching out to touch his chest before he could stop her. "Oh, Jake, you're fabulous."

"Mommy, *want milk.*"

Jake spun around and knew his world had just been destroyed again. Emily, holding Amber, along with AJ, stood in the hallway watching the scene. He pushed Teri away. "Em, no. It's not what it seems."

Em turned and raced back to her bedroom, slamming the door.

"Bastard. We gave you a chance, and you fucked it up. Stay away from her."

He tried to push past AJ but received a punch to the gut instead. Bent over, holding his stomach, swallowing the pain radiating through his midsection, Jake felt like certain moments in his life kept repeating themselves. But this time, instead of Em racing after him spouting her love, she'd been the one leaving.

****

Jake's raised voice in the hallway roused the entire family, and they surrounded Emily in her bedroom, leaving little space for anyone to maneuver. Since the children had also woken, Kate and Megan took the two little girls to put them back to bed. Teri had kept to her room. Probably gloating. *The bitch.*

"I just want to leave. If you don't take me somewhere else, I'm leaving with my daughter."

She didn't care that tears streamed down her face in front of everyone. They'd always known how she felt about Jake. After releasing her anger and mistrust, she'd opened her heart back to him, only to have him toy with her until he could get sex freely from another woman. She'd thought she could win him back. She'd been more of a fool than she'd originally been to think she mattered to him at all.

It had all been for Amber's sake.

"Where would you like to go?" Her father's soothing voice helped slow her frantic mind, her need for escape. "Do you want the HIS safe house in Virginia?"

Where did she want to go? "I don't care as long as it's away from here."

Matt cleared his throat, sat beside her on the bed, and placed his hand on her thigh in a comforting hold. He'd been her only brother to remain quiet about Jake returning and their budding relationship. Knowing what it felt like to have one's heart ripped out by their true love, he'd told her that he refused to offer advice since he had no idea how he'd handle himself in the situation. Only that he wished he had a second chance with Caitlyn. "What about Amber? No matter what's happened, doesn't she deserve a chance with her father? You've seen how attached she is to him."

She bowed her head, placing it in her hands, distraught knowing he was right. She couldn't be selfish and take this opportunity away from her daughter. Not knowing what their future held sent a sliver of fear slicing its way through her body.

"Are we safe here? Are you sure she's not in on it?" She'd worried about that question all day. Her mind whirled around the thought of men swarming the house to grab her and Amber while Teri stood and laughed.

Jesse nodded. "We're sure she isn't part of it. Physically, you're safe."

She noticed how he'd added the one word. Because

emotionally she might not be safe. Not if Jake took up with Teri when everyone slept.

Feeling the sudden tension in the room, Emily looked up, and the loud pounding of her heart blocked out the grumbling around her. At least Jake had dressed, but his rumpled jeans and T-shirt only drew her attention to the body she'd made love to. She wasn't sure she could handle being around him with Teri.

AJ moved in front of Jake, his hand on her newest visitor's chest, preventing him from moving forward. "I told you to stay away from her."

"I need to explain."

Her brother stood his ground. "What's there to explain? We thought you truly cared for Em. But all you did was play around with her feelings and then jump in bed with the next available woman. You've changed more than we thought, and not for the better."

Jake rubbed his hand down his tired face. "Look. I need to speak with all of you. Can we do this downstairs?"

Matt must've felt her trembling because he squeezed her leg as a supportive gesture. Knowing her brothers were looking out for her, and were being overprotective, didn't bother her for once in her life. Facing Jake was the last thing she wanted to do. Collecting her daughter and leaving was her only plan. She didn't want to stay around for the heartache.

"It's important. Just give me a few minutes, and then you can decide what to do with me."

All heads turned to her, effectively putting her on the spot. She didn't want to listen to what he had to say. She looked around wildly for help from any of her family.

Matt patted her leg and stood. "We'll listen to you, but Em needs rest. It's already been a long night for her."

Relieved, she closed her eyes and each of her brothers and her father kissed her on the cheek before they departed the room, warmth began to move back through her. No matter what, she was loved.

****

Seeing Em so distraught, her eyes swollen, red and puffy from crying, knowing he was the reason for it tore at his heart. He was slowly ripping away his chance for true happiness. The loving picture of her in a beautiful silk and lace wedding gown, and his daughter wearing the cute dress he'd chosen for her, crumbled before his eyes.

Fucking Teri. It occurred to him, too late, that she'd glanced down the hall before she put her hand on his chest and purred his name. She'd known Em was there.

He had hoped to speak with Em first to plead his case. When she knew the truth, she would come back to him, and they could return to the closeness they'd found. They'd finally surrender to the heat between them, marry, and maybe even make another child, one he could watch grow up.

"All right, we're here. What the fuck do you have to say?" Brad said.

Six pairs of similar eyes glared at him, burning through his skin, singeing down into his soul. If he couldn't get them on board with the truth, then he had no chance of convincing Em.

Jake moved to the front of the fireplace, the best

position to be seen by all. "I told you it's not what you think."

Brad snorted. "And I'm the fucking tooth fairy."

"You will be when you have kids," Jesse snapped at him. "Let him continue. I'm very curious to hear how he plans to worm his way out of this one."

Jake nodded to the eldest Hamilton brother in thanks, and then cleared his throat, attempting to wipe away any sound of nervousness. He'd done nothing wrong, but the looks from this group would make any grown man cringe. "Look, she came to my room uninvited. I told her to leave. When she wouldn't, I helped her leave." He took a deep breath at the anger still bouncing around the room. "I think she saw Em and put on that little display to get to her."

Blake quieted down the multitude of vocal responses of disbelief to his statement. After that, an uncomfortable silence swooped down into the room.

He couldn't stand it and opened his mouth to try to explain more, but Jesse spoke first.

"Let me see if I've got this right. If what you say is true—"

"There's no *if* about it. It *is* the truth."

"What's she up to then?" Devon asked.

Rubbing his hand on the back of his neck, he shrugged. "I don't know. I think she likes to get to Em. Em told me about how she'd kind of harass her at work and try to show she was superior."

Indecision filled all eyes on him. They were probably like him, wondering why Teri chose him. The room was filled with men and half were actually available.

"Look, I love Em. I plan to marry her as soon as

she'll let me. I wouldn't screw it up for a tumble with that bitch." He pointed toward the stairs, and his eyes followed and widened. *Shit.*

All of the men jumped to their feet.

Swallowing became a chore, painful against the lump in his throat. "Em," he croaked, "how long have you been standing there?"

She stepped forward, a long robe covering what he suspected was the incredibly sexy tank top and briefs she'd been wearing earlier. "Long enough. Do you swear nothing happened tonight?"

He stepped close to her, reached out and held her hands. "I promise you that nothing happened. I know I can't prove it, but I'm begging you to believe me. I wouldn't do something that stupid to ruin my chances with you. I was a fool four years ago, sprite. Maybe I needed some time away to realize that I'd grown to love you, but if I could take it back, I'd have stayed."

Knowing what he needed to do, but this time doing it right, he knelt. "Emily Hamilton, I love you and don't want to spend another moment without being by your side. Will you marry me?"

Chapter Eighteen

Emily drew in a deep breath. *Was this really happening? Had Jake officially, down on one knee, proposed?* A myriad of emotions floated through her. Excitement rippled, but elation led the pack. Something held her back from rushing into his arms. What was it?

She looked around the room and tilted her head to the door for her family to leave them alone. The only movement was a few raised eyebrows or feet spreading apart in a more dominant stance. They weren't leaving. Damn them. She didn't want an audience for this. It was personal. Too personal. Did they not trust Jake? Though she didn't care what they thought. It was her decision, and they'd have to deal with it.

Hesitantly, with her heart pounding and her palms sweating, she asked the question that mattered most, "You truly love me? This isn't because of Amber?"

A broad smile stretched his lips. "Sprite, even without our daughter I'd planned to chase you down when I returned. And, yes, I love you."

She'd waited so long to hear those words, and unlike before, she believed he meant them. He truly meant them. Finally, her dream had come true.

With her heart swelling with love, Emily leaned down and threw her arms around him. "Yes! Yes, I'll marry you, Jake."

The clapping behind them faded as his mouth took

hers in a kiss filled with passion. Never had she experienced such a romantic kiss, one swarming with so much love. She wanted to soak up every moment of it. It was a kiss that sealed their love for each other with a promise of shared happiness for eternity.

When their lips parted, she looked into his eyes and breathlessly whispered, "I love you."

Ignoring the room's occupants, she and Jake left the room. With her hand wrapped tightly in his, Emily walked on a cloud of love behind him to her bedroom.

Her heart was about to burst out of her chest. A lifetime with Jake was all she'd ever craved, and it'd finally come to pass. She'd finally have her own complete little family.

While her doubt that he'd be found alive over the years had wavered, her love never had. It'd been as strong as ever. All of the events since he'd returned washed away in a new beginning. She wouldn't allow anything to ruin what she now had—the man she loved who loved her back.

Jake clicked the bedroom door shut, and she found herself pressed close to his chest. It only took a moment for her to wind her arms around his neck and sink into the embrace. Her breath hitched at the depth of love engulfing his eyes.

Heat blasted throughout her body and a throbbing ignited between her thighs when his hands slid down to her rear and tugged her against him. His hard-on against her belly sent her body into a wild flurry of desire.

He moved his hand to her cheek and lightly stroked it before he cupped it, keeping her face upturned to his. "I've waited so long for you to say yes."

The sound of his husky voice amped up the heat in

her veins. She smiled. "I've waited almost my whole life for you to ask."

His gaze dropped to her mouth. "My little sprite." His lips brushed hers, the mere whisper of his touch sent shivers of delight floating through her.

The kiss changed to warm and potent, and his tongue claimed hers with skilled strokes that melted her from the inside out.

Much to her upset, he pulled back. "Tonight, I'm going to explore every inch of your luscious body." The hand on her cheek moved, and a finger traced a line to the sensitive spot beneath her ear, firing the blood in her veins. "I'm going to take my time, Em. I want to know every mark on your body, your scent and your movements until you are imprinted on my mind."

His hand continued on a path down the curve of her throat to her collarbone and then the top of her breast. There, it hesitated a moment before he gently embraced her, his arms encircling her and drawing her close again, creating an unbreakable connection.

She greedily accepted his mouth, feeling the heat of his lips against hers in a fiery kiss that coaxed a soft moan from her. The fire in her body…the blood pumping fast in her veins…the burning between her thighs…she wanted this man with everything she had.

Separating them, Jake pulled off her robe and the shirt she'd hastily donned earlier. His visual appraisal of her braless interfered with normal breathing.

His heavy breathing matched hers. Reaching out with both hands, he cupped her breasts. "So perfect," he rasped. He lightly massaged them and then pinched her taut, sensitive nipples. Delicious pleasure coasted through her veins. This promised to be one hell of a night.

Surprising her, he removed his hands from her chest and reached down for her shorts, the elastic band allowing him to drop them in one swoop.

Deep need swam in his eyes, and it empowered her, even standing in front of him in only a small scrap of underwear. "Now me."

He caught his breath, looked into her eyes and stepped back, appearing to welcome her undressing him. She followed suit with him and removed his T-shirt.

His olive-skinned chest called to her. She reached out with her right hand and touched him with a light sweep over it. He'd filled back out so well.

Pulling his gym shorts—he'd worn no underwear—over his erection took a bit more work and a light chuckle escaped both of them. His impressive cock stood proudly. She had a hard time taking her eyes away from the object that would bring her so much pleasure.

Wrapping a hand around him, she knew what she wanted to do. She'd only done it that once, but she needed to try again. She looked into his eyes and hoped they told him everything. Since his expression seemed to display a bit of excitement, she knew he understood she wanted to give him all the pleasure she could. She wanted to explore his body too.

Her heart beat fast as her other hand also gripped him and moved them up and down his shaft in tight, slow strokes.

He stayed her hands. "Minx." He guided her to the bed, picked her up and tossed her on it. After her bounce, he settled himself on top of her, pinning her to the mattress.

She wanted to cry out. The pulsing between her thighs screamed for his hard cock, pressed against her thigh, to be inside her, filling and pleasuring her. She sought his mouth and couldn't hold back the hunger in her kiss or the movement of her hips seeking to be closer to his.

Next thing she knew her arms were above her head, pinned by one of his hands.

"Let me show you how much you're mine." His mouth trailed kisses down her jaw, and he nipped her throat with his teeth, his hot breath on her skin as he wound a path down her body to her breasts. His unshaven jaw brushed over her flesh, increasing the heat flashing through her body.

Her lips parted on a shuddering inhale, and a full-body shiver overtook her.

****

Jake halted for a moment and smiled at Em's reaction, almost cocky in his feeling of how he could do this to her, make her come alive.

He licked a circle around a rosebud nipple before taking as much of the breast as he could into his mouth, sucking it back out to the tip, catching the bud between his teeth. He alternated between breasts, making little tugs on the nipple that sent her squirming. She was hot and bothered before he'd even moved lower.

"These have to go." Her underwear had no place in the bed between them. He couldn't believe he'd forgotten to remove them. She'd thrown him for a loop with her hand around his cock. He tossed the offending article of clothing on the floor and turned back to her.

The erotic scent of her arousal called to him, and

he made his way down her body, across her belly to the juncture of her thighs. He inhaled deeply and possessively. *This is my woman.*

"Jake…." Her eyes drifted shut, and her fingers dug into his shoulders.

"Just enjoy." He used a finger and traced her clit and opening, watching her tilt her head back and moan. She may be close, but he wouldn't shortchange her.

Shifting one arm under her leg, he tossed it over his shoulder to open his magnificent view. With his finger, he teased her hot, wet entrance. He loved how it took so little for her to be ready for him. He was the same when she was around. His cock always pointed to her like a divining rod to water.

Reaching under her other leg, he lifted it over his shoulder and settled himself with her prize directly in front of him. She almost catapulted off the bed at the first swipe of his tongue over her blazing center. He continued upward to swirl around her nub, then caught it in his mouth and tugged, catching her clenching the sheets.

Moving back to her euphoric taste, he inserted his tongue into her core and she quivered around him. He mimicked the maneuvers he planned to do with her in a few moments, his tongue thrusting deeply into her and out.

She threw her head back and made a mewling sound that shot a desperate need to his rock-hard cock. And he was only getting started.

He focused his attention on her swollen nub with his mouth, his tongue tugging, his lips suckling, while he inserted a finger inside her velvety heat. She gasped, and her inner muscles contracted tightly around him.

Christ, precum leaked from his erection as he imagined he'd been the one she'd clamped onto like that.

Groaning, wondering how he functioned when all his blood seemed to be pumping so hard to his groin, he continued working his finger in and out of her, seeking her sweet spot and teasing her clit. When she writhed beneath him, moaning, he kept the pace for her to come. Knowing he'd been her only lover meant she'd never come this way, and he'd make damn sure she did this time.

Panting, she bucked against him as her orgasm ripped through her. He kept his movements up to stretch it out as long as he could. When she lay still, a look of pure joy on her face, he slid up her body, kissing his way along the light sheen of sweat that coated her skin.

He nuzzled her neck as she sighed in pleasure. "Good?"

"Hmm. The best."

A man could never hear that enough. "Are you ready?" He hovered over her, poised at her entrance.

Her hand met his chest, and a surge of energy seemed to possess her. "No. My turn." She shoved him over. And he let her, wondering where this might lead.

In reverse positions, her above him, she leaned toward his ear and tossed his question back at him. "Are you ready?" She leaned back and looked him in the eye.

He raised his eyebrows. "Do your worst."

She licked her lips seductively. "Don't worry, I will." Her gaze roved hungrily over his face.

Holy motherfucking shit. He almost came on himself with that look and that voice. Where the hell had she learned that?

His next thought died at the touch of her lips, hot and wet, working down his chest to this tight groin. Hunger ate at him.

She licked down his cock, and his body shuddered in response. With one hand wrapped around the base of it, she licked the tip, and his breath caught in his chest. Starting at the crown of his erection, she slipped it into her mouth, slowly sucking it deeper in a warm, wet slide to her fist, exerting pressure with both her hand and mouth.

When she wrapped one hand around his balls and squeezed, massaging gently, he hardened to stone, and his hips involuntarily flexed forward, pushing him deeper until he hit the back of her throat. His erection was so painful that he wasn't sure he'd survive much more of this. Damn, he wanted to grab her, pull her up and fuck the hell out of her.

She looked up and caught him watching her. Their gazes locked. She continued taking him deep and hard into her mouth and began to hum, the vibrations eliciting a feral growl from him, and his balls drew tight.

Dear God, this woman was trying to be the death of him.

Exhaling in jerky puffs, he pulled her up. "Enough." His hoarse voice broke on the word.

A smile that showed him how satisfied she was with her work stretched across her face. "Are you sure?"

Rolling over until he lay on top of her, Jake settled between her thighs, the tip of his cock at her slick entrance, the heat pulling him toward her. "I love you,

Em."

"I love you, too."

His gaze collided with hers as he eased himself inside her and then withdrew. He tortured himself by sliding slowly into her inch by inch, their invisible bond just as strong as their physical connection. His control nearly slipped. Damn. The woman left him euphoric with her velvety heat flowing around him. If he'd been an uncaring bastard, he would've come at that moment.

"Damn, sprite," he croaked.

Jake listened to a single heartbeat between them. He moved inside her, slow and steady, and she lifted her legs to wrap around his waist, digging her heels into his back. She leaned her head back, exposing her long creamy neck in a most provocative pose. He couldn't resist the playground, and his lips were on her warm, silky skin, kissing and licking his way around her neck to behind her ear.

Her soft moans added gasoline to the brush fire burning in his body. He loved the sounds she made and the look of pleasure on her face during sex. He didn't think that burning need for her would ever go away. She'd be in his blood forever.

Sweating, his heart thundering in his chest, he quickly found a rhythm that sent a tremor through their bodies and set them rapidly approaching a climax. A strangled groan escaped him, and he needed to slow things down, so he stilled for a moment and leaned down to a breast and sucked on the taut bud before him.

"Don't stop."

Like he ever could. He could spend his life in bed with this sensual and responsive woman.

He looked at her flushed face and captured her

mouth in a kiss, his tongue thrust deep, devouring her while he moved again, picking up the pace, taking them on that climb to the cliff. But he held on tight, making sure he got her there first.

Holding back with her slippery friction and clenching muscles was nearly impossible.

Her legs tightened around his waist, and she trembled, her breath panting. He broke the kiss and watched her flushed face as she came apart in his arms, his lips almost too late to swallow her crying out.

The throbbing clench on his cock as she had an orgasm did it for him. He thrust deep and pressed his face into her neck, harshly growling out her name as everything spun around him, and he exploded in an almost unending climax.

He wasn't sure how long he'd been crushing her, but the sudden stillness of her body sobered him. He lifted his weight and looked into her eyes, worried he'd done something terribly wrong. Worried she'd change her mind and not marry him. "What is it?"

"We haven't been using protection."

He chuckled and rolled off her and tossed his arm over his eyes, thankful that it was something simple because he didn't think his brain cells were functioning too well at the moment. "Is that all?"

A hand lightly slapped him across the chest. "Is that all? That's pretty important considering our track record. Don't you think?"

She was right. They needed to do something about it before they were together again, or they'd have a baby right away with as much sex as he had planned for them. They had four years to make up for. "I just thought…. Never mind. I'll take care of it."

They'd use condoms, but they'd have another baby and soon.

****

Jake's hand lightly traced Emily's face, golden from the sun, from her forehead to her cheek to her chin and then to her lips. Thinking about their night together, actually early morning, his cock hardened with a strong need to be back inside her.

He should feel completely and utterly happy, yet he couldn't. There was one thing that held him back. He hadn't planned to fall asleep with her. He couldn't fathom the thought of waking to his hands wrapped around her small neck, choking her again. Yet, he'd been so comfortable that he'd slept. And he'd slept soundly.

Why was he able to sleep the night through last night and not the last time they were together? He'd woken to her arms wound around him, and they hadn't triggered anything. That did make him happy.

Em had been so tired that she dozed before he'd returned with a rag to clean her. If she'd been worried about him having an episode, it hadn't bothered her enough to keep her awake. Or, it had been his outstanding lovemaking. He smirked. Yeah, that was it.

He'd do whatever it took to protect her. Even if it was from him.

Wanting to allow Em to sleep and needing a few moments alone with the guys, he slid from the bed and silently dressed, then closed the door behind him before he trudged down the stairs.

Les, Trent, and his brothers were arguing but quickly stopped talking when he approached. Shit. He'd thought they'd approved. They hadn't tried to talk Em out of marrying him. It was too late. She'd agreed, and that was all that truly mattered. Besides, he had something else on his mind.

Acting as if he hadn't noticed the abrupt silence, he looked around the room. "Good, I wanted to talk with the group." He continued around the kitchen counter and poured himself a cup of coffee. After a welcoming sip, he strolled back into the family room. "It's about Em."

Brad didn't let him say anything more. "Don't fucking tell us now that you've fucked her, you plan to back out of marriage."

He narrowed his eyes at the man. "Fuck you."

The man jumped up from the chair, rushing to Jake and pulling back his shoulders.

Jesse stood. "Christ, Brad, sit the fuck down."

Jake raised his eyebrows and was surprised he hadn't been decked, but he had no time for this bullshit. "I'm worried about this thing with Em. For someone who wanted something from her bad enough to kidnap my daughter, they've laid low. I know the house isn't traceable back to the family, but I'm concerned."

AJ sighed loud enough for him to hear across the room. "Have a seat. There's more we haven't had time to share with you."

A chill froze its way up his spine, but he sat and waited for what he hoped wasn't something to put his fiancée in more danger.

"First, Dad doesn't want to be away from Em and Amber right now. Almost losing his granddaughter seemed to realign his priorities." AJ waved his hand when Jake opened his mouth to speak. "Knowing the potential danger, he led everyone to believe he was traveling abroad, working with foreign country leaders."

Jesse sat. "Although we believe that worked while he remains cloistered here, we're not taking a chance, and that's why we've attached ourselves so closely to her."

A snort from none other than Brad. "Not as close as he's been."

Fed up with the aggression, Jake snapped. "What the fuck is your problem, Brad?"

A beefy finger pointed his way. The man was larger than any of the other brothers, and Jake knew he'd never take him. "You're my fucking problem. You and what you did to our sister. How long will it be before you run away again? How long will she wait next time? You didn't see what she went through when you didn't come back."

Stunned, and knowing he deserved everything that had been said to him, Jake could only stare with no words bursting forth as a reply. What could he say that he hadn't already to make Brad forgive him? Em forgave him so it shouldn't matter what her brother thought, but it did, more than he cared to admit. These men had been his brothers, still felt like them, would be for life. Animosity was not something the family needed.

Matt pushed in between Jake and Brad and shoved his twin back. "Dammit, Brad! This is Em's choice, and if she wants to be with him and forgive him, then we need to do it too. Do you want to push her away by fighting with Jake? That's exactly what'll happen. So drop this bullshit."

Everyone in the room appeared to hold their breath.

The twins had been notorious for fighting over just about everything while growing up, which accounted for the slight bump on their noses where they'd been broken.

Grumbling, Brad took a seat but kept a narrow-eyed glare trained on Jake.

Jesse returned to the conversation as if nothing had happened to the dynamics in the room. "We don't think anyone knows she's here. The home she rented was burned to the ground." He shook his head. "Probably because they are pissed off they can't find her. At least that's my guess."

Absorbing the information and biting his tongue to remain calm, Jake tightened his jaw. "When was this and why are you only now telling me?"

AJ walked past him to the couch. "We only found out a while ago."

This wasn't something she needed to deal with, ever. Not that he'd wanted her to return there, but everything she and Amber owned had been there, all the photos they wouldn't have as mementos when Amber went away to college and married.

Jesse wiped his hand over his face, and Jake noticed how exhausted he looked and worried if there was more.

Jake dropped into a chair. "What do we do now?"

"I was able to pull the data from what Teri had. Now I need Em to help me go through it."

Absorbing Devon's request, he nodded. "She'll help. Are you sure it's him? Randall?"

"Oh yeah. I'm not the expert, but even I can see through their reporting. Each of their SEC filings was signed by one person."

"Paul Thompson," Jake guessed.

Devon nodded. "Bingo."

"And I killed him, making it harder to find out the truth."

"No." AJ shook his head. "He probably wouldn't have talked, anyway. He was in too deep."

Les looked at Trent and with a slight nod, Trent quietly left the room. If Jake hadn't been paying attention, he wouldn't have noticed the gesture, or the man disappear.

"I'm still concerned."

"We all are, Jake." Jesse sighed. "Earlier we were discussing the football game and whether she could go."

"If there's any question, then I'll stay home with her. I won't let her go into danger."

"We won't either, but even if it seems clear and she goes, we've already had some things in motion. The box will be swept prior to our arrival. Security will bring us in the back way. No camera is allowed to point to the box, and every employee that'll be serving us has been cleared, and we'll be double-checking him or her at the door. All the stuff we do automatically for Dad." He shrugged one shoulder. "Except the camera. That was a new one but a necessity to keep her off television."

Jake ran his hand through his hair. Leaning back in the chair, he still felt apprehensive about it all. At least she wasn't pushing to go to the game, or anywhere else.

Les broke into his thoughts. "We need to go. Trent's coordinated transportation."

Jake jumped up, ready to grab Em and his daughter and run. "What's happened?"

"The senator's had a heart attack."

Chapter Nineteen

Jake stood back and watched Em try to hold it together while sitting beside her father's hospital bed. She'd cried most of the ride to the hospital even though they'd been assured it had been a mild heart attack, and her father was doing well. She slid her hands up and down her arms. He should've picked up a jacket or something warm for her. Her short-sleeve peach blouse may be perfect in the summer heat but wasn't even close in the cold room. Of course, it could just be chills from the situation.

"I'm going to be fine," Blake assured his family. "They'll run a few more tests, then I'll go home, so quit worrying."

She reached out for her father's hand. "How can you say that, Dad? You could've died."

Using his free hand, he patted hers. "I'm not going anywhere for a long time." He looked around the room, his sons circling the space, squeezing in where able, and his eyes connected with Jesse, who had managed to get them cleared to wear weapons in the hospital.

At the lull, Jake took the opportunity to ask something he knew would be important to Em. Her father had been there when he'd proposed, but did he approve? What would Em do if her father didn't? Would she back out of things? His heart couldn't handle that. It wasn't an option.

He cleared his throat. "Sir, we'd like your blessing to get married."

Blake looked from him to Emily and then smiled widely. "Nothing would make me prouder." He pulled his hands from his daughter's and opened his arms wide. "Come give me a hug, angel."

With watery eyes, she tried her best to hug him amidst the wires connected to her father.

"Have you decided on a date?" The senator settled back on his bed.

With worry about her father's health, Em had easily agreed to a hasty wedding. That pleased Jake—the quick wedding, not her reason for that decision. He hadn't wanted to wait for some big damn production. He wanted his family together, but he'd needed to leave her options open so he made sure to add a caveat for her. "As soon as possible. We'll have a justice of the peace conduct a ceremony soon, and then if Em wants a big wedding, we can do one later."

Nodding, Blake smiled at his daughter. "I think it's a great idea. Today has taught me that life is short, grab onto it. Get married when I get out of here. We're all together. It's the perfect opportunity."

Seeing a smile and bright eyes on her when they talked about the two of them getting married pleased the hell out of him. That was what he'd been waiting for all of these years to see. He was ready to officially be her husband.

The door opened and Trent walked in with Jesse. When the fuck had Jesse left? He had to quit being lax about his surroundings just because he felt secure with his brothers.

"Ah, Trent."

"How are you, senator?"

"Like I told my boys, I'll be fine."

"Good. Is there something I can do for you?"

Jake wondered the same thing. The room had his children who could do, and would do, anything he wanted, and he'd asked for Trent?

"I need to chat with you." He looked around. "All of you."

Suddenly the elder Hamilton looked much older than his age. Tired lines filled his face and an overall weak aura surrounded him. How had he not noticed it earlier? How long had he appeared this fatigued? Was it just the heart attack? There'd been so much going on that could've triggered things, and Jake's mind had been focused on his small family, not the entire one.

Blake cleared his throat. "I'm going to do something I promised I wouldn't do, but today has taught me a lesson about life. It puts a lot of things in focus, and I won't go to my grave with this secret."

The men all turned their heads back and forth looking at each other as if one or the other might know this secret. Em sat frozen, her hands in her lap, her body stiff as if fearful of what her father was about to say. He wanted to reach forward, pick her up and put her in his lap, hold her close, protect her and maybe he should, but in this roomful of her family, her male family members, it seemed better to let her show them she could be strong on her own. He knew how much she wanted them to think of her as able to take care of herself. He'd let her do that, but it was killing him.

"I don't know the best way to say this, and maybe I shouldn't do it with you as a group, but since it involves all of you, I'm just going to spit it out. About twenty-seven years ago, your mother and I had some marital problems, and we briefly separated." He took a deep breath and released it. "I'm not proud to say it, but I had an affair during that time."

Jake shifted. Em's eyes flicked to Trent.

"Trent, your mother was my assistant, and I took a liking to her. We had a short affair that she was ashamed of and didn't want anyone to know about." He scanned the room, looking at the Hamilton men. "Your mother didn't want it known either."

Turning his head slightly, not wanting to be obvious, Jake watched a large lump slide down Trent's throat and noticed his hands fisted at his sides.

The senator focused his attention back on Trent. "Then she found out she was pregnant. That's when the boys' mother and I had just reconciled." Blake sighed heavily. "She and your father married and raised you as their son. They didn't want you to know I was your father. The only concession was that they would live on the estate so I could watch you grow up."

Looking directly at Trent, Jake witnessed a heavy dose of hostility. Of course, he had no idea what to expect from his friend. What would he feel if he found out his father wasn't really his? That he'd been lied to all those years. He'd probably jump for joy. But Trent had a great life growing up. His father had been wonderful to him.

It would explain a lot, though. Trent's father worked for Blake on the grounds, and they lived in one of the guest cottages. Trent was always involved with them growing up, never treated differently because he wasn't an actual part of the family.

"That makes you all family...my family...brothers

and sister." Blake looked wearily, maybe even apologetically, at Trent.

Jake shifted. He was an interloper in the room. He was not a flesh and blood member of this family. Yet, Blake—the man who had basically raised him—had included him in this emotional family moment. His gut clenched at how this must've thrown Trent for a loop.

Trent had to deal with one monster lie from people who'd loved him. Who did he blame? The parents who'd raised him or the parent who'd willingly refused to acknowledge him?

The newly recognized Hamilton brother stared at Blake through thin slits, his nostrils flaring and red creeping up his neck. His chest heaved. After a few moments of silence, he spun on his heels and stormed from the room.

The family stood in stunned silence. One by one, the occupants turned back to the man in the hospital bed.

"I'm sorry. That's all I can say."

"You cheated on Mom," Em said in a weak, broken voice.

Jake couldn't stand it. He walked to her and lifted her hand in his, squeezing it tight to let her know he was there for her.

"Angel, it was a long time ago. I'm truly sorry for it."

She looked at her father, then stood and led Jake out of the room.

He wondered what the men had to say about it, but his first concern was how Em was handling it.

Reaching the hallway, she continued walking past the HIS men stationed outside the door and to the stairwell. Closing the door behind her, she turned into his arms and burst out crying.

He didn't know what else to do but hold her, so he remained silent and tightened his arms around her.

Em pulled back from him, took a gulp of air and wiped at her tears with the back of her hand. "That's why he never hit on me. I think he already knew." She sniffed.

He kissed the top of her head. He had a feeling Trent had known also. When Jake had questioned him on his feelings for Em, he'd replied that he wouldn't touch his own sister. He had taken it that Trent just wasn't interested in her in more than a sisterly fashion. He since knew better. The question was what was Trent going to do now that it was out in the open?

****

AJ preceded Jake into the living room. The youngest Hamilton brother gave Trent a slap on his shoulder as he walked past him. Trent turned, muscles tense and hands tightened into fists but halted at the sight of AJ with his hands up in a surrender gesture. "Sorry, man. Just came to check on you."

The rest of the family, minus Blake and the children, entered. They'd returned to the house to be with Trent while he grappled with the shocking news. The Hamiltons were a "one for all" type of family. Jake hoped Trent appreciated that.

Growing up, there'd been so many times Jake had felt an animosity from Trent. It'd been at times like when Jake had a big birthday party or received a nice gift from Blake. If Trent had known the truth before today, that would explain the behavior. Jake had been living the life Trent should have. Jake, the outsider, had the love of the family his friend had been denied.

Trent left his spot by the fireplace and sat in a chair. Based upon the changes in his facial features, he appeared to struggle with his emotions. "Don't worry. I'm not asking for anything." Sarcasm laced his words.

As usual, Jesse spoke first. "You know we couldn't give a fuck about that, but just to clear the air on that, you are in Dad's will."

Trent narrowed his eyes at the oldest Hamilton brother. "You knew."

Jesse dropped on the couch. "Of course I knew. Why do you think I watched you so closely with Em?"

Gaped expressions from the family focused on Jesse. A twitch appeared in Jesse's jaw.

Jake couldn't believe it. Someone other than Trent's parents held the secret and had planned to take it to their grave. Why would anyone do that to Trent? The Hamiltons had always treated Trent as if he were family.

A thought occurred to him. If Jesse held this secret, what others were there? There was no reason to keep secrets with this family. They were tight-knit and backed each other with no questions asked.

"Don't you think this was a pretty big secret to keep from us?" Devon asked.

Trent's gaze spun to Devon, anger oozed off him in waves. "This isn't your fucking secret!"

Actually, it kind of was, but Jake wasn't going to toss that in the ring. It was a Hamilton family secret, after all.

"You've known, haven't you?" Em asked Trent.

Jake wrapped his arm around her back, and started at Em's trembling. He'd expected this entire conversation to be uncomfortable, but he hadn't expected her to react physically. He quickly pulled her close and willed his strength to flow through their embrace.

Trent nodded. "Yes."

Em wavered on her feet, and Jake led her to a chair to sit. He stood beside her and held her hand. Her eyes wore a pained expression, and his gut clenched at the fact he couldn't fix this for her. Worse, he didn't know how she felt about it all. She'd been quiet on the ride from the hospital.

"When I was ten," Trent began, but paused and took a deep breath and exhaled before continuing, "I wanted a party at the pool at the big house." He shook his head and snorted. "That's what I called it when I was young. Anyhow, Mom said no, and I really wanted it, so I thought to ask the senator. He allowed me to do everything else all of you did so I didn't see why that would have been different."

Trent looked past everyone and narrowed his eyes as if recalling an unpleasant memory. "He told me that I could on one condition."

Jake stiffened. He had a feeling he knew what it was. A man faced with a son and a daughter not knowing their relationship but living on the same property needed to do something. Otherwise, that could've spelled potential disaster.

"Yep. My *old man* told me that I could have the party as long as I never touched his daughter." Trent shrugged.

Em gasped and Jake squeezed her hand in assurance.

"When I got cocky about it, he told me if I ever

laid a hand on her my family would be out on our ears."

"Oh, Trent." Em's whispered voice broke.

"At first I thought it meant I wasn't good enough for his daughter—being the son of the hired help. Then I remembered bits and pieces of conversations from my parents about the senator and me. It hadn't made much sense at the time. But, adding it to the man's insistence I stay away from Em…."

Silence filled the room wracked with invisible tension. Jake glanced at Kate and Megan doing as he was, remaining quiet. He wondered if they had that queasiness in their stomachs that he had, which proclaimed him an interloper in this close-family meeting. He imagined they shared his thoughts—to be there for the one they loved.

"Why the fuck didn't you say something?" Matt exclaimed. "You're one of us. Why would you hide from that? Are you ashamed of our family? Your family?"

Trent dropped his head back and closed his eyes. "I have a family. I have a mother and a father." He looked back around the group. "I'm a McKenzie, son of Lily and Roger McKenzie. I don't need Blake Hamilton trying to come in and stomp on the memory of the fine man who raised me." Giving no one time to respond, Trent stood. "After Jake and Em get married, I'm taking off. I need to clear my head."

"When will you be back?" Em asked hopefully.

Striding to the doorway, Trent glanced back over his shoulder. "I'm not sure I will be."

Chapter Twenty

Sitting on the couch with her knees pulled up, Emily placed a throw pillow over her stomach and squeezed it tightly. "I can't believe Dad kept that secret from us." She looked up at Jake, who sat beside her. "I can't believe he did that to Trent."

Jake reached over and toyed with a length of her hair. Knowing he was there for her when she needed someone close eased some of her anguish over the situation. His thoughtful gaze filled her with love and warmth. She couldn't have handled pity at the moment.

When he didn't speak, she continued, "I just don't know what to think now. Part of me is angry with my father for the affair, but the other part of me has my heart bleeding for him for not being able to raise his own son. I can't imagine how painful that must've been for him." Against her best effort to fight it, her eyes watered. "But, dammit, he lied to us all. I can't help the pocket of resentment resting inside me, and I don't want it. He's my father."

Jake removed the pillow from her arms, pulled her onto his lap and stroked her back. The reassuring heat of his hand and steady beat of his heart grounded her. He pressed a kiss on the top of her head. "Em, I imagine it's normal right now to have all these conflicting emotions running rampant through you. You just found out something huge that does more than affect you calling Trent your brother."

She didn't want the heated anger that fought to take hold of her senses. Her father had almost died, and she didn't wish to carry the negativity with her. What if she actually did lose him and she'd held on to her resentment? It would eat her alive for the rest of her life. But how did she deal with it now? He'd cheated on her mother. The circumstances didn't matter. If he'd loved her mother, then he would've remained faithful, no matter what.

Now she knew why Jesse and her father kept such a close eye on her and Trent. It made her sick to her stomach to think what could've happened. She'd always thought he would be a great catch for a woman but not for her. Thank goodness.

A tear slid down her face, and she swiped at it. "I don't know what to do, Jake. I can't let myself feel this way. I still love my father."

He lifted her chin so they were at eye level. "These feelings aren't just going to disappear right away, sprite. You need to work through them. Yes, your father cheated. Your mother forgave him. Can you?"

Turning away, she heaved a burdened sigh. "I don't know."

"There's a lot we don't know about what happened during that time. I don't think it's our place to hold him to task for what happened. That would've been your mother's job." He touched her chin and turned her face back to his. "She took him back, and they kept this family together. None of your brothers remember anything but happiness. I know you were too young to remember your mother, but I think Blake loved her very much. He never remarried, and I think it was because of that love."

Em leaped from his lap and stared down at him. "But he lied to us!"

"He did." Jake tilted his head and raised his eyebrows in question. "What lie is it specifically that has you so torn up?"

Needing time to consider the question, she turned and walked to a window overlooking the backyard where her brothers had joined and were probably talking about the same thing. They seemed more upset at Jesse for keeping the secret than at their father.

What secret ate at her the most? Was it the affair? Was it keeping Trent's parentage secret? Was it that her brother knew but also kept it from them? Was it that Trent had known all this time? Hell, it all tore her up inside. Her stomach churned at each question. "I don't know." She glanced back at him and caught his silent approach. "I guess it's the magnitude of it all together." Strong arms wrapped around her waist from behind, and she leaned back into Jake's hard body.

"It is a doozy. Maybe you just need time to come to terms with how you feel about everything."

A comfortable silence descended on them as they stood together. She drew strength from his arms.

Jake kissed her on the cheek. "I can't imagine how hard it must've been for him to have to deny his son."

That was the crux of it. She couldn't imagine not having Amber with her every day. Not being able to claim her would've killed her. It was the knowledge of how painful it must have been that kept her anger from deepening. It had been apparent her father had suffered from keeping the secret all this time. Had that been his penance? If so, it was a horrible one.

She dropped her chin to her chest. "That part breaks my heart and washes away the anger."

He turned her toward him, and she wrapped her arms around his waist. Her head lay on his chest listening to the rhythmic thump of his heartbeat.

"I hope you're able to let it all go. Your father paid for his infidelity with a high price. No matter what, he's still your father. He's still the same man. He just admitted his mistakes to you. That had to be difficult."

She squeezed her eyes closed. "I'll find a way to release it, but I can't do it today." She needed more time to deal with it all. Time to figure out how to react to her father when she saw him next. She shuddered. "Let's not talk about her right now. I know it's just turning afternoon, but can we go to bed? I need to be with you."

He chuckled. "It won't fix anything, but I'll never deny you." Jake stepped back and reached for her hand to tug her along. "Let's go."

She just wanted to lose herself in the arms of the man she loved. Everything would be perfect when they were in sexual oblivion. She didn't have to deal with a thing but the bliss they created with one another.

****

Returning to Em's room, they found Amber asleep in the bed curled up with her thumb in her mouth and her stuffed frog under her arm.

Fingering a lock of Em's hair, the beating of Jake's heart quickened, and every nerve ending tingled with aching need. "I need you. I need to be inside you." He moved her hand to his crotch, clasping it over his growing erection.

She swallowed the lump in her dry throat. "Let's

take Amber to her bed."

"No." He willed his already heavy breathing to calm. "We might wake her."

Em's sharp gaze caught his attention. "We're not doing it right in front of her."

He grunted. No, they wouldn't, but he wasn't waiting any longer. "Bathroom."

She looked back at the doorway, turned back to him and flashed him a sultry grin before she darted for the room.

He looked at his daughter. The sweet innocence of sleep. *Stay that way, princess.*

When he strode through the barrier to the bathroom, his eyes locked onto the fully naked Em waiting for him. That swooped everything else from his mind. He entered the bathroom, closed and locked the door behind him and then divested himself of his shirt.

"I can't make love to you like I want to in here." The close confines called for more of a fuck, and he wouldn't turn it down.

Raising her eyebrows, Em turned provocatively toward the counter, her back to him and leaned over it spreading herself open in invitation.

Fuck. Me. "You don't have to." They were still new in the bedroom, and he didn't want to rush her into something she wasn't comfortable with, but damn if she didn't tempt him beyond all measure.

The seductive grin meeting his gaze in the mirror gave him her answer before she spoke. "I just want you inside me."

He'd be damned if he'd argue with that. Stepping forward, he unzipped his pants, and his cock sprang free. He pushed a relieved sigh from his throat. "Shit.

No condom."

"Who cares? Get those damn pants off. I'm getting impatient."

Laughing, he dropped them and moved closer to her fabulous round ass. With one hand on her back, he reached down between her thighs to prepare her. Impatient also described him, but he wouldn't just thrust into her. No matter how much his throbbing cock demanded it.

"Shit. You're drenched."

She moved her hips against him erotically. "It's all you. Now shut up and fuck me."

"Your wish is my command." He grabbed her hips and guided himself to her center. With one slow thrust, he sheathed himself in her heat completely. "Fuck." Circling his hips, he knew it wouldn't take much to toss him into the abyss. "This will be quick."

Pumping in a hard, fast rhythm, he fought for control with every deep plunge. Balls deep in her, he sat on the ragged edge, holding on by a thin thread to ensure he pleasured her. The sound of his thighs slapping hard against hers did nothing to halt him nearly plunging early.

With the labored rise and fall of his chest, he leaned forward, placed soft, damp kisses on her back, and reached around, grasping one of her breasts and teasing her nipples. She arched her body, tossed her head back, and captured his mouth in a heated kiss. His hand continued its slide down her body to between her thighs. She moaned in his mouth and broke the kiss.

They looked in the mirror, watching each other. It was sexy as hell. Then he dropped his gaze to his cock moving in and out of her wet pussy. Fuck. He rubbed her clit between his fingers and teased it until her face flushed, and her eyelids drifted shut. Her soft moan reached down and tugged at the orgasm building within him.

"Come for me, Em."

He pounded mercilessly, his hand working her nub until he watched, and felt, the orgasm rip through her small body. She tightened around his cock. "Oh, Jake. Yes."

Her legs collapsed, and he clasped her waist to hold her up and thrust two more times before he cried out and spilled himself in a kaleidoscope of red-hot pleasure, colors mingling in his vision, knocking his world slightly out of focus.

With trembling legs, he pulled out of her, stepped back and slouched against the wall, worried he might slide down it before he could catch his breath.

Still coming out of his euphoric state, he hadn't noticed her move, but Em handed him his clothes. "Get dressed."

He shook his head. What the hell was the rush? Did she not enjoy it as he had? If so, she'd still be in la-la-land with him. He hooked his arm around her waist and pulled her to his chest. "No. I think in a minute we can go again."

She reached up and kissed him with passion then pushed away. "I'd love nothing more, but we can't. Amber could wake up any moment."

Fuck. He had to do better as a father. He'd forgotten about the little girl sleeping so close while he had her mother spread out like Sunday dinner on the bathroom counter. So he did as he'd been told and somehow managed to get dressed.

Then Em threw herself into his arms. Now? After they'd dressed? Was the woman trying to drive him insane?

"I love you, Jake Cavanaugh."

"And I love you, sprite." He laughed at the scrunched-up face she made. Before she could put up a fuss, he leaned down and took her mouth in a slow, languid kiss. Their next time would be in a bed, and it would be for a long time.

A knock on the door startled him. "Mommy, *gotta* potty."

They looked at each other, eyes wide, and a euphoric laugh bubbled up his throat.

Chapter Twenty-One

"Guys," Arthur Hall started and then cleared his throat, "and gals, I'd like you to meet James Gallagher, head of the Securities Exchange Commission." The two men had arrived at the house later that afternoon. In the living room, the FBI deputy director took the time to introduce his guest to each family member.

"I'm sorry to hear about Blake." Arthur took a seat on the couch and petted Dottie when she approached him, her tail wagging, and her pregnant belly protruding. "Hey, girl. Look at you."

"She's due any day now." Kate reached down and petted the dog. "The girls want to keep all the puppies."

"Where are those cute little chatterboxes?"

Jesse sat in a chair and pulled his wife down beside him before he answered Arthur. "They're playing upstairs. Do you two have anything for us?"

Arthur chuckled. "So much for pleasantries and catching up." He winked at Em.

Jake was with Jesse on this one. He didn't care about catching up either. He wanted to know what in the hell was happening. What did the FBI and SEC know? Would they make an arrest and get this over and done with?

"We need to speak with Teri Sheppard and see the data she has." Arthur accepted a glass of tea from Mrs. Kessler, who had quietly slipped into the room with refreshments. "Thank you." He took a deep drink. "I miss good sweet tea up north."

"Get on with it." Jake's nerves sat on end. He couldn't give a shit what Arthur missed. Hell, the man hadn't missed him all those months he'd been a captive. Otherwise, he'd have been rescued sooner and wouldn't be going through what he was at the moment. Just having it officially diagnosed as PTSD seemed to ease some of his anxiety.

His old boss raised his eyebrows at him before he turned back to Jesse. "You said she wanted a deal. Does she have anything worthwhile?"

Before they could answer, beside Arthur, James scooted forward. "I have a team that I trust combing through the SEC filings. We have enough now to bring in Charles Randall, but there is so much more, and we want anyone else he might have been working with on this scam. We need a couple more days before we move on him. But, we will move."

"We've added a team to him and his people. I know you've got one on Charles," Arthur said and looked pointedly at Jesse, which only elicited a shrug from the recipient, "which I didn't authorize, but I'll overlook it considering."

The SEC leader smiled at Em. "You were right. It was easy to see right away. Had any of my ethical agents seen the reports, this would've happened a lot sooner." He looked around the room. "I think you all understand that markets go up and down. Not Randall's. His mostly went up. Actually, only about 5 percent were down months."

Blank expressions responded to his statement. The room was not filled with market experts.

James smiled. "To change that to a sports analogy, that's like a major league player batting .950 for a year." He chuckled at the nods of understanding. "Right. Not possible. Anyone who would've looked at this, outside of someone crooked, would've seen the fraud."

Em cleared her throat. "Will people get their money back?"

He frowned. She wanted a dream, but she already knew that Charles had spent a great deal of the money. They'd talked about all his assets. The mansions in the U.S. and abroad. The vacation homes. The luxury cars. The yachts. The jewelry his wife wore. The artwork he proudly displayed. Jake's heart went out to Em because he knew while she was probably ecstatic this was about to be over, her heart broke because the clients would still lose.

James shook his head and with a sad smile answered, "No. We'll get them what we can, but he led an extravagant lifestyle."

"What about Em's boss? We couldn't find him. Did he ever appear?" Devon asked.

Arthur nodded. "We found him this morning. He took the coward's way out and committed suicide. He did leave a note with a detailed summary that implicates Charles. However, he had already made sure any evidence burned with his office." He took a deep breath and released it loudly. "How well do you know Charles's son Brian?"

Jesse raised his chin a notch. "We used to know him well, but we haven't seen him in years. Do you think he's involved?"

"We don't know. He's working for his father, so

that's not good for him. I just wonder if he's involved."
Arthur shrugged. "I guess we'll find out when it all
washes out."

"Fuck! Why can't you just bring Randall in today?
He may not be out and about, but he could be
coordinating with someone to hurt Em and my
daughter."

Arthur raised his hand. "Calm down, Jake. We've
tapped his phones. If he makes a call, we'll know about
it." The man made a good attempt to reassure him, but
Jake couldn't be calmed.

James looked at Em. "This is the largest financial
fraud case in history. Charles will most likely spend the
rest of his life behind bars. Miss Hamilton, you will be
famous as the whistle-blower who helped bring him
down."

Jake saw her visibly shake and took her hand, lifted
her from the chair she lounged in, sat down and pulled
her onto his lap. "Can we keep her identity secret?"

Shaking his head, James gave them a thin smile. "It
won't be possible. The records and trial will be public,
and she'll have to testify."

"Arthur, can't you do something?" Jesse asked.

Heaving a heavy sigh, the deputy director shook
his head. "I could, but he's right. This will be public,
and we don't want to suppress her information or her.
You know if we had Em as an anonymous source,
somehow her name would find its way to the press.
And there is no telling what they'll make up for her
reason for wanting to remain anonymous. It's best we
control it. Otherwise, it may be a scandal you don't
want to deal with. Do you want to hear something like
she heard about it in bed with her boss? You know the

media gets brutal."

Arthur set his glass down on the table beside the couch. "Look, hundreds of people and charitable organizations are going to be devastated or wiped out because of his actions. They want to know who to thank for saving them from further loss. We are doing this, and Emily is our whistle-blower."

Trent spoke from his normal position in front of the fireplace, "Since this person will garner a lot of popularity, to include possible book deals, what if you offer it to Teri and see if she'd consider being the whistle-blower and leaving Em completely out of it. Would that work?"

Em looked at Arthur with a hopeful expression on her face and in her eyes.

Jake wanted to hug Trent for coming up with such a great idea. Of course, Teri would accept it. The bitch would take all the attention she could get.

Arthur rubbed his jaw in a thoughtful gesture. "I'm okay with it. James?"

The SEC leader tilted his head and shrugged. "I guess we could do it since Miss Hamilton didn't actually bring us any hard evidence, only a conversation, and Ms. Sheppard brought us actual records. If the other woman goes for it, I don't see a reason not to do it."

The sense of protectiveness that had woven itself around him to keep Em out of the limelight relaxed. This would easily be a done deal, and his fiancée was free of this obligation.

Jake cleared his throat. "Now, can you find another place for Teri to stay?"

****

A good old-fashioned meal of southern fried chicken, mashed potatoes, corn on the cob and cornbread was served outside at the picnic benches covered with a red-checkered tablecloth. Round paper lights were strung overhead around a pergola to light the area to the descending sun.

Emily watched her brothers and the team rotate in and out, devouring plate after plate, actually piece after piece of chicken without the plate, as if they'd been starved for a week. Mrs. Kessler must've cooked an entire farm of chickens for them.

"You'd best eat up because this is the last time you get this. When the senator gets home, he'll be on a strict diet which means you'll be on a strict diet." Mrs. Kessler pointed at them; her finger moved through the group of Hamiltons, HIS team members, and two guests. "No more fried chicken."

"What?" Les exclaimed. "Come on, Mrs. K. You can't sneak us some on the side? What about when the senator isn't here?"

Emily knew Les was a favorite of Mrs. Kessler's, and she'd cook just about anything for the man. They had a special bond since they were both born in the South.

The housekeeper smiled brightly. "Well," she said and smoothed the country apron Les had given her for her birthday, "I'll cook it when he's not here." She spun and scooted back inside the house with a little pep in her step.

A few of the men chuckled.

"You sweet talker," Matt said.

Les shrugged. "I can't help it if she loves me."

Brad made kissing sounds. "Les and Mrs. K sitting

in a tree, k-i-s-s-i-n-g."

Emily's laughter blended in with the rest of the group's. Hers was at the thought of a twenty-eight-year-old Les and a sixty-something-year-old Mrs. Kessler actually in a tree.

"Fuck you." Les threw his chicken wing bone at Brad, who ducked, and then he turned. "Christ, I'm sorry." He looked at Kate and then at Emily with wide eyes.

He didn't need to worry; the three little ones were attempting to repeat the singsong spelling of kissing that Brad had spoken and probably hadn't heard his cursing. She loved how the men watched, or tried to watch, what they said around the children without being asked.

Looking contrite, he turned. "I'll just go check on the men."

Jason appeared and sat beside Emily. She loved her adopted nephew, and she was happy she'd been able to be here for his birthday party. She'd spent so little time with him before she'd moved. Getting to know him was important to her. He was already a teenager. He'd be grown and out of the house in no time. So would her daughter. She shuddered at the thought.

"Aunt Em."

"Yes, Jason."

He cleared his throat. It was cute that he was nervous.

Since it was serious to him, she wiped the smile from her face and focused her full attention on him.

"If it's not safe, it's okay if you don't go to my party. I understand."

How sweet. He was so grown for thirteen. She

guessed knowing you could die from your leukemia would mature a child. But he'd kicked his disease enough that it was in remission. For now. She prayed it stayed that way forever.

"Turning fourteen is a big deal. I know the party is a month early, but it's your party, and I'd like to be there." She wanted to reach out and touch his face, but she figured that might be considered too babyish to him. "I promise that we never planned on my going to the game if it wasn't safe. We just didn't want to tell you unless it was actually the case."

"Oh." He nodded. "That's good to know. I'm glad." He looked down.

She hoped she hadn't hurt his feelings by telling him about her not going. With what Arthur said, she imagined things would be fine, but she'd still be safe rather than sorry. She needed to bring a smile to his face. "Are you excited?"

As she'd expected, his face brightened. "Am I ever! It's a college football game. And Poppy says he got me into the locker room too. Can you believe it? I get to meet the quarterback."

Laughing, she'd barely caught that Jake had called for everyone's attention. She shook her mind clear and looked up at the man she loved, who stood next to her by the picnic bench, knowing what he was about to say although she thought everyone already knew the news.

He lifted his daughter in his arms, shifted her to his right shoulder, and then with his left hand, he reached down, clasped Emily's hand and helped her to her feet. "Everyone knows how I feel about Em. Well, I've asked her to marry me, and she's said yes. Since you're all here—and since I don't want to wait—"

Laughter interrupted him.

Smiling broadly, he finished his announcement. "We're having a small ceremony, here, after the senator returns home."

Clapping, "It's about time," and whistling came from the crowd. The best part was that when Amber squeezed his neck tightly, and his only reaction was to hug her back.

Chapter Twenty-Two

Jake realized he hadn't had a PTSD episode in a while. The progression muscle relaxation technique he'd learned was extremely beneficial before bed. He'd feared sleeping with Em, but he'd done it anyway because after that first incident, he hadn't any nightmares when she was by his side. Plus, she'd insisted, even though he could see a little bit of concern in her eyes. She wanted to be there for him should he return to the hell he'd lived with. He couldn't imagine anything better than being in her arms should that happen.

He'd listened to the psychiatrist and knew in his heart he could control it. That it was only a temporary thing for him. Yet, Matt had pulled him aside and spoken with him about PTSD and how he might react to certain things. He also told him that it may lessen, but it would never go away, which did worry Jake.

Matt didn't admit it, but Jake guessed the former Navy SEAL must suffer from it. To what extent he still did, Jake couldn't say. But Em's brother rubbed his leg something fierce the longer they spoke about it.

Jake clutched open the directions booklet of the magic kit and refocused on the words as Em leaned close to him to read. His fingers itched to drop it and curl around her soft body. Seeing the old kit on a shelf, he'd come up with the brilliant idea that the two of them put on a magic show for the children. He knew it meant more time alone with Em. He hadn't thought about how close they'd need to get, looking over each other's shoulders, to prepare for the evening entertainment.

He inhaled a deep breath and caught it. Damned if she didn't smell ravishing. Her scent, something with jasmine, kept his dick in a semi-wood state. He wanted to grab her now, toss her over his shoulder and bolt for the bedroom.

Em moved to the table where they'd laid out all the pieces of the kit. "Candy from the drawer box sounds easy enough." She reached out for the plastic component to the trick, looked it over and then handed the box to him. "Do you want to try?"

He knew what he wanted to try, and it had nothing to do with putting on a show for the kids. Instead of doing as he wished, he read through the instructions for the trick, set the booklet down and reached for the trick box. "Looks simple enough."

Their hands brushed, and he clasped onto hers, delighted when she caught her breath.

Clearing her throat, she slid her hand from his and stepped back. "Think you can manage?"

With a quirk of his brow, he smiled, wanting to tease her with an answer that alluded to managing his way around her body. Instead he let her relax. "Let's see what we've got." Flipping the box over, he found the secret hole. No way in fucking hell was his finger fitting in there. "I think my lovely assistant will have to do this trick."

A blush rose on her face as she stared at the hand he held up beside the box to demonstrate his problem.

Well, well. It was pretty easy to get to her. He'd remember that. "Hold out your hand," he instructed.

She seemed to regain control of herself and smiled mischievously. "Your assistant, huh?" She took the box from him. "Since you can't do the trick, I think you should be my assistant."

Jake leaned close, his cheek next to hers as he whispered in her ear, "I'll be glad to assist you in any way I can."

Em pushed against his chest. "Can you get serious for one minute?"

Not wishing to push his luck, he stepped back and nodded with a chuckle, secretly pleased at her erratic breathing. Remembering something he'd seen on the table, he turned away and then back to her. He placed the cheap top hat from the kit on her head and then completed an exaggerated bow. "Of course, oh wise magician."

Her laughter reached in and wove its warmth around his soul. "You're impossible." She shook her head and had to grab the hat to keep it from falling off her head. "We only have a little bit more time before the kids are ready for their show."

He opened his mouth, but she raised a hand to forestall his comment. "I don't want to hear anything dirty. Behave."

"I'll behave." Jake cocked his head and winked. "For now."

"Uhm, okay, let's do this trick." She turned her focus to the box with shaky hands.

Biting the inside of his lip to keep from laughing, Jake picked up the instruction booklet again. He didn't wish to push his luck. "Okay. Put your finger in the hole and then open the drawer."

She looked expectantly at it. "It's empty."

"That's good, Em. Now close the drawer, remove your finger and open it again."

After complying, her countenance flooded with excitement. "It's got the candy." Pride beamed in her gaze. "Look, Jake, I did it."

He didn't have the heart to remind her these tricks were made for eight-year-olds to perform. Seeing her happy was all that mattered. And, he planned a lifetime of making her happy. "As your assistant, I applaud you and am preparing your next trick for our special audience. Do you wish to use your x-ray vision or to multiply rabbits?"

The adults in the Hamilton family plus their houseguests flooded into the room, led by Jesse. "She'll use neither. We've got news."

Jake clutched her hand. He hoped for good news. They couldn't take more bad news.

"That's it," Arthur stated. "Teri has given us enough to bring Charles in, but there's a slight hiccup you should know about. You'll hear it on the news soon enough."

"What the fuck do you mean?" Jake's patience was paper-thin. He was ready to take down this bastard. He didn't trust the man wouldn't find a way to send someone after his Em. Until this asshole was behind bars and someone else was to blame, he didn't think his woman or his daughter were safe.

"He's been ensconced with his attorney all day. We've been informed he plans to turn himself in to prevent our rushing in and arresting him. He'll make a big fucking production of it." Jake's old boss tightened his lips. "My boss has agreed to it."

"Fuck that. Go in and get him. He could change his mind. An attorney can do anything. I don't trust it."

"Jake, settle down," Jesse said from the couch.

The SEC director set down the bottle of water he'd been drinking. "From what we've found, the man's fraud involved around fifty million dollars. The attorney has made a deal that the directors of several agencies have agreed to involve him turning himself in to prevent our embarrassing him by arresting him so there is nothing he can do except put himself in criminal jeopardy. He has until the end of the week to turn himself in."

Brad whistled. "Fifty million. How did he get that far without someone noticing?"

James rubbed his neck with one hand. "I found another agent who helped Paul shuffle the investigations of Randall's firm."

"It'll be a bit of a mess. Randall's wife is already crying she didn't know, and since we've frozen his funds, she says she can't live. It's not fair. The standard excuse." Arthur shook his head in disgust. "She couldn't care less if anyone gets any of their money back."

Jake had a feeling something like that would happen. He was happy the funds were frozen. That would affect the help the attorney would provide. Who would want to work for free? Especially knowing if he failed there would be no funds left to pay him with since they'd all be dispersed to those who'd been swindled.

He didn't really care about that. All he cared about was his family. Would Randall blame her any longer since she was no longer tied to the investigation? Now it was Teri.

"What about Brian Randall?" No one had mentioned him recently. Where did he stand in all this? Jake hoped their old friend hadn't been involved.

"I've got that handled," Jesse said.

With Charles Randall's focus on trying to keep out of jail and on Teri, Jake figured the man would forget about Em, but he'd never let his guard down completely. Of course, he'd always keep his eyes open for danger to his family.

"Let me know when he turns himself in." Jake walked out of the room, tugging his future bride along.

Tomorrow couldn't arrive soon enough. Nothing would ruin their day.

****

Megan leaned against the pillows on Emily's bed and rubbed her belly. "Are you sure you want to rush a wedding. Just have a JP come in? I mean, this is your big day. You shouldn't let Jake dictate it."

Emily had planned her wedding to Jake since she was a little girl. She'd be a princess with her big dress with a long trail, her bouquet of long-stem red roses, her six bridesmaids in their lovely pink dresses. The bridegrooms would be in their white tuxes with matching pink cummerbunds and bow ties, flowers, more flowers, and then there was Jake in a black tux looking like a Greek god wearing a smile that melted her heart.

It was to be the most magical day of her life. A little girl's dream that had turned into a teenager's desire. Was she ready to give it up just because Jake wanted to be her husband now? Because her father had almost died? Because life was too short, as her father had reminded her?

The answer was easy. She wanted to be his wife and all the dream wedding stuff seemed trivial.

"Yes. All I want is my family at my wedding, and everyone is here. You know how hard it is to get the family together when they aren't on a job. Okay, it's a job now, but you and Dad are here too. There's no better time. Besides, I don't need all the frills of a big wedding. I'm a mother now."

Kate looked up from her cell phone. "Everyone deserves frills. Your being a mother has nothing to do with that. If you want to wait, we're behind you. We know how these men can be."

"I just want simple. I'm sure I have something here to wear, and that's all I need." Thank goodness she'd kept clothes here for the parties her father generally had for his elite friends. She had one dress that would work. It didn't matter. She wouldn't remember what dress she wore. She'd only remember Jake saying, "I do." To think it was finally happening. She just wanted to spin around until she was so dizzy she fell on the bed on her back, and then looked at the swirling ceiling until it stopped tilting on its axis.

Putting her phone down, Kate spoke, "Okay, I've found every place we need. Are you sure you're okay for this, Megan? AJ won't be happy."

"I wouldn't miss this for the world. He knows he won't be able to stop me so don't even worry about him."

Emily scrunched her brow at her sisters-in-law. "Missed what?" She worried when the two of them got their heads together. She'd learned that before she'd moved to New York City.

"You're coming shopping with us today."

"I can't go anywhere. I've got Amber. Besides, I thought I couldn't leave the house."

Kate shook her head. "Mrs. Kessler and Kelly have already agreed to watch her. And the men are shadowing us. We'll be in and out of each place, and we won't be unprotected. We're not allowing you to do without frills."

Megan stood. "No excuses. If I'm going, you're going. And," she stated, staring pointedly at Emily, "I'm going."

Knowing she'd lost this battle before it'd begun, she resigned herself to shopping. While most women would love it, since this wouldn't be a normal shopping trip, she wasn't sure whether to love it or dread it. It would be all for her so she loved both of them for that. She'd just rather relax and maybe spend time with Jake and Amber.

Looking at the two women, Emily knew she had no choice. It couldn't take too long to pick out a dress. She wouldn't disappoint them. Besides, it would be nice to find something to make Jake smile at how pretty she was beside him.

"Okay, let's go."

Downstairs they were unexpectedly met with more guests.

There was still a bit of trepidation at the arrival of the Strickland household even though the family had been cleared in the Ponzi scheme scandal. Emily didn't care what the others thought of the head of the family; Sofia was still her friend. And, she'd blown her off in New York City. Emily grimaced at the reminder of her home, now destroyed.

After a tight hug, she turned to introduce her friend. "Sofia, this is Kate. She's married to Jesse. And this is Megan, and she's married to, you aren't going to believe this, AJ."

"No. Not our little 'no woman will ever tie me down' AJ."

Laughing, Megan nodded. "That sounds like my husband. It's nice to meet you."

"How about we go into the living room and get comfortable," Kate offered.

Knowing the house well, Sofia didn't hesitate to lead the way. "That sounds like a good idea because I want to hear why we aren't staying here this year, and why there are more men here than usual for Senator Hamilton."

She flounced on the couch. "You know how hard it is to get a hotel. Daddy had to get someone kicked out in order for us to get a place to stay. Thank goodness Mom decided to stay back this year. She'd have us stay in Memphis, and I wouldn't look forward to that drive every day."

Kate, Megan, and Emily looked at each other. She imaged the question in their expressions was the same—how had the men explained it to Bill? They hadn't asked since their guests had arrived early.

"I've got this." Kate took command and led the remaining group into the room.

Mrs. Kessler miraculously appeared with refreshments and disappeared as quickly. Emily loved that woman. The men had best have been taking care of her when she'd been living away. She'd have to confirm it and kick their asses if they hadn't.

"It's simple really," Kate said. "I'm sure Bill will agree with Blake's change. The FBI deputy director and the SEC director arrived and needed a place to stay, so the senator offered here out of respect for their government rank instead of having them jockey for something in town. Especially since we already have security in place with Blake staying here. We just increased it a bit because they are also here."

Sofia looked doubtful but nodded. "That makes sense. I'm sure Daddy would understand. I'm surprised the senator didn't call him first."

"If he acquired a hotel room, I'm sure he must've." Emily smiled. Sofia had always been a rich, spoiled kid and the small accommodations offered in Oxford were beneath her standards. It must have irked her that she'd been relegated to a level below anyone, no matter who they were with the government.

Adjusting her floral knee-length skirt, her friend acted as if it didn't matter. "What's been happening? Whatever happened with the thing with your home, Emily?"

Emily swallowed hard. They'd always been open, sharing secrets with each other. Sure they'd only seen each other once a year, but they'd talk on the phone plenty throughout the year, keeping up with each other's lives. It was easier to share secrets when one knew someone who wasn't going to spill the beans.

In her standard sitting position of her hand on her belly, Megan smiled. "I bet Emily hasn't told you her good news."

Sofia looked at her expectantly.

Almost forgetting everyone didn't know her big secret, she happily blurted it out, "I'm getting married tomorrow."

"Oh, Emily, that's so great." Her friend looked at Kate and Megan and then lowered her voice. "What about Jake? Have you given up?"

Laughing, she shook her head. "That's the best part. It's him."

Her friend surged up from her seat and hugged Emily. "I'm so happy for you. When? What happened? Tell me everything."

"We're on our way out to shop for her dress. How about you join us, and she can tell you everything then?" Kate offered.

"I'd love to."

Emily definitely couldn't get out of her day of torture. But with her friend along, it couldn't be so bad. Besides, they could catch up on the last year with how her friend's love affair from afar turned out and on her reunion with Jake.

Who knew a simple wedding could still consume a full day? Kate and Megan rushed her through the bridal shop. Exhaustion had set in thinking about the schedule for the day. So much for just a dress.

Even for a small, simple affair, they wouldn't hear of her not having something big to remember.

First on the list was wedding dresses. After that she needed shoes to go with the dress, then flowers, then her hair, then nails, then who knew what else. She feared she'd be too fatigued to get out of bed tomorrow.

"Come on, Emily," Megan said, grabbing her attention, "look at that rack of dresses to see if something catches your eye."

Knowing she'd best not ignore the directive from one of her drill sergeants for the day, she sifted through the clothes. She stopped and pulled out a white chiffon lace floor-length dress. It was sleeveless with wide lace over both shoulders that moved down to cover the bodice. The V-back met small buttons trailing down the back. No train, no frilly stuff. It had a simple, elegant look. It was perfect. "I've found it," she said a bit choked up with the reality that she'd be a princess after all.

The three women swooped to her and gushed over the dress. She tried it on, and the seamstress promised the few alterations would be completed later that afternoon. That assured Emily it was definitely the perfect dress for her wedding.

After Kate paid for it, as her and Jesse's wedding present, they were off to the next store. She'd been wrong, torture it was, but sweet torture she labeled it, as she'd be marrying Jake with this wonderful new attire and accessories. It would be her day as a princess and him her prince.

****

Butterflies in the stomach were supposed to be a woman thing. Weren't they? At least Jake thought so, yet he had a flock of them flying around in his as only one signal of his nervousness. His sweaty palms and slight shaking were others.

In his fantasies, when he'd thought about marrying Em, he'd only thought of her saying, "I do," them kissing, him picking her up and carting her off to bed. His standing in the gazebo in the backyard, decorated by the women, with the entire family watching wasn't part of his dream. It was hot, and he was sweating like a pig in his newly acquired black suit. Maybe he and Em should've just taken off for the courthouse.

No. This was what Em wanted. Truthfully, it was what he wanted too. He wanted this family… his family… around for this. He was marrying the love of his life. It was monumental and having them witness it meant the world to him. Just as it meant the world to her. And he'd give her the world.

He glanced around at the faces. The women were fanning themselves. They could've been considerate and given him one of those things. Christ. But they did take the time to make this as magical as they could on such short notice for Em. Getting to know them when he'd been recovering had taught him they were wonderful, caring women who were tough as shit. They were women that Em would fit right in with. He had also figured out not to get on the bad side of any of them.

His brothers and the HIS men were talking and joking amongst themselves. So quickly he'd grown close to them. Being part of the team was exactly where he belonged. He couldn't believe Jesse had his name on the business from the beginning. His brother's faith in him choked him up. They hadn't stopped looking for him all those years. Then they'd been the ones to rescue him. He turned away, his emotions jumbled thinking about it.

If it hadn't been for Arthur, things would've been different. Like his brothers, he wasn't sure how he felt about the man. They worked with him since that was what they had to do. He knew his old boss had a job to do, and that had meant keeping Jake's whereabouts secret all that time, but the man had seen what Jake heard the family had gone through searching for him, at times believing he might be dead.

Music began playing, and he dropped every thought and turned toward the house. What had originally been a justice of the peace wedding had quickly morphed into a more traditional ceremony. The family had the preacher from the local church they attended when in town agree to do an abbreviated ceremony. The family and Jake agreed that Em deserved to have a memorable event even if she said otherwise.

He froze at the sight before him. Em. Christ, she was the most beautiful woman he'd ever seen. Holding onto her father's arm in a white wedding gown, her hair pulled up, she carried white flowers. He wanted to run the few yards and grab her up in his arms and take her away where it was just the two of them, and they could say their vows privately.

Movement in front of her drew his gaze down to his daughter in the dress he'd chosen. She skipped along dropping rose petals from a basket in piles. If it had been a possible thing, his heart smiled along with him. Amber seemed so proud of her duty.

His little princess stopped beside him. "Daddy, look, look. *I flower gurl.*"

Knowing he had to focus his attention on his daughter, but wishing he could continue to watch Em walk toward him, Jake knelt. He touched the top of his daughter's head, just below the flower ring around it, and moved his hand down her hair. "You make a beautiful flower girl, princess. Turn around and let's look at your momma." He nudged his daughter around and whispered, "Isn't she beautiful?"

She leaned toward him, cupped her hand to his ear and whispered, in a loud voice, "Mommy is beautiful."

Em broke into a huge smile that broadened the one on his face.

This was his family. Em and Amber. He had a large family, the Hamiltons. But this was *his* small family. His to look after, to provide for, to love. And he would do that.

He kissed his daughter's cheek. "Scoot over to Aunt Kate so your mommy and I can get married."

"Okay, Daddy."

Amber scampered away, and Jake stood as his bride approached with her father. She was even lovelier close up. Her bright smile and love in her eyes made him want to rush the ceremony so they could have their wedding night and be alone.

"Jake, I know you love her, but I am giving my only little girl to you. I expect you to take good care of her. She's my heart." Blake leaned over, kissed Em on the cheek, gave her arm to Jake and then walked to a seat. Jake could've sworn he saw tears glistening in the old man's eyes.

The preacher cleared his throat and watched Blake. Maybe they were supposed to wait for that part. He turned back to the couple, and a smile lit the man's face.

Jake's heart pounded. This was finally it, and he was ready. Would Em change her mind? God, he hoped not. He'd waited too long for this, and she'd given up hope on him. *Please let her keep her faith in me.*

He clasped her hand as they took a big step so their life together could begin.

"Dearly beloved–"

The preacher spoke, but Jake didn't really hear the words. He was focused on the woman next to him. He wished he'd been able to watch her walk toward him longer. Would the preacher be offended if he turned and stared at her while the clergyman spoke? Probably.

He squeezed her hand. Was she listening, or was she like him, thinking other thoughts? Hell, now he was thinking of what he'd do with her later tonight.

Out of the corner of his eye, he caught two men striding toward the ceremony. He'd thought everyone was in attendance. Jake turned to get a better view. Brian Randall, with Les tight at his side, stopped on the outside of the guest seating.

Jesse had called and spoken with the man, but they weren't expecting him until tomorrow. They'd been able to discern that, based on the paperwork, Brian had been clueless. Or very clever and allowed his father to be the only one to implicate himself. The family believed he wasn't aware.

Their hope in having him here was to convince him to turn on his father. A big undertaking, but one they planned. Tomorrow.

Today was his and Em's day.

Brian seemed agitated while he and Les whispered back and forth. Les grabbed his arm and began to pull him away.

"Why are you accusing my father of a crime?" Brian said in a booming voice.

The preacher paused at the statement and looked around. "Pardon, did someone have something that needed to be said?"

Jake groaned. Now was not the time. He wanted Em to be his wife. He'd promised the senator he'd marry her right away since Blake fretted for his health after his heart attack. Even though he refused to allow

Em to know.

Les whispered to Brian, and he held the man's arm tightly.

He attempted to jerk from Les's hold. "I don't care. Why should I allow you to enjoy yourselves when you are trying to ruin my family and put my father in jail?"

Dammit, they should've arrested Randall already instead of allowing him his own timetable. And how did Brian realize it was anyone here? Oh, right. Jesse had called. That must've been some conversation.

The SEC director stood and turned.

Brian paled at the sight of the man. "No. It can't be true."

"I'm afraid it is," James said.

Les didn't try to catch Brian as he toppled to the ground like a tree.

Chapter Twenty-Three

"If one more hand reaches in the pan, I'll chop it off," Emily warned her brothers. She'd been fine in the kitchen making the family a big pan of banana pudding while Mrs. Kessler and Kelly chatted on about nonsense which left her to her thoughts. Thoughts of her almost wedding.

Yesterday, Brian's collapse had put a damper on the thing, and they hadn't finished the ceremony. They'd have it again before everyone left. Otherwise, she'd marry Jake without the family. If that was what she had to do, then she'd do it. They only needed Amber.

Arthur and James, along with Jesse, had taken Brian off to the local FBI office for questioning. Jesse returned later that night and let them know Brian had taken a deal to speak against his father. He hadn't known, but they did think he suspected something was wrong. Who wouldn't? No one was that lucky.

She'd been keeping occupied while Jake attended a PTSD group meeting. She'd done well until five of her siblings, sweaty from their afternoon workout, invaded her workspace. "Couldn't you have showered before you came in here?"

AJ grabbed the empty box of vanilla wafers and tossed them back on the counter in disappointment.

Trying to hide her smile, she pointed the knife she

was using to slice the bananas toward the pantry. "I had Mrs. K. pick up an extra box."

"Hot damn!" AJ bolted from the room, ignorant of the smiling faces and shaking heads left in his wake. She wondered how Megan kept that man fed.

Jesse stuck his finger in the pudding and earned himself a slap on the hand. He'd been damn lucky she'd just finished cutting a banana and that hand was free, or the odds were fifty-fifty whether the hand with the banana or the one with the knife would've connected with his.

Emily set the cutting utensil on the counter and wiped her hands on the apron she wore while she collected her thoughts. They'd arrived en masse. It had to be for a reason, and she knew it wasn't to have an early taste of dessert. They didn't like the banana pudding that much. "What is it you want?"

AJ walked toward them, his hand stuffed in a box of wafers, and stopped close to her. Brad, Matt, and Devon pulled out bar stools across the counter from her. Jesse brought up the other side. Damn. They'd closed her in like penning a wild animal. They weren't letting her get out of this. Whatever this was.

Her legs wavered. Please let this not be them coming to give her bad news. "Has something happened?" She wanted to race up the stairs to check on Amber but somehow knew she needed to hear them explain first.

"No, nothing like that." Brad reached across the counter, pulled a banana slice out of the pudding and tossed it in his mouth.

She didn't care at this point. Maybe it wasn't her baby, but something was wrong. "What is it then?"

Maybe Jake?

Jesse cocked a half smile. "We need to know your plans."

Confused, she could only repeat him. "My plans?" What was he talking about? Now? Later today?

"Yeah." AJ tossed a wafer in his mouth. "Your plans after this," he said around chewing.

Those plans. She and Jake hadn't really spoken in depth about what they'd do once they left Oxford. Truthfully, they hadn't spoken more than generally about their future. She was embarrassed to say that she had almost married the man and had no plans past the day. Actually, she wasn't embarrassed. They were in love. That was all that mattered. The rest would work out.

"Um, Jake and I haven't worked everything out yet."

Since he'd be working for her brothers, they'd live somewhere near Baltimore. That she knew. With his having nearly four years of paychecks that had banked, buying someplace shouldn't be too hard. If it did, she had some of the trust fund from her mother remaining. She'd spent some on college. Her plan was to leave what was left to Amber and any other children they had, but they could draw from it if necessary. Amber needed a home.

They didn't need anything fancy. Sure they'd grown up in a nice home with lavish things, but the two of them never needed those things. Actually, none of the kids needed them. They lived around things their mother had put in the house that their father refused to remove or change. They cherished the items but never wanted anything so grand for themselves.

She cocked her head at Jesse and drew in her brows. "Why?" She reached out her hand and slapped Brad's, who she'd caught in her peripheral vision snagging another slice of banana. Mother reflexes. They'd learn not to mess with her. She turned her head to him and narrowed her eyes in challenge. "Mrs. Kessler, would you be so kind as to finish making this pudding for me?"

Brad's jaw dropped open and then he looked to almost pout before a sullen expression appeared on his face. He watched the housekeeper carry the dessert dish off as if he'd not eaten in a month. Emily shook her head, pleased to see something other than anger on his face. She wished she could heal the pain that had dug deep inside him.

She returned her attention to her oldest brother.

Jesse was having a terrible time suppressing a laugh at Brad's antics. His eyes brimmed with it. He straightened and looked at her. "We want you to come work with us."

A stroke of anger flew through her. How dare they? "I don't need you to feel sorry for me. I'll find something on my own. I don't need you." She turned away, only to bump into AJ's chest.

He set the box of wafers on the counter. "This isn't charity, Em."

"Let me pass, AJ. I appreciate you helping me with this problem. I couldn't have done it without you, but I don't need you bailing me out of every little situation." This was why she'd moved away, well partly. Part was memories of Jake, and part was her overprotective brothers. They didn't think she was capable of doing anything for herself. Now they didn't think her capable of finding employment after she'd screwed up her career in New York City.

She spun around on her three brothers at the counter and pointed her finger. "I think you've forgotten that my name has been left out of this situation. Only a few people have any idea that I was involved. This will not impact my ability to find work. And until I do, Jake can take care of me and Amber."

Matt cleared his throat. "Em, this has nothing to do with what happened, except the fact you showed us what you can do. You blew us away with your skills. We need that. Dev can manipulate data like no one's business, but he can't break down the financials like you did. Do you realize how much asset work we do? How much financial research we do?" He leaned forward on his forearms. "Em, like AJ said, this isn't charity. We truly need you on the team."

Choked up at Matt's words, she looked at her brothers. They thought she was good? She'd blown them away? Why hadn't they said so? Maybe they had said something, but she'd thought they were pandering to her at the time.

From what she'd learned from Kate, Emily would love the jobs the team worked. She'd get to play with the types of financials she enjoyed. Solving the types of problems that intrigued her. But she'd have to work for her brothers. It was a quick pipe dream shot down to hell. "I don't see how it would work."

Devon's wide eyes locked on her. "What do you mean?"

She shook her head. "I want a job where I'll be treated like a colleague, a partner, not like a kid sister who needs help with everything. That's how you guys treat me. I wouldn't enjoy that day in and day out. So, I can't do it." A hand squeezed her heart. It would've been fun working beside Jake, her brothers, and Kate. She knew she'd be inside with Devon all the time, and that was fine with her. The others could keep the fieldwork.

The men laughed. Actually laughed at her. Fucking assholes. She spun and pushed at AJ's chest. She'd had enough of them.

He grasped her arms. "Calm down, Em. You misunderstand. We're laughing for a good reason."

Emily snatched out of his grasp, harrumphed and then put her hands on her hips in anger. "What is it then?"

"We want you as a partner. You know, part of the Hamilton in Hamilton Investigation and Security," Jesse said.

Stunned, she stared at him, her mouth agape. Did he really just say partner? A partner with her brothers. Not a kid sister, a true partner. She scanned their serious faces. Each one turned to a welcoming smile. "Truly?" she asked in awe.

"Actually, your name has been on the business as an owner since we started it. Everyone in the family was. Dev, Matt and I wanted it to be a full family business when we started it, and we knew that each family member would join when the time was right for him, or her. The time is right. Say you'll join us, Em."

Jesse made one hell of an argument. That was for sure. They'd wanted her from the beginning. Why the hell hadn't they said anything? These damn men were confusing as hell. But she loved her brothers.

She threw herself into her oldest brother's arms.

"Yes."

"Hey, it was my idea too," AJ whined from behind her.

Originally, she'd thought that she would discuss a job opportunity with Jake before taking it, but she was pretty sure he wouldn't mind her taking this one. Since they'd both be owners, he could kiss her ass if he did have a problem with it.

Each embrace from her brothers lifted the worry clouding her mind. She and Jake were meant to be back in the fold of the family. Things were going to work out the way they should.

"What about Trent?" Em asked.

Brad chuckled. "Funny you should mention him."

She looked inquisitively from Brad to Jesse.

"We wanted to talk with you a second and then go ambush him. We just needed to know your take. The six of us, Jake included, want to offer him a partnership. We think it's bullshit what happened to him. We know he had a great life, but he is a Hamilton. You're a partner, so you have a vote. You have to agree since it'll split ownership and profits."

Shocked, she couldn't believe he'd ask her such a thing. "How could you think my answer would be anything but yes we should offer it to him?"

AJ, already munching on more wafers, said, "We didn't. We just had to ask. It's part of treating you like a partner instead of a kid sister." He shrugged, tossed a wafer in his mouth, chewed and swallowed. "Jesse made us do it."

Emily laughed so hard tears came to her eyes. Honesty was something her brothers had never grown out of, and she loved them for it. She swiped at her eyes. "Well, let's go find Trent."

"I'm right here. Why do you need to find me?"

She spun around so fast at the sound of his voice that she almost fell. How long had Trent been there? Surely if he'd overheard, he'd have said something before now.

He reached into the refrigerator, pulled out a bottle of water, screwed off the cap and took a drink. At least he'd showered after his workout. Now she understood why her brothers had rushed in to see her without cleaning up as usual. They needed time with her before Trent came downstairs.

"We need to chat about something. Want to go to the living room?" Jesse asked.

She worried for her friend. This situation wasn't easy for him. She didn't understand why, but she knew it wasn't her place to question. If he wanted to talk about it, he would.

Trent shrugged and led the group out of the kitchen. Behind her AJ followed, crunching on those damn wafers.

Taking a space on the couch by Matt, Emily waited for Jesse to speak. Sometimes allowing her brothers to take the lead wouldn't be so bad. She'd push them to treat her as an equal another time. In this instance, she didn't want to start the conversation.

With Trent's jaw tight enough teeth should be cracking, and his fists clenched as they were, she'd prefer to stay out of his path.

"Don't worry, we're not here to talk with you about Dad," Jesse began.

Something that sounded like a growl emanated from Trent's direction.

Uh oh. Not a good start.

Jesse sighed. "Trent, this is about HIS."

Trent said nothing but nodded.

Okay. Good sign.

"Well, whether you want to recognize it or not, you are a Hamilton," Jesse said.

"Look, no disrespect, but I'm a McKenzie."

Emily shook her head unable to remain quiet. "We're not saying you aren't. We're saying you are also family to us. Trent, you have always been family to us. You know that."

He smiled at her before turning back to Jesse. "What's this got to do with HIS?"

"It's simple." Jesse leaned forward, his forearms on his thighs. "We want to offer you a full partnership as a Hamilton."

Trent stared at him.

She could only imagine what was going through his mind. Would he accept it, or would he fight it? She knew he wasn't angry with them. But he seemed to be angry all together, and it was really starting to get to her as well. She missed the man she knew. Oh, he was still there, but this Trent just wasn't happy.

Would this finally get him to commit to staying with them? God, she hoped so. She feared if he took off, he might not come back. He really didn't have any other ties here. They were all he had. That might not be enough.

"Why are you doing this?"

Trent's question caught Emily off guard. What had she missed?

"What do you mean why are we doing this?" Jesse demanded. "We're your family, and you belong with us at the family business. That's why we're doing this."

Shit. Her oldest brother's temper was beginning to flare, and it wasn't always a pretty sight when that happened.

"Most of you didn't even know I was your brother until a few days ago. Now all of a sudden I should be a partner in the business where I worked for you?"

"Fuck, Trent," AJ said. "You know we've treated you almost like a partner from the beginning. You've never just worked for us."

"What the fuck is the problem?" Brad exclaimed. "We're giving you a fucking partnership."

Trent jumped from his chair. "That's the fucking point. You just give me things. Give. Give. Give. That's what your life has been all about. You've been given things. Now you want to give it all to me." He jabbed his thumb at his chest. "I may have Hamilton blood, but I'm a fucking McKenzie. I earn what I get." He spun on his heels and stormed from the room.

Emily thought about it. He was right in that they'd been given just about everything. But they'd worked for the family business. One that was incomplete without Trent.

Mrs. Kessler walked into the room carrying a tray with dessert dishes on it. "I thought you might need the banana pudding early. I guess I was right. Give him a bit of time to cool off. It's new to him." She unloaded the dishes and turned to the kitchen. "Oh, and you should let Emily be the one to talk with him alone if you want him to listen."

****

Jake couldn't believe he'd allowed himself to get roped into driving Arthur and James to the Memphis airport. There was no damn reason the two men couldn't drive themselves. Or someone on the team could've done it. He'd not wanted to leave Em's side. Sure, Charles had turned himself in and blamed Teri so things appeared safe, but he just wanted to be with Em. It seemed he'd lived a lifetime without her.

The drive was the perfect opportunity to make his peace with Arthur, though. He really shouldn't fault the man for believing his agent's lies that Jake was doing fine. Bryant had been the senior agent.

The Hamilton brothers' rescuing him still filled his body with the love and warmth only a family could generate. He gulped. Damn, it'd been close.

"We haven't been able to talk alone, son."

Jake looked over at Arthur in the passenger seat. No, he'd made sure they hadn't been able to do so. Until now. He turned back to the road in front of him. "Nope."

"I heard you joined HIS."

"Yep." Hell, he knew where this was going. He hoped he wouldn't have to argue his decision.

Arthur harrumphed. "I guess that means there is no use in trying to talk you into coming back to the bureau."

"Nope." The decision to never go back to what he'd thought was his dream job growing up, hadn't been as hard as he'd expected. He fit with the Hamiltons.

In his peripheral vision, he saw Arthur nod. "You'll do well with them."

Yes, he would. So would Em. He was thrilled her brothers planned to invite her to join. He'd made sure he hadn't been present when they'd offered it to her. It had been important that she realized her brothers, not just him, wanted her to join. He knew she needed to feel appreciated by them.

Now he had to work on a place to live. Jesse offered the extra rooms at his home until they found a place themselves. Jake wanted something close to the oldest Hamilton brother so Amber and Reagan could see each other often. Of course, they could just bring her with them when they were at headquarters. He nodded to himself. That was the way to do it. The kids could play under Mrs. Kessler's watchful eye while they worked. When they were on assignment, Em and Devon would still be there so nothing really changed. Except he'd have a cold bed at night.

"We haven't talked about your assignment since you left Maryland." Arthur's words broke into his thoughts.

Jake glanced at his passenger. "I thought all the debriefings were done." He didn't want to talk about that job at all. He was done with it. He didn't want anything to bring up memories he longed to forget. Memories that brought out his PTSD. "Besides, I'm not with the bureau any longer."

Arthur shifted in his seat. "True, but we should discuss a couple of things."

Spearing a glance at the backseat passenger in the rear-view mirror, he wondered what needed to be discussed so openly. Although James was checking messages on his cell phone, Jake imagined he was hearing everything.

He shook his head. "I don't want anything else to do with it. I did my part." He turned to Arthur. "More than my part." Being a prisoner, beaten and tortured regularly, and about to lose his life gave him a pass to do more. Although he had the desire to jump in and obliterate the group for what they'd done. But they'd captured the leaders and the ones who'd treated him thus. Had any of them still been loose, his answer might be different. Paybacks could be hell.

"You're right," Arthur said, his voice resigned. "Just keep an eye out."

He fought slamming on the brakes and pulling to the side of the road. "What the hell is that supposed to mean?"

Arthur looked uncomfortable.

Clenching the steering wheel, Jake gritted his teeth. "Has my cover been blown?" Christ, he couldn't bring this to his family. Not after what they'd just gone through. And, he'd never allow them to go through what he had. He'd kill every man who tried.

"No." Arthur tried for a calming look, but it failed to comfort Jake. "Like I told you when you resigned, this is what I tell every agent after an assignment. As far as we know, you're safe."

Jake quickly studied the man. He appeared to be telling the truth. Maybe Jake was just jumpy. "Would you tell me if you thought someone knew?"

The passenger turned to him and nodded. "Of course."

That was all he could hope for. An uncomfortable silence made the remainder of the drive seem longer than it had been. Jake still wondered about whether he should worry. No one had known he was FBI except Bryant, and he hadn't spilled the beans.

Still pondering what Arthur had said, Jake frowned when traffic slowed to a near stop on Highway 6E. The game traffic. He hadn't expected it to be backed up this badly. Maybe there was an accident?

Whatever the case, he'd never make it back to the house in time to leave with the family. Em would not be happy.

Chapter Twenty-Four

Jake hadn't returned home yet. Dammit, he'd promised. Why hadn't they left for the airport earlier? Then he'd be home. Heck, it wasn't like the traffic was a surprise on game day.

Dressed in her Ole Miss jersey, looking more like a college student than the well-dressed women who attended the game, Emily smiled like it didn't matter she would be alone, but she had a feeling her family didn't believe her. Oh well. "Jesse, I promised I wouldn't go if I was still in danger. So, what's the verdict?"

She knew everything had been cleared, and she and Amber were finally safe. Thank goodness. But, she'd made that promise to her brother and wanted to allow him to be the one to release her.

Her brother shrugged. "We look good. Randall is in custody. He hasn't been blaming you. He now blames Teri. And, we don't think he worked with anyone else. He never called out any threats as far as we can tell."

"So I can go?" Hope filled her. Jason would love it if everyone attended. Including Jake.

He'd been reluctant to drive their guests, but had finally agreed when she'd pushed him. They knew everyone was safe, and he could take the time to speak with Arthur. Maybe he'd finally forgive the man.

Although her brothers hadn't forgiven Arthur yet, so it might be more than she should expect.

He nodded. "Yeah. I'm keeping the guys around since we have Dad, even though he doesn't demand it. A few members of the team will get to enjoy the game, but some will be on duty. The others are taking a much needed day off at the ranch." He ruffled her hair. Something she'd told him she had hated since she'd turned ten. "Oh, expect Jason to keep an eye on you. He's decided he wants to be part of HIS instead of a quarterback when he grows up, so he sees it as his duty to protect you, even though we told him you were safe." Jesse chuckled. "That's after he goes to the locker room to meet the team and quarterback."

Emily attempted to put her hair back to rights. She should've worn a ball cap, but she'd chosen to at least keep her hair down to somewhat appease the high-faluting women, who'd put their noses too high in the air if she did. She probably earned it since she'd already breached the attire rule. She didn't want to embarrass her father too much, but she wouldn't give up the jersey, though. It was one of her brother's old ones. Matt and Brad had attended Ole Miss and played football. Each year she switched out which brother's jersey she wore. This year it was Brad's.

Besides, it was much more comfortable than the heels and dress clothes many of the women wore to the game. Whoever heard of tailgating the way these people did it in The Grove was beyond her. Yet it was constantly noted as one of the best places to tailgate nationwide. She'd had great catered food in the past. It was just that if she wasn't spoiled otherwise, she'd probably enjoy it. But she liked the grill and her jersey.

She couldn't wait until Jason saw the difference. It was a pity they weren't going to The Grove today. They were bypassing it so he could go to the locker room. "That's okay. I would love to let him feel important. As long as you really think there's no danger. I'd hate for him to get hurt."

Tossing his arm around her and walking her toward the door, Jesse laughed. "Not only would I not put my son in danger, but Kate would have my ass. Trust us, sis."

"I will as long as you don't make me ride with AJ."

While laughter rang out in the room, she heard said brother protest from somewhere behind them.

The excitement of the game bled into the box, even to the women, although Megan's excitement meter seemed to be waning. Emily smiled at how AJ fussed over his wife. Who would've thought the player that he'd been would have ever been this way. Then again, who would have ever thought Jake would've fallen in love with her.

He still hadn't made it. At least he'd called. There had been an accident and depending on the time he actually arrived, it'd be a last minute call on whether he'd make the game.

"Are you listening to me?" Sofia sat beside her at a bar table.

Emily shook her head. "I'm sorry. I was thinking about Jake." She couldn't help but smile. It didn't matter that she was disappointed he might not make it. She'd see him later. She missed him, though, and it had only been a few hours.

"Ah. The smile returns. Will he make it back in time?"

Emily rolled a glass of water in her hands. "I don't think so, but he's going to try." She took a swig. "What were you talking about?"

Her friend laughed. "You had asked me about the man I'd been seeing since we'd never finished our conversations before."

"Oh yeah. You said he was married, but that was to change. That's why you moved to New York City. To be by him."

She smiled. "You were listening." Sofia turned to Jason, who had stuck to Emily like glue although his eyes had remained mostly on the game.

To keep him from missing out, she had stayed mostly outside in the seats below the enclosure. She'd recently walked inside and sat down to cool off for a few minutes.

Sofia cleared her throat. "Jason, dear, would you get me a water, please?"

Bobbing his head, Jason stood and moved to the refreshment area.

"I'll tell you all about him. He's someone you know."

Intrigued, Emily leaned her elbow on the table, closer to her friend as if waiting for a secret. She hated that she wouldn't be living in New York City with Sofia. She and Jake would live somewhere near Baltimore. If only her friend had moved there sooner.

Jason appeared with the water, and Emily lost track of her conversation with her friend. This was her nephew's day.

"Okay, my protector." Jason blushed and Emily hid her smile. "Now, let's get as close as we can and watch the rest of this game."

"Thanks, Aunt Em."

She almost grabbed his hand to lead him, but caught herself knowing he was all of thirteen going on fourteen, and wanting to be part of the grown up HIS team, and holding hands with one of the women was not going to fly.

"Did you see that pass? It was a perfect spiral, and it was easily sixty yards," Jason ranted, excitement flowing through every word.

Emily listened as he commented on every play during the game. She tuned out half of what he said as he didn't stop talking about every move the quarterback made while including all the locker room chat. It was nice to see him like this, though.

She couldn't wait until Amber got as involved in something. She wondered what it would be that piqued her interest. She hoped it'd be volleyball as she enjoyed watching the games, plus they were indoor. Weather controlled. Until she decided on beach volleyball.

They sat down after an Ole Miss touchdown. "I'm so happy Poppy brought me here today."

Thank goodness Jason had finally stopped his unwillingness of calling his grandfather Poppy. Emily agreed with him that it sounded like a girl's name, but her father felt it special since he'd been named that by Reagan. He'd made his grandfather so proud by doing it. "I think he's happy too. He's enjoyed spending the time with you. I don't think I've seen him smile so much in a long time."

"This family has been so good to me." Jason looked around the box behind him.

Emily smiled, and her heart contracted. He'd seemed to be part of the Hamilton family forever.

Nothing would change the love they felt for him.

"Em." Matt leaned down and said in her ear, "I need you to remain calm."

Every muscle went on high alert, and her heart beat rapidly sending pulsing through her veins at a speed that throbbed throughout her body. When someone said that, there was a reason not to remain calm. Dear God. Amber. "What?"

"We need to go home."

She closed her eyes. He didn't have to say it. She knew her little girl was in trouble.

****

Trent wasn't waiting around for another wedding. There was no telling how long it would be before they decided it appropriate to take the plunge. He needed to leave. The senator, his father, wanted to get close with him, and he wasn't ready to forgive the old man for lying to him all those years. He had to get away to figure out how he wanted to proceed with the Hamilton family. He guessed nothing had to change, but everything actually had changed. They wanted him to be a partner with them. To be one of them.

It was the perfect time to leave. Em and Amber were safe, and the men were preparing for their next mission. None had seemed to mind their precious break between assignments had been spent protecting the Hamiltons.

It was still hard to believe that he had brothers and a sister. Sure he'd known it a good part of his life, but to hear it said aloud, and for them to know made it all the more real. But they'd always felt like brothers and sister. It was his damn father who was the problem.

Trent needed to go to his mother and father's

graves. The father who'd raised him. The man he truly called and felt was his father. He had to speak with Roger McKenzie, even though the man was dead.

He needed to know what to do about Blake. Did he give him a chance to be the father he'd been denied? Or did he continue living the lie his mother had wanted them to live? It had been her secret to begin with. She'd never wanted it revealed, yet his dear old dad had decided every-fucking-body needed to know. Trent knew that was what really pissed him off more than anything. The man had ripped away something his mother had held dear. Something she'd been too embarrassed to reveal to the world. Blake had just tossed it out there like it was nothing.

He jammed another T-shirt into his suitcase then walked to the window. So lost in thought, he'd missed the beauty of the day. He could've been in the middle of a sea storm instead of a bright, sunny cloudless day.

Running his hand up and down the back of his neck, he heaved a burdened sigh. Where to go from here?

After a visit to his parents' graves, he thought maybe he'd take a nice long drive. He hadn't been to the beach in a while. Vacations on the coast with his family had been a highlight of his summer while growing up. Maybe he needed a bit of nostalgia.

He would miss hanging with his brothers and the men. He'd miss Em and Amber the most. The bonds he'd formed with them had been strong. Many had worried about that bond, but since he'd known from the beginning of their true relationship, he'd ensured it'd been platonic in nature. Still, they were close. And he loved that little munchkin. She was a ray of sunshine.

A knock on the door caught his attention. "Come in." His unfocused gaze continued to look out the window.

"There's an FBI agent here to see Jake."

Trent spun around and raised his eyebrows at Danny, an HIS team member. How interesting. "When is he due back? Didn't he call earlier with an ETA?" He'd tried to make the game, but traffic hadn't cooperated, and Trent couldn't wait to see the groveling he'd have to do to make that up to Em because she'd been looking forward to attending it with him.

"He's just down the road. Maybe five minutes."

"No problem. Check his badge and let the agent wait." The more he thought about it, the odder it seemed since Jake had just driven the FBI deputy director to the airport. Why would they want to speak with him now? He shook his head. Damn feds and not communicating.

"We did check *her* badge. It looks authentic. Les is with her by the pool. It took some convincing to get her to go where no one else was around."

Curious, Trent leaned against the window frame and folded his arms across his chest. "Why's that? If she's FBI, why not bring her inside to wait instead of standing in the heat?"

"Well, Les stopped me midway down the walkway to the house and took over." He shot Trent an incredulous look. "I know we aren't on duty, but it's hard to stop."

Trent nodded. True. They all seemed to be in protective mode 100 percent of the time.

"Anyhow, Les caught how her suit jacket fit weird. She's wearing a bomb vest."

"Fuck!" Trent pushed past Danny and snatched his weapon off the dresser on his way out the door, urgency in each step down the stairs. The entire time he attempted to think of a plan. What the fuck could he do? He wasn't a bomb expert. He didn't have a vest to protect him from a bomb blast. Hell, he was in shorts and tennis shoes. He really couldn't do anything but get his ass blown to smithereens.

Danny halted behind him before he reached the back door. "Would you like your earpiece to know what the fuck is going on? You forgot to grab it when you took off like a bat out of hell."

"Thanks, man." Trent held out his hand and then inserted the piece of equipment in his ear. Hearing nothing, he searched Danny's face.

"It's quiet." The man cleared his throat and continued, "They ran into someone along the way, and the woman insisted the three of them stay together."

Trent's heart palpitations went almost out of control. There were only two people Danny would warn him about since the family was at the game—Amber and Reagan. *Christ.* "What happened?" he asked in a raspy voice, sure it sounded as broken as he heard it.

The vein in Danny's neck pulsed rapidly. That was the only visual sign Trent saw that warned him he wouldn't like the man's response to his question.

Trent's breathing grew erratic, and he took a couple of deep breaths in hopes to calm it… calm himself enough to handle the situation correctly.

"The men rushed in to collect Mrs. K. and the girls, but before they reached them, Amber broke off running to Les to tell him about Dottie's puppies. It was too late at that point. We don't know the blast radius."

Shit. He couldn't just stand here. "Come on, let's get where we can see what's happening." There had to be something he could do. Standing around here chatting wasn't going to solve anything.

"Wait." Danny grabbed Trent's arm, squeezing taut muscles to restrain him. "Do you think I want to stand here longer than necessary? Fuck no. But you need to know. The woman wants Jake to watch his daughter die."

Trent made to break free of the grasp and get to Amber. To pull her from the crazy woman's grasp.

"Wait, dammit. Jamaal stepped closer to grab Amber, but the bitch showed us the dead man's switch and threatened to use it. You know we couldn't care less, but our angel was in there and without protective gear." Danny tightened his jaw. "We just couldn't risk it. He had to back off and leave it to Les."

Holy fucking Christ! He'd heard enough. "Grab another earpiece for Jake, meet him and bring him around. Quietly." Trent slipped through the house and out the back door. What good was he going to be? He just had to keep the woman occupied for five minutes. Until Jake arrived. He could do that.

****

Skidding the car to a stop, Jake almost jumped from it before he put it in park. Danny held out a Glock, body armor and an earpiece for him. He shoved the earpiece in his ear, grabbed the weapon and shook his head at the body armor. He needed to move, not take time to don the vest.

He couldn't believe someone had his daughter. Fuck! They'd thought everyone was safe. If only after Arthur had said something about watching his back he'd called and had the men protect Amber and Em, this wouldn't have happened. The woman never would've gotten near his little girl.

It was his damn fault. He had to figure out a way to fix this. "What's Les been saying? Does he have a plan to save them?"

Danny sighed. "Nothing yet. We've been chatting, and so far we've got nothing. He just pushed to get them near the pool. We can't shoot her with that switch."

Fuck. "How the hell did she get through?"

"Calm the fuck down, Jake. She had an authentic FBI badge. We may have been off-duty, but we aren't that stupid. And, her suit jacket hid the vest well. Les just happened to catch something with it from afar."

He took in a deep breath. Christ, his heart raced dangerously fast. "I'm sorry."

The HIS team member nodded. "It's best if we go through the house. It'll allow you to arrive without her knowledge. Trent went to keep her occupied, hoping to get her to release Amber."

"Fuck! What the fuck is going through her mind? Why is she here? Who is she?"

"We don't know. She's not speaking except to say she wants to see you and that she plans to take away your little girl like you took away some asshole in a raid. We can only guess she's from your FBI op." He turned back to glance at Jake. "She's wearing a hijab."

In all situations Jake had been taught to remain cool and calm, to keep his focus on his actions, not the individuals. He couldn't do it this time. His body and his mind were wound tight, the reactions within him, the racing pulse wasn't due to the pending action, it was due to fear for his daughter's life and the prospect of losing her. He couldn't fuck this up.

"What about the rest of the team?" He needed his brothers to help with this one. He also needed their bomb expert.

Nearing the back of the house, Danny lowered his voice to answer, "They're on their way back from the game."

"And Em?" She'd been through enough.

"I doubt they'll keep her in the dark on this one."

Shit. She didn't need to see their daughter in this situation. She definitely didn't need to lose Amber like this. He'd make sure she wouldn't lose her.

Jake stopped. Power snaked through his veins from his head to his toes, giving him a feeling of control once again, the knowledge that he no longer feared losing this battle. He turned toward the pool with no particular plan in mind. All he knew was that he would be there to help Les save Amber's life at all costs.

Even though he knew what to expect, turning the corner of the house, he saw something that would be ingrained in his memory for years to come.

Amber, holding her stuffed frog, crying and calling out to Les, who stood a few feet away, and attempted to pull free.

What would happen if she got loose? Would the woman blow them up without knowing he watched?

"Jake, give us a minute. Stay put." The voice in his ear angered him. Stay put? His daughter was being held by a madwoman intent on killing her, and they wanted him to stay put?

"Once Trent is in place, then you can talk to her." He sighed. He'd missed what place Trent needed to be in, but he understood that he didn't have to remain hidden for long. He would save his daughter. The HIS family would help him save his daughter.

Trent stepped into full view and called to Amber, "Hey, munchkin, be still and hold the nice lady's hand for me. Afterward, we'll have some cookies and ice cream. Can you do that for your mommy and me?"

The little girl stilled, her crying stopped, but tears still streamed down her face. She sniffed. "*Pwomise*?"

Trent leaned down, set his weapon on the ground and then took two steps forward. In his ear, Jake heard a man talking to Trent about the best spot to be close to Amber and the bomber to help calm his daughter and hopefully save her. "I promise. And you can have the big bowl if you want."

The woman held up the hand not holding Amber's, displaying a device Jake assumed was the dead man's switch Danny had warned him about. "Stop where you are or I'll let go of this button."

Trent stopped and raised his arms in surrender. "I'm just trying to help calm the child for you. To make it easier while you wait for Jake. If you let me closer," he said and then gestured with his head to where Les stood, "by him, I can help you keep her calm."

Maybe the woman noticed how compliant the child had become—Jake didn't know the reason—but she allowed Trent to join Les. Walking slowly with his hands in front of his shoulders, he stopped with his back to the pool. "Since I'm just arriving, why don't you tell me what's going on? And, would you say it where it won't undo what I just did." Amber might try to run to him, and they couldn't have that. Not right now.

The woman looked down at the child and then up at him. She narrowed her eyes. "I'm Zainah Jalal."

Jake thought the name sounded familiar, but couldn't be sure. He hadn't met everyone at the compound.

"Abdullah Alim Shah lied to us. He was really this Jake Cavanaugh. This FBI agent who had Mohammed bin Shakaran arrested, and we couldn't complete our mission. America deserves to be cleansed."

Fuck. Someone in the FBI had given him away. Bryant? Probably. That bastard. He'd have to have a chat with Arthur about this as soon as he saved Amber's life.

Trent looked down at Amber's wide eyes and trembling body. "It's okay, munchkin." He turned his gaze back to the bitch and didn't seem to care if his hatred bled through his stare. "That's enough. You're scaring her."

Jake noticed the little girl squirming. He knew that movement. *Shit. Not now.*

"*Gotta potty.*"

"I need you to hold it until your daddy gets here. Can you do that? It won't be long."

He hoped she could do that. She was only three fucking years old. Did they have that much control? Please don't let her make a fuss.

Amber nodded. "*I twy.*"

"I can get a shot of her hand, but I can't guarantee the bomb won't go off so we're better off waiting to see if our bomb expert can give us any insight." Trent heard one of the team sharpshooters, Neftali, state in his earpiece.

"Rob should be here in three minutes," Danny

responded.

That meant the group from the game was close. Shit. He wanted his brothers to help, needed them, but damn, he wished they didn't have Em with them. He had to try before she arrived. If he failed, she couldn't witness it. *No!* He would not fail.

Jake leaned his forehead against the cool barrel of his weapon in his hand and said a silent prayer. He had to find a way out of this. These men were the best there was and with them, this had to be possible. He lifted his head and looked at Danny.

Danny frowned but nodded.

Stepping from his hiding place, his pulse racing, Jake moved forward and spoke aloud, "I'm Jake Cavanaugh."

Chapter Twenty-Five

Emily sprinted into the backyard behind her brothers with her heart pounding against her ribcage, threatening to escape her chest. Her daughter was in danger once again. The men had been vague, but she knew it was bad, or they wouldn't have been so tight-lipped about the situation. The worst-case scenarios ran through her mind. The danger to her from Em's job had been resolved so it couldn't be that. She'd overheard part of a conversation, and she'd discerned Jake wanted them to keep her away. Like that'd happen if her daughter was in trouble. She'd walk if she had to get there.

Since they'd run the way they had around the house, her first thought was that her daughter might've drowned in the pool. AJ's arms reached out to stop her forward momentum, almost knocking her on her ass she stopped so fast. Her gaze snapped to his face. How dare he stop her when she needed to get to Amber? Her pulse jumped up a notch at the angry look on his face. She followed his gaze and reached up and covered her mouth with shaky hands. *Oh God.* Fear sliced through her, leaving behind a stomach ready to heave, limbs that weighed a ton and a pounding of her heart that surely could break through her chest.

A woman with a bomb vest held her daughter's hand with Trent and Les about six feet from her, and

Jake stood about forty feet from it all. None could save her daughter.

Swallowing past the large lump in her dry throat, she managed to speak, "Who is that?"

Her brother closed his eyes for a second and sighed before he refocused his gaze on the scene before them. "She's someone from Jake's past. From when he was undercover." He reached down, grasped her hand, gave it a gentle squeeze and released it.

"Is that a bomb?" She prayed for a different answer than what her eyes told her.

"I'm afraid it is."

Her knees buckled, and AJ wrapped his arm around her, catching her before she dropped to the ground. Her baby. *No. No. No.* "You have to do something, AJ," she begged in a weak voice.

"Em, we're working on this. We'll figure it out. Trust us."

Starlights swam before her eyes. The desire to slip into oblivion, to pretend this was a bad dream was overpowering. But she knew it wasn't a dream. It was fucking real, and that bitch had her daughter. Something snapped in her and anger rolled back and forth through her veins heating her blood, bringing it to a near boil.

"No, let Jake keep trying to talk her down."

She knew AJ spoke to the team, but it almost sounded like he was directing her. She wished she knew all that was being said between the men. Or maybe she didn't. There were things that might break her new resolve to believe this would end happily. Her brothers would save her daughter. Her little Amber.

"What's the plan?" she asked.

Putting his finger to his lips to silence her made her want to slap his face. He'd just spoken. Her brothers always had special rules that applied to only them. Then she understood why he'd done it.

"Zainah, you don't have to do this. You can take me instead," Jake said.

Emily gasped, and that newly found resolve took a hit. The thud of her heart sounded loudly in her ears. She didn't want to lose either of them. She needed both Jake and Amber in her life. It wouldn't be complete without them.

"Leave the little girl to her mother. That woman has nothing to do with this."

"But she does," the woman hissed. "She must mean something to you to have a daughter. She should suffer also."

"She was nothing more than a one-night stand. She means nothing to me."

Even though Emily knew it wasn't true, it ripped at her heart to hear the words she'd feared all of those years. And it'd been her fault she'd been the one-night stand. The one with consequences.

AJ leaned to her ear. "You know he doesn't mean it."

She sniffed. Christ, had she started crying? "I know."

"I want her here as well. I want you to see the pain on her face too," the crazy woman told Jake.

The arm that had stopped her from rushing forward before was back.

"Let me go." She pushed against AJ's blockage.

"No." AJ shook his head.

"She's not here," Jake said.

High-pitched laughter pierced the humid afternoon air. "I know better than that. In fact, I believe I spy a blonde head among all of the dark heads watching us."

Jake jerked his head around, and when he saw Emily, an acute pain swamped his eyes. He closed them for a moment and then turned back to the bomber. "No. This is between you and me. Now, trade me and my daughter."

"Mommy," Amber cried out and reached toward her with her free hand. "Mommy."

That was enough. She was going to get her daughter.

"Try to calm down, Em."

"Calm down! Calm down! My daughter is holding hands with a terrorist with a bomb strapped to her, and you tell me to calm down. Fuck you, AJ. I'm going to get her." She shoved past her brother and ran out only to be halted by Jake.

"Stop or she'll blow it up. I know she's not faking."

"Munchkin, munchkin, I need you to look at me." Trent tried to gain Amber's attention, keeping her from attempting to rush to Emily. "I need you to stay with us for just a bit longer before we go to your mommy and daddy, okay?"

Her daughter stared at her uncle with fearful, confused eyes. She tried to jerk her hand free from the bomber, but the woman held on tightly.

Emily's heart broke. "Amber, just stay with the lady for a minute while Daddy and I talk. We'll be there shortly to get you. Talk to your Uncle Trent and Uncle Les, okay?"

Amber turned to her mother, tears leaving streaks

down her red, puffy face. "Okay. Hurry, *I gotta potty*."

"We will." Her gaze not leaving her daughter, she spoke to Jake, "Why don't they just shoot her and get this over with?"

"They can't. She could still blow up."

"Oh God. Now that she's got both of us here, she's going to—" She couldn't finish the thought as a sob fought its way to the surface. "Tell me you've thought of something, Jake. Tell me you've thought of something to save our daughter."

When he didn't answer, she looked up at him and noticed his gaze flicked to Les and Trent. Maybe they did have a plan after all. Her heart lifted. Yes. She knew she could count on them to save her baby. Then she saw him visibly swallow hard, and a sense of fear made the hairs on her arms prickle.

By the pool, Trent and Les no longer watched the bomber. Hell, every other eye was on her. They seemed to be in a non-verbal conference where their expressions held a great deal of resolve. They looked from Amber to the bomber, and then Emily understood. Her hand flew to her mouth. *Oh God!* "No. There has to be another way," she whispered in a wavering voice.

Jake reached out and squeezed her hand. "There's not. Rob says it all looks legit."

"No, Jake. Find another way. This can't be the only way. Shoot her."

"Em. Do you see her other hand? Can you guess what happens if her hand comes off that switch while our daughter is there? No. We can't shoot her unless Amber is free of her."

She wavered on her feet. Options. There had to be options they weren't considering. *Think.*

311

"Zainah, I'm asking you again. Please take me instead of the child."

Emily couldn't believe how her world was crashing down around her. With a sinking stomach, she looked at Trent and Les again. It was her daughter, but she couldn't allow someone else to possibly sacrifice his life for Amber's. She knew Jake was right; they were pretty much out of options and time had run out. The woman had them both, which was what she wanted. But, what if they didn't survive? They had to keep thinking. Only time had run out.

Jake pulled an earpiece from his ear and handed it to her. "Les wants to speak with you."

She sobbed and her hands shook uncontrollably. She couldn't grab a hold of what he was attempting to discreetly hand her.

"Here. I'll hold it near your ear."

Emily sniffed and shook her head. She didn't want him to take it away before she heard everything. Reaching out, she managed to calm her hands enough to grasp it and then place it in her ear. In a very low voice, she heard Les speak, almost as if mumbling to himself. And, he was since he was so close to the woman. Only the bomber's focus was on Jake. "It's the only way. You know that, Em. This is what we do. We all know the risks. Any of us would take them, especially for our family, and she is our niece. Blood or not."

Jake touched her arm. "Em, you have to hold it together. You're scaring Amber, and she's trying to come to you."

She took a deep breath and held it at his words, hoping to stifle her sobbing. She couldn't help it. She loved Les. Like he said, he was family. Wiping the tears under her eyes, she continued to moderate her breathing. Looking at her daughter, she brought a smile to her face. "I'm okay. Just one more minute, and I'll be over to get you."

"Mommy, I *caired. Want* you and Daddy."

Of course she was scared. She was three years old and a strange woman wouldn't release her. "Just one minute, Amber."

Jesse gave some direction to the men in the earpiece, and it made it so final that it was difficult for Emily to fight the clawing dread of what was to come. They talked of potential death as if it was normal operating procedure. The task delivered calmly. She was freaking out inside, and they acted as if it were another day at the office. Even Les appeared fine with his decision to possibly die in a few moments. If he couldn't grab her hand fast enough….

Everyone seemed to understand what was happening except the bomber. She remained focused on Jake and her need to make him pay. She spewed consistent nonsense at him. The hatred in the woman's eyes made Emily want to rush forward and scratch them out with her bare hands.

The earpiece needed to be returned to Jake so he could be prepared with proper timing. She couldn't release it before she whispered, "I love you, Les. God bless you."

He gave her a barely noticeable nod, and then murmured, "Gulf Bravo." The phonetic for good-bye. She bit her lip to control it. If he died, she'd hold on to this guilt forever, knowing she'd allowed this man to sacrifice himself for the life of her daughter. She prayed the bomb was a dud, and they would all be safe.

All she knew was that she would know right away if this worked and her daughter survived. Goose bumps coursed over her skin at the thought of the word *if*. It was one hell of a risk, but she understood it was the best chance they had. If they didn't at least attempt something, the psycho woman could blow Amber up without thought. They'd lose her for sure.

The earpiece exchanged, Emily waited on pins and needles for everything to happen. Trent and Les took simultaneous deep breaths, and she knew it was time.

The next few moments, second, minutes, hours, she didn't know, but they seemed to move in slow motion, constricting her heart and making it difficult to breathe. Before Jake threw himself over her, she caught Les reach for the surprised woman's hand, and Trent yank Amber from her and spin, wrapping one arm around her little body and one around her head. Then she saw nothing but the green grass where Jake had pushed her down.

An explosion. A splash. And then a moment of quiet. But only a moment. Men were yelling, and Jake was off her and gone. She jumped to her feet, frantic to check for her daughter, a bit fearful of what she'd find but determined to search. To find her.

Through the ringing in her ears, Amber's sputtering, squalling voice came through loud and clear. Rushing to the pool, she was halted midway by Jake, who placed a soaked Amber in her arms. He hugged them tight, and then kissed them both on the cheek. "Get her to the house." He jogged away.

Finally, she held her daughter, whole but scared and crying for her mother. The child wrapped her arms around her, choking her a bit, but she wouldn't complain. It meant Amber was alive.

Emily glanced across the pool, bile formed in the back of her throat when Jesse covered Les's face with a shirt, and she quickly pivoted so her daughter's face was averted. A tear slid down her cheek. She'd always grieve for him. Of the men on the team, he was one of the closest to the family. He'd be missed for a long time to come. Missed as a family member. She'd known the level of love these men had for her and the family, but this went beyond anything she'd ever expected.

Red in the pool caught her eyes. A great deal of it. She ran her free hand over her daughter, double-checking for any injuries. Nothing.

Trent. No. No. No.

Some of the men gathered in a circle around what she could only assume was Trent lying on the ground. With them kneeling down, she couldn't get a peek at his condition, and she couldn't bring Amber over to ask. In fact, it was almost as if they were blocking her view on purpose.

She wanted to thank Trent, but that could wait until they doctored him up. There certainly had been a lot of blood, though. The plan had been that he put himself between Amber and the bomber before he took to the pool to try to prevent any impact of the blast to her daughter. She hadn't considered the fact that the back of his body would be exposed in the meantime.

She walked through the back door. *Please let it not be serious.* She couldn't handle two sacrifices.

Her knees buckled, and she collapsed in a chair when ambulance sirens rent the air.

****

Jake hadn't known what to expect when he'd approached the pool, but he had prayed his daughter would be alive. He'd never expected some fallout from his undercover assignment. Arthur's intel sucked. He should've known the man was giving him a hint that the deputy director didn't want to say aloud. Fuck.

How had they found him? Surely Arthur's trip hadn't been secret, and they'd discussed the operation, which probably went into reports his old boss filed. Did the terrorists have more people in the FBI who believed in their cause or was it just Bryant getting information out?

At that moment, he couldn't care less. Christ, his daughter had almost died, and it was his fault.

Thank God for Les and Trent. They'd made a sacrifice that stood for their love of this family.

He swallowed hard at the thought of Les, and the fact nothing could be done for him.

Jake should've been the one standing there protecting his daughter. Now someone had given his life to save Jake's family. How did he ever repay that?

Watching the ambulance cart Trent off, Jake's heart bled for him. He might not have wanted to have the family pull themselves around him, but he'd learn that this was his family.

Jake had hated walking away from his little family, tossing his wet and crying daughter at Em to take care of after everything had happened. The men had needed him, and he couldn't turn his back on the man who'd saved Amber's life.

"How is he?" Em asked as he caught up to her in her bedroom.

He pulled her tightly into his arms. Damn, she fit

so perfect with her head resting on his chest and her arms wrapped around his middle. "It's not good, but he'll survive," he said past the growing lump in his throat. Was he choked up about Trent's injuries or about what happened to Amber? Either way, he found it difficult to breathe.

Even through his damp shirt, her tears touched him. He remembered the closeness she had to Trent. The closeness that had once almost driven him mad with jealousy.

He glanced at the bed. "How's Amber?"

She sniffed and stopped her weeping. "I rocked her to sleep. She's scared, but she doesn't quite understand." Em stepped back and looked longingly at their daughter. "She asked for you."

Not realizing it, she'd deliver a significant punch to his gut. Trent told him to take care of his family, but he'd refused to part from his friend all the while telling Trent that he was family. Jake also knew that Em would understand and take care of their daughter. He knew that she'd be strong until he was with them. He'd just hoped that he'd be able to hold them both tight before Amber fell asleep. Another time. "I'm sorry."

"Don't be." She smiled brightly, and her eyes glistened with the tears she'd left unshed. "It's where you needed to be. I'm not upset. You'll be here when she wakes up, and that's what will matter to her. She just needs to see you."

What did he ever do to deserve this woman? Thank God, he'd come to his senses. Thank the Hamiltons he had his life to live with her. "Em, I'm sorry about it all. This is my fault."

She placed her forefinger on his lips. "Shh. You

couldn't have known."

Grasping her hand, he kissed each finger and then her palm. Most women would've gone berzerk on their man had something like this happen. But not his Em. She didn't blame him for what caught up to him. Maybe she'd seen enough with her brothers and knew his being an FBI agent brought its own trouble. "I won't let anything like this happen again. I'll keep you safe. I love you."

She whispered, "I love you, too."

"*Luh* you, too, Daddy."

****

Jake and Emily arrived at the hospital hand in hand, joyous that Amber woke before they'd left to visit. Their daughter hadn't understood exactly what had happened so they hoped she'd be able to keep her curiosity away from it. They didn't want to answer questions about Trent and Les right away.

No matter their happiness from their home life, they wore a heavy heart for this visit. How did Emily repay a man for something as precious as saving her daughter's life? Family, friend or team member, Trent had risked his life by walking into it knowing he could be the only chance to save Amber, if she could be saved.

Inside the ICU waiting room, a group of men stood restlessly or sat fidgeting, not huddled around joking as usual. Her brothers and the team members' actions twisted a knot in her gut. How bad was he? Les had been one too many. Not Trent too. She couldn't handle it.

Jake steadied her, and they walked into the room and approached the group. Her gaze automatically zoned in on Jesse. "How is he?"

The pained look on his face worried her. They'd said he'd live or else she would never have delayed their visit for Amber to be loved on by Jake. She'd expected him to be in emergency care, and there'd be nothing she could do. *Please don't let things have changed.*

"He's heavily medicated, but he'll be okay."

A pent-up breath whooshed from her lungs. When her brother's expression changed, she leaned back against Jesse, knowing she'd need his strength. Had he lost limbs during the rescue?

"He's lucky."

AJ jerked up from a chair across the room. "How do you call having shrapnel pulled from you and being that extensively burned lucky?" The painful emotion in his voice tugged at Emily's heart.

Jesse narrowed his eyes at his baby brother. "He's lucky he's fucking alive. Scars are nothing compared to dead."

Emily gulped, trying to pass a tennis-ball-sized lump down her throat. "How bad?"

"It's significant." Kate, sitting next to her husband, leaned into Jesse. "But, like Jesse said, he'll survive. It'll be tough and painful for him for a while."

Jake's arms wrapped around her, anchoring her body to him, and warmth seeped into her veins. On one hand, she agreed with Jesse—be thankful he has his life. On the other hand, she agreed with AJ—this was nothing to be happy about if it was to be as extensive as they believed.

The quick, tight squeeze with his hand told her how hard this was for Jake. He blamed himself. She'd tried to convince him otherwise on the drive to the hospital with no success. It didn't matter that it could've been anyone that threatened their daughter. Hell, they'd recently had their share of trouble. But, Les and Trent had known the risks. They'd taken them. Without them, she and Jake wouldn't have their daughter at home, playing with her cousin.

A doctor entered and scanned the room. "McKenzie family."

The entire group moved forward. "Hamilton," Jesse growled.

Bewildered, the man shook his head. "No, I'm looking for the McKenzie family."

"You've got us. But, he's a Hamilton." Jesse crossed his arms over his chest in his don't-mess-with-me stance. She wanted to roll her eyes, but she was too curious about what the man had to say.

Reaching a hand out, the man spoke, "I'm Doctor Walker." He shook Jesse's hand and must've decided that was all that was necessary because he didn't offer it to anyone else. "I understand Nurse Fulton updated you on his condition. It hasn't changed except for he's awake. He's asking for Emily and Jake."

They stepped forward in unison, her desire to thank Trent and see how he truly was raced through her body.

"I'd rather he went back to sleep to deal with the pain, but he refuses until he speaks with the two of you."

Emily nodded. "We'll be quick." She reached for Jake's hand before anyone noticed the slight tremble that had overtaken her. Would he blame them for his injuries? He had every right.

A nurse provided them protective clothing and

waited while they donned it. The woman spoke non-stop on the trip to the ICU, but Emily didn't hear the words. Her thoughts were on Trent. She feared what she'd see. How he might look. Walking in and witnessing all the machines hooked to him and people caring for his burn wounds buckled her knees. Jake caught her midslide to the ground.

Trent lay on his stomach, his back and legs partially covered in cloth instead of the hospital gown and sheets. Her hand flew to her mouth, and she choked back a sob.

"Em, don't cry." Trent's weak voice jolted her gaze from the injuries to his face. "Come here."

Safe in Jake's arms, they moved to the head of the bed and a sleepy man. "Trent…" she started but couldn't finish. No matter what he said, tears began a slow slide down her face.

"How is she?" Her brother closed his eyes for a moment, and she noticed a shudder rack his body.

Emily almost broke down. Despite his significant pain, he wanted to know about their daughter. "She's fine."

He nodded as best as he could against the pillow. "Good. I'm sorry if I frightened her."

A small smile made its way to her face. "She did say something about not going swimming with you again."

His light chuckle did wonders for her heart even though she caught him still himself rather quickly.

"Trent, we can't thank you enough." Thank goodness Jake had the ability to put words together and say what they'd come here to say to begin with.

"Think nothing of it." A yawn escaped the patient.

Jake cleared his throat nervously. "I'm sorry. I never expected… I never meant for anything like this to happen—"

"Don't worry about it. You didn't do this. I'd do it all over again to save her."

Clasping Trent's hand, a small part of his body not covered with bandages, she avoided the IV and squeezed it a moment before just holding it in hers.

"I wanted to tell you two something." His lucidity visibly began to waver as his speech became somewhat slurred. "Don't hold off the wedding for me."

Emily glanced at Jake then back at Trent. "Of course we'll wait for you. You're family, and we want you there."

He closed his eyes, and she thought he'd dropped off to sleep. "Blake is right—life is too short. You've waited too long. Marry him now while you have everyone who loves you around you. They'll be leaving again soon. Don't waste this chance. Just remember me in spirit." A smidgeon of a smile fixed on his lips.

"Trent McKenzie, you're crazy if you think I'd have my wedding without you there."

"Don't wait for me, Em. After I get out of here… I'm leaving, and I'm not coming back." He dropped off to sleep.

Chapter Twenty-Six

"Emily, stay still so I can finish these last few pins in your hair." Megan poked Emily's head again in her attempt to control the elaborate hairstyle she'd created for the occasion.

Stuffed in a small hospital bathroom preparing for her wedding ceremony, Emily obeyed fearing she might mess up her hair, and they'd have to start all over again. She appreciated what her sister-in-law was doing for her, but she didn't see the need for it since her hair would be completely covered anyway.

She and Jake had finally given in to Trent and decided not to wait to marry, but they'd made a couple of private concessions. The big one was that they would not leave the man who'd saved their daughter's life out of the family affair. Because he was family whether he liked it or not.

Sure, squeezing the entire family in the tiny burn ward waiting room hadn't been her plan, but she wouldn't have this day go any other way. Thank goodness her father knew the administrator and had convinced him to allow them to put on this production. Even if he had nixed the chapel with concern on moving Trent that far.

Kate grinned at her shifting in the seat. "I think it's a great thing you're doing by having your ceremony in the hospital so Trent can be there."

A light mist filled her eyes at all that he'd been enduring. "We want him to be part of it, and we didn't want to wait." Her heart broke for her brother. With the public revelation by her father and then the bombing, he had a lot to deal with emotionally and physically. He had a long road to recovery ahead of him with possible skin grafts and such. After that, he planned to leave and never come home, but she wished she could convince him to stay, or at least return to them one day. She'd help him through anything she could. He'd been there for her so many times when she'd allowed Jake's absence to affect her. She wanted to repay the favor.

But Trent had been right. If she wanted her entire family present, they needed to do it now as her father had an overseas trip planned, HIS had a scheduled job, and she knew in her heart that Trent would leave before everyone returned. Emily would have him at her wedding. Hence their not waiting.

Sadly, she thought that someone else was missing. Someone she couldn't pin down like she was doing with Trent. Les. They'd laid his remains to rest, but the loss still had a profound impact on everyone. Emily held onto the guilt knowing he'd sacrificed himself for Amber. All the men assured her that they would've done the same thing. It didn't help her feel any better about it. Though every time she held her daughter, she sent up a silent prayer of thanks to him.

Megan dropped her hands and nodded. "Finished."

Relieved to be brought back to a happier topic, and to have her head stop feeling like a pincushion, Emily turned to look in the mirror. "Wow," she said in awe. "It's beautiful, Megan." Small pearls dotted her blonde hair. It was a shame she'd have to cover the hairstyle with a hospital cap, but if they wanted Trent to be part of the ceremony, they had to don full hospital scrub outfits. There was still a chance of infection in his back, backside and thighs so there was no other way to ensure he participated.

With her hair styled as it was, she felt like a princess.

And she was ready to marry her prince.

Finally, after all these years.

Her brothers laughed at her when she'd been six years old and claimed Jake as her husband when she grew up. They'd picked on her mercilessly. But she hadn't cared because she'd known what she wanted. No, who she wanted. Throughout the years that yearning never changed.

All the waiting and heartache faded away. They were now together and nothing would change that.

A knock sounded on the door. "He's here," her father's voice boomed. "Are you ready?"

Trent must've been wheeled into the room. They'd refused to begin until he showed. Heck, they were here for him anyway. He had tried to back out since Blake would be in attendance, but she'd convinced him how important it was to her.

Emily hugged Kate and Megan, her heart bursting with love for the two women. They'd again tried to make the day extra special for her. Thankfully, there hadn't been a full day shopping excursion. "Thank you."

Kate reached for the doorknob to exit, but Megan touched her eyes with a tissue and sniffed. "I'm so happy for you."

Weddings were a time for joy and sometimes tears,

but her sister-in-law's emotions were all over the place lately. Emily remembered pregnancy hormones. "Don't cry or you'll make me cry." She had to escape before she walked down the aisle with tears streaming down her face.

"I'm sorry. I can't help it." Megan blew her nose, took a deep breath and straightened her spine. "Okay. Let's do this."

Emily wiped imaginary wrinkles from the white scrubs she wore and then followed Kate out the door to stand in front of her father, who had chosen a charcoal gray set of scrubs.

He'd also introduced a woman named Nancy to everyone earlier. Emily wondered how serious their relationship was. Her father had introduced them to women before, but only at events they attended together. Never had he brought someone into the family setting.

"You look breathtaking, angel." Pride, love and tears glistened in Blake's eyes.

Fighting to hold back her own tears of joy, she hugged her father. "I love you, Dad." His embrace filled her body with warmth. Forgiving him had been easier than she'd expected. Jake had helped her realize she had no right to hold those actions against him. Especially since it all happened before she'd been born.

He pulled back. "I love you, too. I wish your mother could see you now. She'd be so proud." He offered a weak smile. "She'd also be bawling her eyes out."

Emily chuckled at that. Heck, she was close to bawling herself. Just like she'd known her mother had been there to look over Amber when she'd been kidnapped, she knew her mother was beside her today. She just believed in it.

With a wide smile, her father pulled up his mask; then he offered his arm. "Let's get you hitched."

Megan helped her with the hospital cap, and then she slipped into the room.

Emily tied on her mask and placed her hand on her father's arm. They entered the waiting room, which had been opened to them for the ceremony, to music playing from AJ's cell phone. The small room was filled with her family.

At the back of the room, she spied Trent lying there, face down in a hospital bed. She wanted to cry because she knew he must still be in pain. He winked and nodded her forward.

Emily turned and gazed ahead at the love of her life. He waited for her at the front of the room wearing black scrubs and an expression of undying love. Definitely the Greek god she'd dreamed about when she'd been so young. He may have at one time broken her heart, but he had also fixed it.

The family, all dressed in hospital garb, stood around the room. Everything blurred as she breezed past them to reach Jake. She wanted to do a happy dance since her happily ever after was occurring.

Her father kissed her and moved to stand next to Nancy. Amber came running to her, excited about the Dalmatian scrub shirt she wore. She kissed her daughter through their masks and took her back to AJ to watch.

Throughout the ceremony, Emily's focus remained on her husband-to-be while thoughts of their wild lovemaking took center stage. They had years of lost time to catch up on in the bedroom, and they were trying to make up for it. Her cheeks heated thinking of some of the things Jake had shown her.

Then she was caught off-guard, and her focus surged back to the ceremony.

"I understand you wrote your own vows, Jake," the family preacher said.

Jake turned to her and clasped both of her hands in his. *Oh no.* Her mind raced. She hadn't prepared any vows. What was he doing?

"Em, I don't expect your own vows as this was last minute. I just wanted to speak." He squeezed her hands and warmth flooded her. "There was a time in my life when my best friend's sister used to follow me around telling me she would marry me when she was older."

A light chuckle passed through their family. She couldn't help but smile at the memories.

"I remember watching you grow up from that little girl into a beautiful woman. What I didn't realize was that during that time, I'd fallen in love with you. I'm sorry it took me so long to realize what you mean to me." Jake lifted their entwined hands to his chest. "You are my heart, sprite. I need you as I need my next breath. I never want to be separated from you again."

He took a step closer. "I pledge to be the husband you deserve, and the father our children need until the end of time. I love you, Emily Hamilton."

A tear slipped down her face. Her heart overflowed with happiness and love. No words had ever sounded sweeter or more beautiful.

She had to say something. He'd opened his heart. She only hoped she didn't sound like an utter fool. "Jake, I've loved you since the day I met you. I've always known you were the only man for me. It's not important what happened in the past because now we are together, and that is all that matters. I love you, Jake Cavanaugh."

The next steps, rings and I dos, passed in a blur until she heard the clergy's final statements.

"I now pronounce you husband and wife. You may kiss your bride."

His eyes lit with a smile before Jake lowered his head toward hers. It didn't matter that they wore masks, didn't matter that his lips wouldn't be pressed directly against hers. All that mattered was that he was finally hers, and they'd have the rest of their lives to be the family she'd dreamed about since the day she met him when she was six years old.

A note from the author...

Thank you for reading *His Return*! If you enjoyed reading Jake and Emily's story, I would appreciate it if you would help others enjoy this book, too. You can do that by recommending it to friends, readers' groups, and discussion boards. It would mean a great deal to me if you'd take a moment to write a review and share how you feel about my story so others may find my work. Honest reviews help bring my books to the attention of other readers.

A word about the author...

Sheila Kell writes about romantic men who leave women's hearts pounding with a happily ever after built on memorable, adrenaline-pumping stories. Her debut novel, *His Desire* (HIS Series #1), launched as an Amazon #1 romantic suspense bestseller, later winning the Readers' Favorite award for best romantic suspense novel.

As a Southern girl who has left behind her days with the U.S. Air Force, and as a University Vice President, she can usually be found in South Mississippi, where she lives with her cats and all the strays that magically find her front door. When she isn't writing, she has her nose in a good book, is dealing with the woodland critters who enjoy her back porch, or is wishing she had a genie to do her bidding.

Ways to connect
SheilaKell.com
facebook.com/sheilakellbooks
goodreads.com/sheilakellbooks
bookbub.com/authors/sheila-kell
I'd love to hear directly from you, too. Please feel free to email me at sheila@sheilakell.com.

Don't miss out on new releases, exclusive excerpts and giveaways!

Join my newsletter:
www.SheilaKell.com/subscribe

More from Sheila Kell at The Wild Rose Press
Deadly Betrayal
Read Between the Lines